Other works by S.M. Sykes:

Eyes of Blue (book 1 of the Blue series)

Loss of Blue (book 3 of the Blue Series)

It's my body, I'll haunt if I want to

Life of a Lycanthrope

Message on the Wind

Every review helps immensely. If you enjoy this book or not, please take the time to leave a review @ Amazon or Goodreads. See the Qr above for links.

A Dim

Blue

(Book 2 of the Blue series)

S. M. Sykes

Printed in the United States of America
First Printing, 2024
Ingram Spark:
ISBN 979-8-8691-7044-6(paperback)
979-8-8693-3212-7 (ebook)

Amazon:

ISBN 979-8-3964-6584-8 (paperback)

979-8-3235-9181-7 (widespace)

ASIN- B0C84SRVMZ (kindle)

S. M. Sykes Books
27196 Indian Meadows Cir
Millsboro, DE. 19966

Table of Contents

Dedication

To my loving wife and son. You put up with me talking incessantly about this story. Most likely to the point that you never want to read it as you know everything that is going to happen. But then you read it and edit it for me. Then read it again to make sure I got it right. These stories would never come to life without both of you.

I can never thank you enough.

Prologue

Ava seems to think a lot more about my story than most people probably will. I have been through a lot and learned a lot along the way. Pain and loss are good motivators to learn from your mistakes and do better the next time. I have a lot of scars that prove that maybe I am not the fastest learner.

Ava was young and immature in the beginning. She did not completely comprehend the imminent threat and danger that the virus and the deaders could become. Youth and inexperience can cause you to walk through life with rose-colored glasses. This is not a bad thing in any way. We should all hope to keep the weight of the world off our shoulders for as long as humanly possible.

For others, our glasses were ripped off and thrown to the ground. I had to make hard choices and do things that I never could have believed would need to be done. Let alone need to be done by me. I have had a few bright spots of hope along the way too. Made some good friends and happened to be in the right place when people needed me.

My story is not all doom and gloom. There are a few bright spots. My biggest reason for agreeing to write it down is so that future generations can know what we endured. They can learn from first-hand experience the danger that this creature poses. They can learn what I know of its habits and the differences in each and every one. These creatures are not as simplistic as first thought. They do not follow all of the tropes that the old zombie movies created for them.

They started out human. Each human with their own vices, intelligence and abilities. These creatures inherited some of this from their host and expanded upon it. Each one differently than the next. Hopefully, our trip to South Dakota will be a success and this will just be a historical record of the creatures that tried to eliminate the human race. But if we fail. I really hope we don't fail. If we fail then please understand these creatures. Understand how to stay away from them and make a life for yourself in this forsaken world we now inhabit.

We fight for survival every day, but just surviving is not enough for the human race. We need to live and experience life in new ways. That is why we are taking this journey. That is why I became the soldier that I am today. We are trying to give the human race a chance to be human again.

Running….

Again with the running. Always with the running. I remembered a time when I actually enjoyed running. Enjoyed the rush, the wind and the feeling of my legs, strong, propelling me towards the finish. Then it was fun. I ran with my sister, with my team and for our school. I loved the competition and the feeling of getting stronger and faster every day. I could feel myself getting better and having more endurance.

That was high school. In college, I felt like the coach had me running every day with no end in sight. Between my senior year and my freshman year of college, I trained for the upcoming cross-country season at home. I did not start college until the middle of August, so all of my June and July running was done at my pace and when I felt like running. I had just come off my senior season of lacrosse, I felt like I was in good shape. Lacrosse was more like cross-training. You had to sprint and turn along with taking and dishing out the appropriate body check. Cross country was just running distance. I had done it all four years, it would be easy.

I showed up in Daytona Beach, Florida and was shown just how wrong I was. I was not fast and not in shape. I was a walk-on to the team so I needed to be faster and stronger than anyone there. I was not. Not even close.

I did not run cross country during my freshman year for the Embry Riddle Eagles. I watched from the sidelines. I was discouraged because I was not good enough to make the top squad. The coach saw the potential I guess because I had been able to train with them. It had shown me how lazy my training was before and made me feel better about not making the team. It also made me a better runner in the end.

It definitely helped me get in better shape for my freshman lacrosse season. I did make that team, although on the practice squad. I'll call it a red-shirt year.

Running in July of the following year made me rethink running cross country at the college level. I had not gone home for the summer, as most college kids did. I had gone home only for a short break but returned in the middle of June to train. I had planned on getting an apartment with a couple of the guys from the team for this year. I just got in on the apartment early to put in the work.

Coach had lived near the college so he had seen me working and came out three times a week to put me through it. I had to run 5 days a week, but the three he was there were the toughest.

So now that you have a bit of my history, you're probably asking who I am.

Well, we have never officially met, but I think you had heard of me from my sister, Ava. My name is Matthew Francis Washington. It's a name that sounds like it should have a third after it or something, but I am the first and only of my name.

At the time of the Fall, I was 19 years old. I had my whole life ahead of me. It was my second year in a college degree, majoring in Unmanned Systems. I was learning to pilot Unmanned Aviation Vehicles (UAVs). Pretty cool right? I was living on my own and the whole world was my oyster. Something my Grammy used to say, I personally do not like much seafood and hate oysters in particular. Never really got the reference.

College was great. The training during the summer was not so great, but it would lead to me making the team and maybe impressing a few of the girls around campus. July and August kinda flew by in this way. I worked a lot to put money in the bank to pay for my apartment. I did not have a scholarship, so the tuition was already going on student loans, I tried really hard to not put room and board on there too.

When I wasn't working or training, I was trying to enjoy the sights and sounds of Daytona Beach. I had grown up on the east coast, actually in a resort beach area, but that did not compare at all to what Daytona Beach brought to the table.

Before I knew it August was half over and school was back in session. Then it became school, training and work. No time left for anything else. Going to one of the most prestigious aviation colleges in the world tended to mean harder classes and even harder expectations. That was before trying to win a spot on the sports teams.

Sophomore year should have been an easier adjustment, I knew the campus, people and a lot of the teachers. So the implementation of a CDC mask mandate right at the beginning of the year had thrown me for a loop. We were told to wear them inside and out. They even made us wear them while we were running. This of course caused the college to suspend a lot of the fall sports and activities. It was not really safe to run in 90-degree weather with 100% humidity with a mask on. It was a total bummer to lose the season after training so hard all summer, but people had been passing out and falling during their runs from wearing the masks.

The news said that there had been some meteorite strike in Russia over the summer which was spreading some sort of pathogen. It was causing sickness to spread across the entire planet. There were multiple deaths attributed to this spread. Our professors were worried and spent most of the classes showing news feeds from around the world. Things looked bad. People stayed inside and avoided others like they had the plague. Which in a sense they did.

Soon after the CDC mandated that people stay indoors and away from each other. The university decided to err on the side of caution. They made everyone leave campus and the university started holding classes virtually. Students that lived in the dorms had to get out. They either had to go home or find an apartment out in town. The school recommended the former.

At first, I thought this was great, it allowed me more time to work and train. Since I lived off campus anyway there was not much of a change for me. Online classes were usually taped to be watched by those that could not be on during class hours. This allowed me to watch them whenever and do the assignments as I pleased. Not that there were many assignments. The professors were too involved with current affairs to care much about homework.

Momma had called a couple of times asking me to come home. I told her that this would all blow over and I did not want to pay for an apartment I was not living in. Mostly though, I just wanted to stay and party with the college co-eds. Well, that and playing online games with my friends back home. Surprisingly, internet companies boosted their speeds during this time of crisis. It made gaming so much better with way less lag.

A little later the CDC came out with a new mandate that shut down all non-essential businesses. This meant retail stores and most small businesses. The closings gave me even more time since I did not have to work any longer. I decided to use that time on the beach and at parties.

About this time we had heard about shootings, stabbings and your everyday beatings in the streets. The mask and quarantine mandates had people panicking to the point that they were rioting, protesting and looting. It brought criminals out in droves. Almost everyone was out of work. The government said that this would keep people out of the streets and harm's way until a path forward could be carefully considered and enacted. This was just a written invitation for the criminal element to take what they wanted and shoot, beat or stab anyone in their way.

I put training off for a bit, now that the season was canceled. I was not allowed on the track at the university to train properly and I was not supposed to be out on the streets per the CDC. Yet, I lived in a college town, so we were not about to stop having fun because the world stopped spinning. We figured it would all blow over in a couple of weeks.

A week or so later I was at a party and one of the dumbasses overdosed on some new drug that hit the streets. I guess in the areas around the equator the poppy plants started to produce twice the number of seeds and were growing at a ridiculously high rate of speed. This made the opium that came from the seeds a lot more potent. It was being made into a new designer drug called "Blue Lightning". It supposedly let you see blue lights emanating from anything electrical, including people.

Well, this guy decided to try some and took way too much. He ran around for a while like some whack-job. Touching people's faces and making weird noises. We all ignored him for the most part until he touched the wrong girl and one of the football players from a rival school, I guess this guy thought he was a knight, punched him so hard he fell in the pool.

When the guy fell in, he flailed and couldn't swim. A couple of people tried to jump in and pull him out, but he fought them and sank to the bottom. He passed out from lack of oxygen before anyone was able to get near him and pull him out. By the time he was rescued his heart had stopped. 911 was called and the party broke up.

I am not sure what happened after that. I was underage at this party and did not stick around to give my statement. That was one thing about me. I liked to follow the rules and I was not a real risk-taker. Even when I went to these parties I kind of sat at the edge of everything and people-watched. I did not get adventurous on the dance floor or flirt with all the pretty girls. I most definitely did not drop it like it was hot. I liked the music and the atmosphere, I just didn't feel comfortable in the mix of everything. So when things like that happened I just faded away into the background and left.

Since the party was a bust early in the night I decided to go back to the apartment and get online to do some gaming. I was playing in a heated battle of Call of Duty when my social media started to blow up. Apparently, the guy at the party was not dead, just passed out. The guy came to a couple of minutes after everyone left and started running around again. But this time he was hurting people when he touched them and his eyes had an odd blue glow to them. The pictures could have been photo-shopped, but they came from so many sources in different positions that I did not think so. This was one hell of a drug I guess. The police finally showed up and took the guy into custody, but only after hitting him with a taser. People said that seemed to make him stronger. This is why I have always stayed away from drugs. No telling what was in those things.

I stopped playing and got lost in the social media rabbit hole. Before I knew it my game was ruined. I had been kicked out of the room with my friends and others had jumped in. I couldn't get back on. Then everyone in the lobbies were talking about incidents just like that guy throughout their hometowns. I decided to get off the game and watch a movie instead. I stayed current on social media but sometimes it was just too much. There had been a couple of movies that I had wanted to watch but hadn't given myself the time for. One bag of popcorn, a large soda and a small couch took care of the rest of my night.

I had to turn off my phone during the movie because the social media platforms kept blowing up with a lot more incidents like the pool party. I could not fathom that this drug got out to the rest of the country so fast and that so many people were overdosing on it. Kind of told the story of our society. Everything was an escape from the harsh bitter reality of life. That is why I tried to enjoy life where I could.

The rest of September got really weird, really fast after that. The regular media started echoing the bloggers and talking about corpses being reanimated and terrorizing major cities around the world. People were being killed by these things without a mark on their bodies. Some doctors were saying that they were having fear-induced heart attacks. Even though a lot of the deaths were in young healthy people.

All travel was shut down across the world. People were stuck in a lot of places that were not their homes and having to try to find a way back. It was ok if you were at least on the correct continent, but some did not even have that luxury.

People were leaving the American big cities to go to more rural areas. They felt that fewer people made it safer. I thought about heading home myself, but with only one major route out of Florida from Daytona Beach, I knew it would be a nightmare in traffic until I got to Georgia. I decided that I was safe as long as I didn't go outside without my mask and I avoided the major areas, like supermarkets. Luckily I loved macaroni and cheese and had stocked up on the last trip. I could hold out for a while as things sorted themselves out.

A lot of my friends had the same idea, so we just stayed in and played games. Some of the streaming platforms designed a watch-group function. You could turn it on in different homes and watch the same movie at the same time and talk about it like you were in the same room. This was really cool, especially for someone like me that liked to be in my own comfort zone. This is something that should have existed long ago. We took advantage of this a lot and tried to ignore the happenings of the world until it blew over.

Lights

The lights started going out across the world in early October. It started with the third-world countries, ones that had sketchy electrical grids, to begin with. It was soon followed by eastern European countries, then the western ones. India, China and Japan lasted longer than most, but it still seemed like they would succumb to the darkness soon too. North America could not be too far behind them, could they? It was already happening in certain towns and cities. There were three areas in Florida alone that were reportedly out of power. Miami, Jacksonville and most of the Keys.

This ended the fun times we were having. It made us all think that the apocalypse idea was not too far off. Even if the undead were not walking the streets, darkness and loss of electricity would cause panic. The rioting and looting would only get worse. I decided then that I needed to get back home, bad traffic or not. It was an 850-mile trip from Daytona Beach, Florida to Millsboro, Delaware. I needed power to fuel up along the way. If I waited any longer I may not make it back.

The next day I packed up my Jeep Liberty and headed north. The situation was becoming a real danger and my family and I would need each other during this time. I mean people had hoarded toilet paper so badly that you could not find a single roll on a shelf at the local Walmart for god's sake.

On a good day, the trek would take 14 hours, not counting stops for food and gas. With the country falling apart I did not know how long it would take. Most retail stores and fast food places were closed due to the CDC order. Gas stations were reporting that people were hoarding gas by filling up everything including Ziploc and grocery bags with gasoline to take home. The prices started to skyrocket because of the lack of availability of oil from other countries. We definitely relied too much on foreign oil from the Middle East and Eastern Europe.

My SUV got decent gas mileage for its age, but that was still only 15 miles to the gallon. With traffic sitting at a standstill on most highways in Florida, I would have to shut the engine off every chance I got. Then I would have to navigate around on side and back roads. Luckily the GPS satellites were still working and I would not get too lost. This would just add miles and time to my trip. I already had to stop three times for gas on the way home. It would be more like four or five with the round-about way I would have to go.

I did have an extra gas tank I could fill, but it was only five gallons. I figured anything would help in the end, so I went to the closest gas station to fill it and my tank up for the trip. I drove the mile or so it took to get to the closest Wawa gas station. Since this was also a convenience store, I figured I'd grab some food and snacks for the road. There was no telling where I would be able to stop. I did not have much at the apartment, mostly macaroni and cheese, so I needed a quick resupply.

Well, quick would not be the operative term in this scenario. It took fifteen minutes to get into the parking lot. I had passed a couple of Sunoco stores too and they did not seem to be any better, so I stuck with my original plan.

Once in the parking lot, it took another forty minutes just to get to a pump. In this time frame, I saw three beatings, one stabbing and a full royal rumble at pump 3. None of it was over the gas itself, it did not seem, just over people taking too long or leaving their car at the pump while they went inside to get food. I decided then to get gas as quickly as I could and leave. I would get food at the next stop. Maybe somewhere more civilized, like Gotham city.

The gas pumps were running slow, which probably meant they were running low on gas, so it took a bit longer to fill up. The natives behind me were getting restless and I would hate to see what would happen to this place when the gas stopped pumping. Hopefully, I would be on the road before that happened.

What felt like a year later, the Liberty was all fueled up and I headed down the road. It took another twenty minutes to pull away from the pump and get to the road. People were not patient and were taking risks with their cars and SUVs that they wouldn't normally do. This caused backups at every single turn.

Later, I heard on the radio that the fuel at the Wawa and the other local gas stations did run out not too long after I headed out. The scene that the announcer described was very grim and gory.

Apparently, someone or a couple of someone's had been using Blue Lightning because the reports told about glowing blue eyes and impossible feats of defying death. One of them told about a guy that got set on fire and he just kept walking down the road. Weird.

I was on the road and the traffic on Rt. 95 was moving at a slow but solid pace for the scenario. I decided to jump off and take the smaller Rt 100 over to Rt17 once I got there. Most people were looking for the most direct route, so if I took a roundabout route it should mean less traffic. While I was right about there being less traffic, there was still traffic to contend with. I coasted in neutral as much as I could and was even able to turn the engine off a couple of times to conserve fuel. The trip was looking OK, but I did not think about the problem with taking RT 100. It put me right downtown Jacksonville. There was no way around it on this route.

For those of you that do not know, Jacksonville was a very populated city in Florida. The people were young and liked to party. The cost of living was low and things seemed more affordable than in other areas of the state. These things combined made for an atmosphere best described as YOLO (you only live once).

During the end of time and the fall of our society, things there fell a bit quicker it seemed. This was one of the cities that had lost power. The city was lost. Cars blocked streets, either partially or completely. I had to turn around more than once. On the plus side, there was no traffic. People meandered about in some areas, seeming lost or in a daze. In other areas, the people were running and terrified, while others ignored everything around them to loot and steal what they could.

I refused to stop and do anything outside of my car. I kept the radio low as I drove through so I could hear the yelling and fights in the street. I thought that listening for the loud sounds in the streets might give me a warning and let me turn off before I ran into those areas. The quiet areas were better. Fewer people and more room to navigate. The going was slow, but not as slow as the interstate would have been. Although twice someone with glowing blue eyes stepped in front of my car and I had to slam on the brakes to avoid hitting them. Then what did they do? They put their hands on the car hood and glared at me like I was wrong. They then looked to the sky as if in euphoria. One time I guess I hit the brakes too hard because the truck started to lose power as I sat there. I had to goose the gas and swerve to get them to take their hands off my car. Dang drug addicts.

Luckily I was able to put Jacksonville in my rear-view mirror sooner than later. I was able to get onto Route 301 and head north, out of Florida. The traffic seemed to clear out on my side of the road at this point. I don't know if Jacksonville was a choke point or if people just stayed on RT 95 to avoid the smaller roads.

I traveled through a couple of small Georgia towns along the way. None of which seemed too changed by recent events. The gas stations were operating, so I filled up when I could, and the people seemed really friendly when I stopped for food. Apparently, even the apocalypse takes longer to reach the south. I knew this would probably not last when I reached a major city like Savannah.

Once out of Florida the 301 freeway had cleared. Another plus of the happenings was that speeding was not really a big concern to the police at this point. In all actuality, I had not seen a cop at all in the hours that I had been on the road. I took this as a sign to drive as fast as I could, below the speed of reckless abandon of course. If I wrecked, there would be no one to help. The end of the world meant the collapse of local and federal governments. First responders would most likely be the first casualty of the fall. Either figuratively or literally.

Once I got close to Savannah, I had a choice to make. I could hope that RT 95 was clear now that we were farther north and jump on there. Or stay on the smaller routes and go directly through the city. Any other road would take me out of the way and I would lose too much time. I decided to stay off the major routes a while longer and try the city. Savannah had always been a relaxed type of place. Maybe the people there were like the other Georgians that I had met and were still doing ok. Plus I needed to rest. I had been on the road for almost eight hours at that point. Usually a four-hour drive, but the day started off slow.

It was sunset as I rolled into the city. The day had been stressful and even on the clear roads, I was amped up waiting for the other shoe to fall. I never really felt like I was seeing everything out there. Something dark seemed to be on the horizon. Either way, I knew this was not going to be a one-day trip with everything going on, so this seemed like as good a place as any to stop and rest.

Savannah

Savannah, as it turned out, was not like the other small towns I had run through at all. This city made Jacksonville look like Smallville. When I filled up in Hinesville there had been a few whispers from the locals to avoid Savannah. I ignored them. as a 19-year-old will often do. I knew better than them. They probably did not like the city much, to begin with, I thought. Well, I found out they had their reasons.

The radio had been spotty for the last hour or so of the trip. I had my Spotify in offline mode and just let my playlist carry me through the miles of roadway. As I entered Savannah though I figured it would be prudent to look for a local radio station and see what kind of news was coming out of the city. No point rushing into a bad situation if at all possible.

I should have known that something was wrong when I did not get any radio station on the AM or FM bands. I had just figured that maybe something was wrong with the towers or there was no one to man the stations. A lot of the radio stations had sent their DJs home during the pandemic and they ran their shows from there through the internet. The issue with this was that the internet had to run and the towers still needed to be maintained on-site. If anything went down the whole station would stop functioning.

As I entered the area surrounding the city, I found that there were several cars abandoned on the road. Some had been involved in accidents, others just left with their doors open wherever they had stopped. Maybe they had run out of gas, or maybe something else had happened. There were several times that I had to get out of my car and move another vehicle out of the roadway. I left my car running and got out quickly to put the other car in neutral. A couple of times I found that the keys were in the ignition and the car was able to be started, so I could drive it out of the way. Other times the batteries were dead or the keys were missing. I started to wish that more people had driven manual transmissions by this point. I did not need the keys to move them. I had no idea what would cause people to abandon their cars in the middle of the road, but it made me uneasy. The roadway was slightly blocked, but mostly by the cars that seemed abandoned. It seemed like they just took off on foot and left.

There were a few times that I found a dead body on the road or in a car. One vehicle, in particular, had a person in the back seat, raging on some kind of drug. He banged on the windows of the car trying to get out like he was locked in somehow. His eyes had that blue glow that I had started to attribute to Blue Lightning. He must have been so high on this drug that he could not figure out how to open the door. I mean even if the child safety locks were on in the car he could have climbed into the front seat and opened that door.

Further down the road, I came across a police car that had crashed into the jersey barrier on the side of the road. The car was still smoking so I thought that it may have been recent. I stopped to check on the cop to see if he was ok. The police officer in the driver's seat seemed to be dead. The accident did not seem to have been bad enough to kill on impact so he must have died before the crash. When I opened the door the officer was definitely deceased although there were no apparent injuries to him. He must have had a heart attack or something while driving.

As I was checking for a pulse someone in the back of the car jumped at me and hit the cage. I jumped back so quickly that I lost my footing and hit my head on the jersey barrier. I saw stars and hoped that I did not give myself a concussion. Luckily the cage held and the person was not able to get to me. The only thing he seemed to be able to do was reach one hand out toward the officer, but he could barely even touch the headrest with his fingers. I had a feeling that the area was unsafe. The problem was that there were no roads connecting to this section of the roadway. I would have to turn around and backtrack several miles to find another way around. The time and loss of fuel would make the trip even longer and harder. It was possible that whatever had happened on this part of the highway was over and whatever caused it was gone. I had never been in a situation as stressful as this before and I was probably just overreacting.

This thought was negated by the time I reached the next exit. That exit had a military blockade blocking the entrance to the city. There were no soldiers around so I found a way past the vehicles and started down the off-ramp. Once I got past the blockade I could see that there had been some type of altercation. There were several dead bodies and a lot of empty shell casings on the ground. Something bad had gone down there. Instead of trying to figure out what, I decided to haul ass and leave the area immediately.

The next mile or so after that was clear. Obviously, the previous congestion was from the blockade. People probably ran from the altercation that was happening. The cars were left anywhere and everywhere as people ran for their lives. Most people were not brave in the face of danger. I could say that as I was one of those people. My fight or flight was usually the latter. I decided that staying in this area for the night was probably not a good idea. If this bad of an altercation happened, it may just be a matter of time until something popped off again.

I checked all of the following on-ramps to Rt 95. All of them were blocked to the point that I could not get the Liberty through. There were no soldiers or people around but they were impassable. I continued into the heart of the city to find my way through. Hopefully, the other side of the city was not as inaccessible as this side seemed to be.

The sun was completely set and darkness had settled in by the time I reach the city proper. As I got into the heart of the city, I started seeing people milling about in the building lobbies. The power seemed to be out, like Jacksonville, so people were hard to see, especially since headlights only illuminate directly in front of you. I took it slow but steady. The people did not seem bothered by me or had any indication of running out of the buildings and in front of my car as they had before. The city must have had a curfew set because I did not see a single person on the sidewalk or the street.

It started to seem more and more ominous the more I looked. People were in the building's lobbies like they were at a Christmas party. But no one was outside smoking or walking home. Some of them were pressed up to the doors and windows like they wanted to come outside but they couldn't remember how to open the doors. Some were dressed nicely, others were in jackets and shirts that were torn and ragged.

I saw that a lot of the lobby doors were bolted or chained shut. The people looked like they were trying to get out because they were. Was this for their safety or was someone in charge that did not want people on the streets? The people were pushing on doors and windows trying to get out to the streets.

Suddenly, I heard a big boom and the sound of glass hitting the pavement. One of the building's glass windows had shattered and fell to the sidewalk. The people inside came running out of the building in droves. The closest ones turned toward me and my truck and ran toward me with reckless abandon. I did not wait to see why they were acting this way, I hit the gas and left them in my rear-view mirror. I was no longer taking this city slow and steady. I needed to get out fast. Something was wrong here and I did not want to stay and find out what.

After making a few turns down side streets I seemed to lose them. I continued on my way out of the city. A lot of post-apocalyptic movies had scenes where a gang of people would pull someone out of their car through smashed windows and busted doors. I would not be able to make it home if that were to happen to me. The Liberty was my sole source of safety and transportation. I did not want to see if the movies had this part of the tropes correct.

Finally, I came to a bridge on the north side of the city. As I came up to the area I expected this bridge to be blockaded. Apparently, my luck had changed and it was not. I crossed the bridge and left Georgia, their martial law and that weird incident behind me. I would love to say that I would avoid populated areas from there on out and especially stay away from the cities. The truth was though that the eastern seaboard was full of cities all up and down Rt 95. I would need gas, food and eventually a place to rest. I would have to risk those areas again. Hopefully, the next one would still have the lights on.

Gas

A little while later, I was almost out of gas. When I arrived in Savannah I had been close to empty. When I vacated the city I stopped and put the full five gallons in my reserve tank. Rt 95 was clear. The road was desolate and lonely. Not a bad thing when the world was falling apart. It meant less opportunity for trouble.

As I approached Walterboro, SC I was praying for nice people and working gas pumps. Mainly just working pumps. If I did not get gas there I would have to start walking home or find a hose and start siphoning gas from vehicles stranded on the road. There were not too many of those on this part of the highway, so it would be slim pickings.

I knew that the area had power, I could see small towns and areas of light from the road and the signs were lit up on the highway. I had been taking it easy and had slowed my pace to conserve fuel. It took me about two hours to get just outside of the small town. I did not know much about this town, but since it was right on Rt. 95 it had to have gas stations. That would have been its biggest draw in our society.

I stopped just outside of town and turned the radio on to scan for stations. Instantly music came through the speakers. No warnings or static clogging up the airways. This seemed to be a good sign. I decided that at least this town wasn't under strict martial law. There were lights, music and a distinct lack of Army blockades. Already better than Savannah.

As I pulled into the town I could see all of the gas stations had pulled the pricing off of their signs. I pulled into a Shell station to see why. There was a sign stating that they were completely out of gas and had no idea when another shipment was coming through. The next three stations I checked had the same notes in their windows. It was a quaint little town with a nice main street. A couple of people were out walking on the sidewalks and I could see others looking out of their windows at me as I drove slowly past.

I had started to lose hope of finding any gas when I happened upon a small gas station. It was most likely owned and operated by a small-town family man. It had only four pumps with a small convenience store at the center. The sign still had prices and I saw people sitting by the pumps. As I pulled in I could see the people all stand up and turn toward me. I could also see that all of them were armed. One had a rifle, another had a shotgun and the three others that I could see had sidearms on their hips.

As I came to a stop an old man approached my car.

"You from out of town?" he asked as he leaned on my door.

"Yes sir"

"You need gas?"

"Yes sir."

"You got cash?" He was a man of many words.

"Yes sir." So was I it seemed.

"We won't let any of you city folk come here and hoard our gas any more. That's why we alls out here. If you just passing through I'll let you fill your tank, but no extra shit. Got it?"

"Yes sir."

He then showed me to the pump and I gave him my cash. He counted out what it would cost and actually charged me the going rate of about $4.50 a gallon. That was a lot cheaper than the gas I got in Daytona.

A younger fellow filled up the tank and closed my gas cap.

"Ok get on outta here. You need to get somewhere quick and get off the roads. It ain't safe out there." He warned.

I waved at him and said thanks, then headed back towards the highway. It had been an odd transaction, but I had a full tank and could probably make it to the north side of North Carolina. All I had to do now was get up the road a bit and find a small area to pull over and sleep until dawn. I could feel my eyes starting to get heavy. I couldn't just stop to get a cup of coffee and a Monster energy drink anywhere, so I had to make due the old-fashioned way. Sleep.

A couple of miles later there was a truck stop pull off and I used it to my advantage. I parked under a tree in the shadows. I sat there with the engine running for ten full minutes. It seemed like it might be a waste of precious fuel, but I was trying to make sure the area was clear. I did not see anything that drew my attention so I shut off the engine and climbed into the back of the truck to lie down. I locked all of the doors and felt reasonably safe for a world that had started to get turned on its head.

Sleep came quickly. I was asleep long before I thought I would be. A long, stressful day of odd things and driving long distances must have taken it out of me. I dreamt of eyes glowing blue. Of people walking in front of my car and not caring if they got hit. I then dreamt of cities on fire and people dying by the thousands.

Quicker than I would like the sun came beaming in my windows and woke me up. I tried to turn over and sleep a few more minutes, but my bladder had other ideas. I got up and unlocked the door to get out and pee. I walked a little bit into the woods line to relieve myself. Why? Why not just pee next to the truck, You may ask? Maybe old habits die hard. I am not sure myself. Believe me, I ask myself this a lot now. As soon as I started to go, I heard the doors open and people jumping into my truck. I yelled at them and started to run back when I heard the engine turn and the gear drop into drive. They sped away, heading north with everything I owned.

I stopped at the side of the road and watched my car drive off. I had not even known there was anyone around me. I did not pay attention at all to my surroundings and paid dearly for my mistake. I felt like I was safe because I had not really seen anyone at all on the road outside of the towns. I let my guard down and I was left with nothing. No water, food, or transportation.

Damn, I was stupid.

Walking

Do you know what is worse than running in sweltering August heat, in 100% humidity, with a coach yelling at you for hours on end? Walking down the road knowing you were a total dumb-ass and you caused yourself to have to walk for 600 miles to get home. I still couldn't believe that someone was able to jump in my truck the second I got out. They must have been watching me for some time to gauge that timing so well. I know when I pulled into that truck stop area that there was no one around. I took the appropriate precautions. I thought it would be safe. I guess I hadn't figured on someone passing through while I was asleep.

I was walking down the interstate and off ramps to try and find an area with some kind of population. Maybe someone had seen my car or could find me a way to get around. Unfortunately for me, since I was trying to avoid populated areas, I had only success in that area at this point in the trip. So much success that I started wishing that this area of the highway was not so desolate. I could have gone for a bunch of cars blocking the road with their keys hanging in the ignition. I'd even try one of those new electric cars right about now if it ran. Another way that humans tried to save our world. We didn't see an end of times coming that was not global warming. Well, welcome to the new age.

Before I knew it, the sun was setting on the first day without my car. I figured I had walked about twenty miles that day. Checking the off-ramps and side streets took a lot of time off my travel north. At this point, I had to try and find an abandoned building or something to keep me safe for the night. I was a boy scout when I was younger. Actually made the rank of Eagle before my 18th birthday. I had slept in the woods and made my own camps, but I usually had some materials to work with and a sleeping bag. October nights got chilly. All I had was the t-shirt and jeans that I was wearing in the truck. Luckily I had gotten out with socks and sneakers on or I would have been royally screwed.

As the sun set and darkness set in, I had still not found any homes or places to get under a roof for the night. I am not sure why, but after the strange happenings over the last couple of days, I did not want to be walking on the roads after dark. I saw an intersection off the major highway coming up. I decided that if I could not find a roof, I could stay under the overpass for the night. I would be protected from the rain and maybe I could find some material and get a fire started. Just as I thought about a fire the sky rumbled and rain started down. I was soaked in seconds. I was so worried about getting a roof over my head for the night that I completely forgot to check the sky for clouds.

I reached the overpass just after true night had set in. I got lucky and found some papers and dry wood. It looked like a few pallets had fallen off a truck, or other people walking had set them up for themselves. I hoped that they did not feel like coming back here tonight. I really did not want any company. I was shivering from the cold and the rain, but I got to work to get the fire started.

An hour after I found the materials I had the beginning of a fire going. I felt like Tom Hanks in the movie Castaway by this point. Very proud of myself for making fire with no matches or flint. I had done this one time before in Boy Scouts, but it was a long time ago and I had to remember how to get everything set up. In the end, I had taken the shoelace out of one of my shoes to get the sticks moving right. I fed the fire slowly even though I needed it to grow fast. If I fed it too fast it might go out and I don't know if I could get it started again. My hands were sore and starting to cramp up from the previous effort and the cold rain. As it got built up I figured the fire would keep me warm and fight off the fear of the dark that I was suddenly getting. My sister was always the one with the big imagination that jumped at sounds in the dark. She always thought some big monster or crazed killer was hiding out there. Man, she would not like it out here all by herself.

The fire would also attract attention if seen by anyone passing by. While I knew I needed help, I did not want to attract any at night. I had recently started to get a bad feeling about people, I was usually open and willing to meet new people. Whatever was causing the lock downs and shortages was causing people to react in ways that were not consistent with how I thought of them. Instead of coming together, people seemed to only look out for themselves. For instance, they stole my truck right out from under my nose. But, my need for survival over ran my new fear of people.

So I kept the fire going. Something in the back of my mind was very fearful of freezing to death.

As I sat by the fire trying very hard not to think about food or my stomach gnawing on my backbone, I realized that I had to find water tomorrow or I would be in seriously bad shape. I hadn't seen a single car drive up or down the road today. I had stayed on the interstate as much as I could hoping to see someone that may be able to help me out. During the drive from Georgia, I had not seen many cars, but there had been some. I wondered if all of the gas stations in this area were out like the ones in Walterboro. That may have explained the lack of traveling. Conserve what fuel you have, or horde it for another day. If no one was on the road tomorrow by noon I would have to get off the main road and try a few of the smaller roads to find a house or a store where someone could help me. At least I could find a house or store with some bottles of water. I thought about the fact that I would not be in such dire need of water if I had my truck and some supplies. With the rain, I could collect it with a sheet of plastic or a rain jacket. Sadly, I had neither of these and my shirt was not too good for water collection.

These were the thoughts that I had as I fell asleep in front of the fire. I woke up a couple of hours later in the pre-dawn light, shivering. My sleep had been dreamless, as it usually was. The fire had died out, pallet wood burns hot, but it burns fast too. The coals were too dead to try and restart the fire easily, so I decided that the other way to warm up would be to get on the road. The rain had stopped sometime during the night so nothing was keeping me under this overpass.

I stood up, put on my sneakers, stretched, then took off in a northerly direction. I had hoped that I would find something that would help me live another day. Noon came and went faster than I would have liked. I had not seen another soul or a building in the distance. I guess it made sense too as most people did not want to hear the highway as they sat on their front porches. I had to find a road off of this interstate if I was going to find help.

My mouth was a desert prairie. I was starting to feel light-headed and sick to my stomach at the same time. Being in shape helped me keep moving and helped me work through the slight dehydration that I was feeling. My legs were hurting and I could tell that I was slowing my pace. Nothing in my training had prepared me to walk for two days straight with no food or water.

As I was lost in thought, I saw a small road intersecting with the interstate. As I came upon it I could see there was a small farmhouse within sight. There did not seem to be any movement there from this distance, but it was the first thing I had seen but farmland and road for the last day and a half. I'll let you know that I felt a little elated at this sight. A farm had to have a working well or people on it that would help me out. The other part of my brain was warning that farmers also tended to be loners and liked to keep to themselves. They may not want people coming onto their property possibly bringing disease and trouble.

An hour and twenty minutes later I was standing at the driveway to the little farmhouse. I had argued with myself the whole time. I had eventually decided that I could die here, be run off, or get help. If I did not get help and was run off I would likely die in the next day or so from dehydration anyway. I was not sure how much longer I could keep walking without food and water. I may not be able to make it to the next farmhouse or town down the road.

The farmhouse had several outbuildings but no movement or sound. There weren't even chickens clucking in the yard. With some reservations, I walked up the driveway to the house and slowly walked up to the front door. I was cautious and listened for any sound, especially a sound of a shotgun shucking a shell into the chamber or a rifle breech being sent home.

There were several windows on the porch, all of them were shut tight with blinds and curtains drawn. This did not bode well, but I knocked anyway. I waited a minute or two and knocked again. When there was still no answer or sounds from inside. I decided to try the door handle. It turned, but the deadbolt was set, and the door didn't open. Thinking that maybe they were in one of the outbuildings I walked around the side of the house and yelled a hello. I asked if anyone was around and if I could get some help. There was no answer. What I did see was a well pump in the middle of two of the outbuildings.

Now I would like to tell you that I calmly walked up to the well pump and tested the water properly before having a drink. I will not lie to you though. I ran with what energy I had left to the well pump and stuck my head under it as I pumped it as fast as I could. So fast, as a matter of fact, that I almost drowned myself before I got it under control. I am not sure if it was delirium or not, but this water tasted like it was straight from the gods. It could also be that I had spent the last years living off bottled water to avoid the stuff they called tap water in Florida.

After I sated my thirst, washed my face and hands clean of the filth of the road, I looked around again. There still did not seem to be anyone around. No movement or sounds from anywhere around me. I decided to try the back door to the home and see if there was any food that I could take with me and maybe a couple of bottles for the delicious well water.

As I walked up to the door I knocked again just in case someone was there. I then tried the handle and the door gave and swung inward on silent hinges. The sight I beheld when the door finally swung all the way open made me glad that I did not have anything but water in my stomach. I saw the terrible aftermath of a brutal killing. There appeared to be three people in the kitchen. All of them were cut and bloody. My sister loved horror movies. The campy slashers were her favorite. I was never much of a fan but would watch them for the comedic value and to spend some time with her. The movies never got the amount of blood and gore right. They were never subtle and they liked to overdo it. This scene may have been straight out of a Jason movie. Blood was splattered across cabinets and appliances alike. So much that there could not have been much left in the bodies themselves. Someone or something enjoyed these kills.

There was also no way that these scenes would ever prepare you for the smells that came with it. They must have been in that kitchen for several days because the overpowering smell of death and decay hit me hard. I fell off the steps and regurgitated all of the precious water that I had just drank. As soon as my stomach would let me get back into a standing position, I went back to the water pump and tried to drown the images out of my brain and the smell out of my nose.

Hint—it didn't work.

I guess I then knew why no one was around or answering the door. I also knew I still needed food and a couple of containers to hold water. I decided that I would have to brave the outbuildings and hope that there was no more carnage and no killers lying in wait for their next victim. Great I started to act like my sister. I was jumping at my imagination.

Luck struck in the first building that I came across. I found, not only a country kitchen but one that held thermoses and lunch boxes. There was a jacket that just about fit me hanging on a coat rack and a bag slung over the back of a chair. I grabbed all of this and raided the cabinets for some food. The only things that were any good were some granola and protein bars. These were dry but would keep me alive for a while longer. I had never really liked granola but seeing the bars made my mouth water. I took several, opened them and scarfed them down as fast as the dry grain would allow. Sufficiently sated I headed back to the well to wash the remaining bits out of my mouth and throat. I filled a couple of thermoses and returned to the kitchen where I then loaded the rest of the bars into the bag.

I thought about leaving then. Hitting the road with my food and water and walking up to the nearest town for some help. I am glad that I did not listen to my first instinct because the prize behind door number two was almost as good as the food and water containers. In the second building, I found an old dirt bike. It was a 250cc bike with a kick start. That meant it did not matter if the battery was dead on the thing or not. I could get it started. Well, I could have if I had gas. I checked the tank and it was dry, but under a tarp tucked into the corner behind the bike were two gas cans, both of them full. If I could get this running I wouldn't have to walk the other 560 miles or so home.

I would like to tell you now that I got this thing started on the first kick and was on my way. Well, that didn't happen. It took me the rest of the day and into the night to get the thing to fire. Apparently, it had sat there for a while and had not been used. There was also the fact that I was not very mechanically inclined. I usually tended to run things from a keyboard. I worked with remotes and codes. Gears and spark plugs were not my thing. I did eventually get it running and got the hang of how to kick-start it without falling over and pinning myself under it.

That only happened once! And my foot slipped on the dirt.

By the time I got all of this under control, it was too dark to head out for the night. I decided to just stay in the outbuilding with the kitchen. There had been a small cot in the room that I could sleep on. I could also, eat some more food and get water from the pump to get me through the night. I would head out in the morning. It bothered me a bit that the back door to the house was open. Wild animals might get the smell and start feasting on the family during the night. I decided to go out there and close the door before that could happen.

I found a flashlight in one of the drawers and walked out to close the door. As I got there I could see the bodies again. I tried not to concentrate on them or the smell and reached in quickly to shut the door. One odd thing though was that I could have sworn there had been the remnants of three bodies in the house when I saw it earlier. I had only seen two this time, both of them decapitated. I guess I did not see it really well the first time and my imagination was playing tricks on me. Either way, I went back to the building at a very quick pace. No, I didn't run, ok maybe I did. But I then closed the door tight and locked it the best I could. This trip was starting to really freak me out.

Learning

Learning to ride a dirt bike for the first time with twenty pounds of stuff on your back is not the easiest thing in the world. Yes, I had never ridden a motorcycle before, especially a dirt bike, the opportunity never came up before. Did I mention that I preferred computers? After the first thirty minutes and no complete wipeouts, I felt like I had a handle on it and was ready to get on the interstate and ride north. It was scary getting up to speed, but I couldn't ride the rest of the way at 20 mph. What made it even scarier was that the first bit of the interstate that I had to ride over was a two-mile bridge. No pressure there right?

The twenty pounds on my back was food, water, a sleeping bag and gasoline. I used a couple of water containers for gas. I knew these things got decent gas mileage, but they had small tanks. I also grabbed a part of a hose and a knife out of the shed so I would be able to cut gas lines or siphon fuel out of abandoned vehicles along the way. Not usually my style, but desperate times call for desperate measures.

I had found an old dirt bike helmet in the back of the barn. I had been looking for anything usable late last night. I had trouble sleeping, just thinking about the days to come and the days past. The helmet, and the jacket I had found earlier, had been the only useful finds after the bike, food and water. Not quite as important, but for a novice like me, this may save me from some unwanted road rash or head trauma.

The loss of my Jeep was still weighing on me. This bike was a great find and stopped me from relying on others or walking the rest of the way home. But it was not as comfortable and it limited the load capacity, I could only carry what I could fit in my bag. The seat on this bike was small I had to keep the bag on my back, I couldn't even strap it to the seat. This changed my weight shift and caused my back to get sore very quickly.

Another issue with the bike was how to keep it safe. I think I was starting to learn how society was reacting to this pandemic. If I left the bike to use the bathroom, or sleep at night, someone could walk away with it. Even without the key, I was sure someone could get it started. Or just throw it in neutral and load it up. Even if I stayed with it all the time I couldn't see a way to keep it safe, I was not a fighter and if someone wanted to take it they could. There would be nothing I could do about it. I was still a ways away from the Delmarva Peninsula, let alone Millsboro. The fear of losing my ride again weighed on me. My mind was lost in this possibility for so long that I guess I zoned and only came to when the bike started sputtering. This caused a new fear to blossom in my soul. What was wrong with the bike, I had just gotten on the road and now this?

After pulling the bike off the side of the road, not sure why but it was just a habit. I pulled the gas cap to check the most obvious concern. The tank was empty. So nothing really wrong with it. Good. I poured the gas into the tank from the containers that I had on my back. It was only about a gallon total, so only half the tank. Luckily, I was just outside of a small town. I would have to go and see if they had fuel, if not I would have to resort to theft to get back on the road. I figured I still had about 400 miles to go, I couldn't get there on a half-tank.

I pulled into the area around the town. It looked deserted. I didn't see any cars moving on the road or people walking around. It was still early in the day, so I did not have to worry about night setting in on me, I decided to hide the bike just off the overpass and walk into town. I only needed about another gallon of gas at this point to fill the tank. I could carry that easily.

I stayed on the side streets and tried to not look suspicious. If I was starting to gauge society properly, suspicious activity may very well be met with gun violence. Shoot first ask no questions later type of vibe. I walked towards the first gas station and could see signs stating that they were out of gas and closed. I stopped and tried to get my bearings to see if there were any other gas stations nearby. That was when I saw a set of curtains close quickly. It was on the second story of a small house just off the road. The movement caught my eye, so it could have been the wind that moved it. I had not seen anyone in the window, but I figured there was someone there. I moved to another side street and started checking for abandoned vehicles along the street. I got the feeling that I needed to get out of this town sooner than later.

The next street I turned down had a bunch of cars on the side of the road. It didn't seem that anyone of them had been moved or touched long before the pandemic hit. Most had flat tires or were pulled into the yards of the homes. I hid beside a tree and watched the houses along the road for about 20 minutes. I did not see or hear any movement at all. I decided it would be safe to check a couple of the cars and siphon some gas out of one and get back on the road.

I quickly slid under the back of the first car I came to and tapped on the tank. Hollow. No gas there. Then the same with two, three and four. Finally, the fifth car seemed to have some gas in it. It was an old 50's Bel Air. It looked like it had been restored, maybe for car shows. My dad would be pissed if I cut the gas line on a vintage car like this, especially one that had been painstakingly restored, so I decided to use the hose and siphon some out.

I had seen this done in movies and understood the concept, but had never attempted it myself. I put the hose down into the tank and got a couple of bottles ready to put the gas in. I then put the hose in my mouth and sucked on the end to try and get the gas moving. The concept was easy, once flowing the gas would move from the tank into my containers as long as they were lower than the tank. Gravity and science at work.

What I did not count on though was not removing the hose from my mouth quickly enough and getting a mouthful of gasoline. It hit me so quickly that I think I swallowed some. I was cognitive enough to put the hose in a container before I started coughing uncontrollably. The coughing was racking my chest so bad that I lost my lunch, or was it breakfast? Both had been granola bars so it really did not matter. I stopped paying attention long enough for the gas to overflow my container. By the time I realized and started to put another container under the hose someone spoke behind me.

"I would stop what you are doing boy."

I quickly shifted the hoe to the other container before I turned around and saw a large man with a very large caliber pistol pointed directly at me.

"I, I am sorry. I just need some gas to get home." I stammered

"So stealing is the way to go. Looks to me like you ain't too good at it as you caused all the commotion of coughing and puking up the gas that you swallowed." He stated.

"First time actually. I am not really sure what I am doing. Is this your car? I could pay you for the gas."

"Ain't my car, but I cain't stand a thief. Figured you may try to steal more around here too."

"I just need some fuel and I'll be on my way. I am trying to get north and my bike ran out of gas. I can only carry so much at a time and no gas stations are operating." I pleaded.

"True, we been outta gas for a while now." He said as he lowered the gun.

By this time the next container was overflowing. I pulled the hose out of the tank and laid it on the ground. I was still too scared to stand up. I noticed that some of the gas had dripped on the paint below the gas cap on the car. I pulled my shirt up and wiped the car down. It was dusty but I did not want to ruin the paint by letting the gas sit on it. Again, old habits.

"I don't want any trouble and I am not here to cause any. I just ran out of gas and needed some. I am sorry for the theft." I pleaded with the guy as I tried to tuck my shirt back in without standing.

"You seem to be sincere. Plus it seems you really care about other peoples property. You could have just cut the gas line and did not have to wipe off that drip. So I'll do this. You get your stuff together there and walk directly back out of town the way you came. But stay to the middle of the streets this time. I have been watching you since the gas station. You aren't very sneaky. And tellin' the truth, if you were any good at this you would be doin' it at night. You need to be more careful or you be endin' up shot before you knows what was happenin'" He put the gun away and opened his stance so I could get by him.

"I had the same thought earlier. I am sorry, it was just a necessity. I'll be on my way." I apologized.

"See that you is."

I packed up as quickly as I could under the stern gaze of the mountain, which was a man, at my shoulder. Put my pack on my back and walked down the middle of the streets back to the overpass. I looked back several times but never saw the man again. I did see several people looking out of their windows, but none approached or left their homes. Society was definitely not the same as it was just a couple of weeks ago. There seemed to be a mistrust of others now, more so than before. There was still power here and yet people still cowered in their homes, not trusting their neighbors and especially not trusting outsiders.

The trek out was much quicker than the trek in. There was no sneaking and honestly, the fear of that man and his pistol made me walk a lot faster. I never had a gun pointed at me before. I hoped to never have one pointed at me again. I had shotguns and liked pistols, but being on the barrel end made you feel a little different.

I got to the bike, luckily it was still there, and gassed it up. I was hoping to get a little more and keep a couple of bottles in my bag, but I got enough to fill the tank and get on the road without getting shot. It was a win in my book.

I kick-started the bike and got back on the road. From what I could see there was nothing in my path for miles. I powered on my phone and checked my GPS to see just how far I still had to go. It was enough that I would have to risk fueling up again at least once more before I even reached the peninsula. I checked the internet, just to see, but it only showed the oops something went wrong symbol. I powered my phone off and stored it back in the bag.

I was feeling a lot more comfortable now and poured on the speed. I wanted to get home more than I had before. I needed to get off these roads before something bad happened to me. A couple of more hours and it would be getting dark. I would need to get more gas before then. Hopefully, I could find an open gas station or some cars left on the interstate. Something that would let me avoid a situation like the last. It may not go the same way twice.

Surprise

A couple of hours later, I stopped on the interstate to grab a bite to eat. I had been trying to keep my rationing low so I could conserve what food and water I had for as long as I could. Another disadvantage of riding a bike instead of my Liberty. I could not eat while driving. I am sure there were people out there that could, but I was not even trying that. My water supply was depleting. I would have to find someplace in the next day to replenish. I used what I had for now and worried about later when it came around. I tried not to worry about things that I could not control.

I had been able to stop about 30 minutes before and grab some more gas out of an abandoned car on the interstate. I had not passed many, but it still had some gas and was a safer bet than going into a town. As I ate I poured some of the gas into my tank. I was keeping it topped off as much as I could every time I stopped for something. No point in running it dry again.

I had been traveling for about two hours since the last little town. I figured I had put another 120 miles behind me. I was on the home stretch. I also figured that in about another hour I would have to start looking for a place to sleep for the night. It was starting to get really cold at night. With the loss of my blankets and other gear, I needed to find somewhere sheltered from the weather. The jacket and sleeping bag made it a little better even though the bag was a summer bag. I needed to find an abandoned farmhouse or something like it. Preferably one that did not have dead bodies decomposing in the kitchen this time. I still say there were originally three bodies when I first looked in.

As I thought about this I walked around and started looking down the embankments and surrounding areas. Walking felt good. Being on the bike all day was starting to hurt. I was nervous most of the time so I could not really relax like I could in my truck. I was just taking in the scenery when to my surprise on the side of the embankment about a mile or so away I saw a vehicle over the embankment. It appeared to be a Jeep Liberty. It was my Jeep Liberty too!

I know what most people would say, there was no way to tell from that distance if it was mine or not. I could tell it was mine though for a couple of reasons. One, it was an odd brown color that was not very popular. Two, the rear quarter panel was painted red, I had to have it replaced after a small accident with a concrete piling, long story. It was hard to tell if that quarter panel was red from where I was because it was sitting in high grass, but I thought that it was. What would be the odds of another Liberty having the same colors and quarter panel replacement? For that matter what were the odds that I would come across my stolen truck 200 miles down the road?

I quickly stuffed the rest of the food in my mouth and got the bike started. I pulled up along the road above the embankment where I thought that I saw my truck. I did not want to walk away from the bike, so I just turned it off and walked it to the side of the road. From here I could tell that it was mine. The panel was red and my star wars sticker *Come to the Dark Side, we have cookies* sticker was on the window.

The truck had seen better days. These thieves really did not take care of it too well. It had apparently rolled down the embankment, the roof and sides were dented. It had landed on its wheels though. It also looked like all of the windows were intact so it might still have been drivable.

I made the quick decision to backtrack a bit. I had seen an access road back a little ways that would allow me to get down to the embankment's bottom level. This would allow me to ride through the grass and come up on the Liberty from the same level. When I got near the truck, I rode out wide to see if anyone was near it. I pulled about 20 feet in front of the truck before I stopped and got off. Close enough to get back quickly and close enough to keep an eye on it. Far enough that I should not be surprised if someone was in the area.

As I walked up on the Liberty I could see that it had been through more than just a roll down the embankment. The front windshield had bullet holes in it. The same with the front grill and hood. These guys were definitely driving at someone that was shooting at them. The next thing I saw was probably the two car thieves. They were both in the front seats of the car. The driver was not moving, he appeared to have been shot in the face and throat multiple times. The passenger though seemed to have only been wounded. He was moving and thrashing around but didn't seem able to get out of his seat belt or open the door.

I called out to him to see if he was ok, but he just kept moving around. I walked up to the passenger window to check on him. His eyes were blue and the look on his face was one of pure pleasure, like someone eating a sandwich after starving all day. Was this another guy that had overdosed on Blue Lightning? This stuff seemed to be everywhere.

I decided that if he was high there was no real helping him, besides he had not cared about stranding me in the middle of nowhere. I just went to the back of the truck and opened the hatch. Luckily it could still open, although not very easily. I asked the guy again if he was ok, but he seemed to be ignoring me now.

The guys had not touched most of my stuff, so I grabbed a few things that I needed and walked back to the bike. I felt kind of bad about leaving the guy there, but he was the druggy. I was more worried about whoever had been shooting at them. The car engine seemed to be cold so hopefully whoever it was had left a while ago. But maybe I needed to find a different route.

I rolled up my blankets and tied them to the back of the bike and put what food and water I grabbed in my bag. I pulled up my phone for a second to see if maybe there was an alternate route I could take from there without heading into a town. A quick look showed that I really could not without backtracking and going along a very windy route. I could not do this without getting lost as my battery was very low and I could not read the GPS while riding the bike. I decided to risk staying on the interstate and started the bike.

There seemed to be no access back to the road from where I was, so I backtracked again. As I got back on the highway I stopped and looked around. There was an overpass just past where the Liberty had stopped. If they had been driving down this road the shots may have come from there. I had not seen anyone when I was here the first time. Maybe they moved on. I decided to take the risk and started back up the highway, heading home.

The first shot rang out about thirty seconds later and ricocheted off the pavement to my left. Shit! I hit the accelerator on the bike. I hit it a little too hard and lifted the front tire off the ground. I was not this good yet, so I let off the gas and it slammed back to the ground. This caused me to swerve and almost go over the handlebars, which probably saved my life as the next shot hit the pavement directly behind me after I heard it whizz by my head.

The shots had to be coming from the overpass up ahead. They had not been there or had not shot at me when I had stopped next to the Liberty the first time. Why were they shooting now? Maybe they had not heard me coming the first time? Well, they knew I was there now. If I could get there without getting shot I may have a chance to get past them. I was not sure what they wanted. There was no town or anything to protect anywhere near this location. It seemed they were just taking potshots at anyone that happened by. Another breakdown in society I guess. No police force to come to stop them, no court systems currently running to convict them and no correctional facilities to put them in. Even during the height of our society, we had psychos that would do this type of thing, the Washington sniper comes immediately to mind. The lack of everything just made it easier so more could allow these feelings to dictate their behavior.

The only choice I saw was to hammer the gas, easier this time, get up to a high rate of speed and weave along the road the best I could. As I got closer I would be an easier target, but hopefully between the angle increasing and the speed they would not be able to get a clean shot on me.

This idea worked, mostly. As I was getting within feet of the overpass a bullet hit the pavement to my left, as I was weaving in that direction. I could not correct the other way without wrecking the bike. I was already going way faster than I should have been going with my lack of experience. The bullet hit me in the left calf. Luckily it did not hit my shin and I think it lost some speed as it ricocheted off the ground. The pain was not bad at first, I just felt the impact. Then a couple of seconds later I was under the overpass and hit the brakes to get stopped before I exited the other side. I think this kept my mind off the pain.

I remember thinking, this isn't so bad. The movies really made this out to be worse. As I stopped I put my feet down to steady the bike and the searing heat and pain hit me. It was so bad that the bike fell over and almost caught me underneath it. I knew that I needed to stand it up again, but I could not get my body to respond. A couple of minutes passed and I got the pain under control. I reached into my bag and grabbed an old shirt to wrap around my leg. I had no idea if the bullet was still in it or if it was a through-and-through shot. Every time I went to look at it a wave of nausea would wash over me and almost cause me to pass out. I decided to let it go and just wrap it to stop the bleeding. I thought about the fact that I had a true first aid kit in the back of the Liberty. I had not grabbed it to save room in my bag for food and water. I was not going to go back for it now though.

Two thoughts weighed on my mind. Who was on the overpass and would they leave it to come to finish me off? They obviously knew where I was and that I did not suddenly disappear. They probably didn't know I was hit though, that would work in my favor. They also had not left to finish off the passenger in the Liberty, but since he never got out of the truck the shooter may not know he was alive. I did not have a weapon of any kind. Without my truck, I did not even have a tire iron. Guess I should have grabbed that. On the plus side, I did have a working bike that somehow came out of a shooting unscathed, unlike me of course.

I had about fifteen minutes before it was completely dark. The interstate was wide open from the overpass as far as I could see. I figured if they did not come at me before then, I could shoot off at full speed. It would be harder to get a bead on me in the dark. It was not the best plan and it still figured on them not coming down off their perch before then. I tried to stay off my leg, but I was able to get up long enough to get the bike righted and on its kickstand. I then moved all of my food and water to the back of the bike and tied it down the best that I could on the small seat. I put anything heavy and hard in my bag on my back to help protect me if a shot did find me. I had grabbed a couple of books and electronics from my Liberty. Anything would help.

I also noticed that the guard rail did not extend fully under the overpass. If I walked my bike over to the southbound lane and shot off from there, it may confuse them long enough for me to gain some distance. Unfortunately, it was only a two-lane overpass so the shooter would easily be able to get to the northbound side to get a shot at my back.

The time passed slowly, but sooner than I thought night came. I waited past dusk for full night. The temperatures were starting to cool, or I was losing more blood than I thought. I had not seen or heard anything from above me. I moved the bike over to the southbound lane and got on prepared to start it up.

It took me two tries to get it started because I had to use my left leg and I could not get enough push through the pain on the first kick. Once it was started I revved the engine up a couple of times to echo under the overpass. I knew that I could not hide the start-up of the bike from them, but I hoped this would confuse the sounds and not let them know where I had moved. I closed my eyes and counted to three, released the clutch as I hit the gas. I shot out into the night as fast as I could accelerate. The front wheel came up a little again, but I kept my cool and let the acceleration take it and set the wheel down easily. I had never driven like this and I was actually enjoying the speed as I cleared the concrete pillars of the overpass and shot into the night.

My predator had not left as I had hoped. As soon as I cleared the pillars I heard a shot ring out. The shot came from my right so I must have confused them by moving to the other lane. They were not set for me. The second shot made impact with my bag. I felt it kick to the left as I swerved in that same direction. This threw off my balance a bit but I was able to keep moving.

I poured on the speed and shot through the gears like I was racing for my life, which I literally was. A minute later I realized that had been the last shot that I had heard. They must have lost me or figured I was leaving their area and conserved ammunition. Even with this realization, I kept the speed on for another ten minutes.

I stopped and let myself breathe for a second and catch my breath. I got off the bike and went to my knee. Adrenalin was leaving my system and I was crashing from the rush. I had never had to go through anything like that before. I pulled off my bag and reached in to see what was hit. I pulled out my phone to turn on the flashlight and realized that it had taken a hit directly to the middle of the screen. It was useless to me. I thought about it for a second then tossed it to the ground. No use bringing it with me any further. I was never really attached to it too much anyway. It was just a way to connect to the world and listen to music. The internet was down and the battery was almost dead. I grabbed a car charger, but I did not have anywhere on the bike to charge it.

I dug into my bag a little further and almost began to cry. The bullet that had destroyed my phone had also destroyed my laptop. I had just gotten it back from the back of the Liberty and it was now destroyed. All of my work and research had been on my computer. My work from school and all of my art was stored there too. It was what I used to game and connect to the virtual world, which to me was more important than the real one. As I opened the top I could see that the bullet was still lodged in the keyboard. It most likely hit the solid-state hard drive and stopped. This meant that the memory was shot and could not be recovered. I dropped it on the ground alongside my phone. One tear may or may not have dropped to the pavement alongside it too, I will never tell.

I figured I was just a couple of hours outside of Delmarva by this point. I needed more than anything to get home. I was hurt and I didn't have any medical supplies with me. I had probably lived through the worst experience of my life up to this point. I was swirling out of control emotionally and I needed to get home. If I drove through the night instead of stopping I might be able to make it tonight, as long as I found the fuel that I needed.

I used what little gas I had in my reserve tanks on the bike to fill up the tank. Luckily they had not been hit when my bag was shot. I would most likely still need to stop one more time before the bay bridge tunnel and then again on the shore, but these should be easy stops. I would most likely pass a few cars between here and there. I hoped my leg didn't get worse and make me stop.

I got my resolve all set and got back on the bike to head home. My leg hurt like hell but getting home and having people there to help would make a big difference. A couple of more hours, then I would be fine.

Delirium

An hour into the ride I had to stop and change the bandage on my leg because it was bleeding through. I knew a little about first aid and surmised that the bullet must still be in my leg if it kept bleeding like that. Every time I moved my leg to shift or stop, the bullet was tearing the wound open again.

I thought about stopping and trying to remove the bullet. If it was too deep or if I pushed in it further I would be in worse shape. I also had the problem of almost passing out every time I looked at it or tried to see into the wound. I needed to carry on and get home as quickly as I could. Someone there should be able to patch me up.

An hour after I got back on the road my bike started getting low on fuel. I had not seen any cars on the road in the last hundred miles. At least I didn't think I had. My mind was starting to wander a bit. I was losing focus and driving all over the road. I needed to stop and rest as much as I needed to get off the road near a town and siphon some gas.

I started looking for signs for the next large town. That is when I realized that I had missed all of my turns for the bay bridge tunnel. I was coming up to Richmond, VA. I had to turn off fifty miles back to get to the exits for Virginia Beach and the bay bridge tunnel. A hundred miles is a huge detour. Damn, I should have been paying better attention. I was too used to my GPS telling me where to turn. I must really be losing it. There was no way I should have missed the signs to the tunnel. This detour would take me at least two more hours and another tank of gas to get home. The other problem was having to go through Washington D.C. Before the news cut off and I lost my phone I had heard stories from D.C. that were not good. Something about corpses walking about and killing people. It seemed like some Night of the Living Dead bullshit, but after what I had seen already on the road, I figured that even if a little bit of it was true I would be in danger.

On the plus side, it seemed like a lot of Richmond had working lights. I saw a low glow on the horizon as I started to get close. Maybe I could get some medical attention there instead of waiting. As I exited the interstate I saw nothing but total chaos. There were cars abandoned everywhere. Windows were broken out of every building. Bodies were laying dead in the streets. I slowed my bike and stopped near one of the abandoned cars. I figured that some of them had to still have gas in them. I was not sure what happened to cause this type of destruction. My best bet was to get gas fast and get out of there. I could wait a little longer to get someone to look at my leg.

I hid my bike behind the car and crawled underneath to cut the gas line. It would have been faster and easier to do than siphon. Except that I forgot about my leg and I could not push myself under the car very well. After some finagling and some cussing, I made it under the car and cut the line. The car had a full tank of gas. I filled both of the tanks I had on me quickly. I then kinked the line and rolled out from under the car. I limped back to the bike and filled the tank. I was just turning to go back to the car and fill my reserves once again when a figure appeared out of nowhere.

It was a tall man, over six feet tall. He was wearing clothing that looked like fatigues and a mask over his face. He seemed to be looking for something. He was walking slowly and looking around and below the cars. He must have come down the street and I failed to notice him while I was working on getting the fuel. He was too close for me to make a run for it, I would never get my bike started and get away before he noticed me. I decided to hunker down near my bike and hope he found what he was looking for before he came across me.

As I had that thought his words rang out.

"Boy, I saw you out here. You can not really hide the sound of that motorcycle in the silence." He said

I waited in silence, now scared to death as he was looking for me.

"Come on out. I am not going to hurt you., Quite the opposite. You looked hurt. I was up in that building over there." He pointed to a building with lights on down the street a ways.

"It is a clinic, I am a nurse. I know the hospitals have all stopped taking patients. So I opened my apartment to people that are hurt. The ones that don't have the illness. There are more people there and a couple of EMT's that help me. The fire station and ambulance teams have shut down. Trying to contain the spread of this virus. What ever it is. So they decided to help me. We all know there are a lot of people that refuse to leave their houses but are hurt or sick. We can't help all of them as they refuse to open their doors or ask for help. But when I heard your bike I looked down and saw you limping. We can help you."

I am not sure what it was, but this man's voice held sympathy and empathy for my pain. He felt real and sincere. I stood up and looked towards him. He must have sensed the movement because he turned towards me as soon as I stood up.

"There you are. What is wrong with you? What can we do to help?" He asked

"I got shot. I think the bullet is still in my leg. I can't stop the bleeding." I said as I pointed to the bandage around my left leg.

"Well we can help with that. Come over here, let me help you. I can help you walk to my place. Your bike will be safe where it is. We can come back and get it after we see what we can do to treat your leg."

He stooped down and helped me push my bike down the road into a parking garage. I went with him to his apartment. The stairs were not fun with my leg, but he let me lean on him which helped a lot. The apartment was set up like a doctor's office. There were chairs and people in them wearing masks. Some were helping people with burns and cuts. Others were wrapping wrists and legs for broken bones.

The nurse took me to the back of the apartment. He had a surgical table set up.

"This is Doctor Stephen. He is a surgeon. He comes here and helps us on his off time from the hospital. He can look at your leg and then we can get you all stitched up." The nurse told me as he started to put on rubber gloves to remove my bandage.

The doctor looked familiar to me, but I could not place it. I jumped up on the table and laid down so they could look at my leg. This whole thing was incredible. Not only was I found by a nurse who ran a clinic out of his apartment. I was here when a real surgeon was here for them to operate on my leg and get the bullet out. All the time I had been on the road I had not had any help or seen anyone that was not trying to steal from me or hurt me. Like the nurse had said before, most people stayed in their homes and refused to have contact with the outside world.

The doctor then put a mask over my mouth and told me to breathe in. It smelled like gasoline, which seemed weird. The smell made me groggy and I started to fall asleep. As my eyes started to close I could swear I saw a cape appear on the shoulders of Doctor Stephen. Then black.

I have no idea how long I was unconscious, but I was rudely awoken by someone shaking me. I was back on the road and the sun was in my eyes. All I could see was a silhouette of the person trying to wake me up.

"Who are you? Where is Doctor Stephen? Why am I back outside?"

"Look man I don't know what you were dreaming, but I was walking by and I found you laying half under this car with gasoline dripping down into the can next to you. You trying to steal our gas from around here? Anyways I tried to get your attention and you would not wake up. You said something about a doctor and a cape. That's when I tried to wake you up. I been shaking you for five minutes."

"No that's not right I was taken to an apartment by a nurse and Doctor Stephen worked on my leg to get the bullet out."

"Look man your leg is soaked with blood and there aren't any nurses or doctors around here any more. They all left and got out of the city. You must have been dreaming."

That's when it hit me who the doctor looked like. He looked likc Doctor Stephen Strange. A real doctor turned master of the mystic arts in the comic book named after him. That's why the mask smelled like gasoline. I must have passed out under the car while pulling the gas.

I sat up quickly and looked for my bike. The guy that woke me up jumped back just as quickly. I stood up too quickly and almost fell back to the ground. My head was swimming and I couldn't see straight for a couple of seconds.

After that cleared I could see my bike where I had left it. The guy looked at me and said. "You sick or something? Do you have that living dead virus thing? Man, I was just trying to see if you were dead. I am outta here"

He ran down the street and away from me as fast as it seemed he could go. That was more on course for what I had seen of people this last week. As he ran away I took stock of my situation. My hair, jacket and shirt were soaked with gasoline. I would never get this smell out of any of them. I looked for the apartment of my dream. I could see the building and the window that I had dreamt of was my saving grace. There did not seem to be anyone there, nor any lights on at this time of the morning.

Morning. It was morning, I had lost the whole night under that car. Not much to be done about it, but to finish my task and get back on the road. I was still wobbly on my feet, but I made it back to my bike. I checked my leg and found that it had at least stopped bleeding, although it hurt worse than it had before. It was red and swollen, not looking good at all. I was probably getting an infection from it too.

I looked in the tank and found that I had filled the first tank and the tank on the bike. I must have fallen asleep on the second round. Good, at least it was done. I raised my leg to get on the bike and about fell to the ground.

I was light-headed again and my other leg felt weak beneath me. The smell of gasoline was settling in my nose and making it hard to breathe. I finally settled on the bike and was able to get my senses back. Riding was going to be dangerous if that kept up. When I tried to kick-start the bike I am pretty sure I passed out again for a split second, But the engine caught and I was on my way.

Richmond was only a four-hour drive from home. The good night's delirium sleep may have helped heal me a bit, but it left me foggy and distracted. I needed to keep my speed low so I could keep my attention focused. That would add to the time, there was no help for it. I knew that Rt 95 ran along the James River. I figured once I got close I would stop and wash my hair and jacket. I had one more shirt in my bag so I would just throw this one away. It would take some time and time was one thing that I seemed to be running out of. Besides the fact that the bullet in my leg was slowly killing me, I had very little water and food left in my bag. I had the sneaking suspicion that the guy that woke me up helped with those deficiencies. I needed to get home and get help but I had to clean up a bit first. It probably wouldn't hurt to clean the blood off my leg too.

It was not very long before I could see the river next to the road. I pulled off and stripped down to my boxers. My leg looked worse but there was nothing I could do about it. I took a couple of minutes to try to clean up the best I could with no shampoo or soap. I then dripped dry as best I could and got dressed and got back on the road. One plus of a fallen society was that you could do pretty much whatever you wanted whenever. No one was really going to stop you.

The water seemed to help clear my head and got most of the gas smell out of my hair. I still had to stop a couple of times over the next hour when my head would get heavy or my vision would get dim. I tried to eat, but my stomach was not liking that very much. I had trouble breathing and my heart rate kept jumping through the roof. I knew I was in bad shape, but I had to keep going. Washington, D.C. was just around the next bend. I had to hope that there were no people there and I could just get through. If that occurred I could get across the bridge and get home.

Thirty minutes later I knew that my time had just run out.

Washington

This city was named after one of my oldest ancestors, President George Washington. Not all Washingtons are related to one of the greatest men that helped form our country. My family is. We had some genealogy classes in high school and with the help of some websites and other resources, I found that we were direct descendants of our first president. Does not mean much in the end, but a cool fact otherwise.

As I turned off the 95 interstate onto the 495 to head East to the Bay Bridge, I ran straight into military barricades. All traffic was stopped. Luckily I had a bike instead of the Liberty, one advantage, so I could go through the middle and down the shoulders. It looked like this had happened a little while ago because there was no one in any of the cars that I was passing. The barricade up ahead was manned though, unlike the ones before. I slowly worked through the traffic jam and up to the barricade.

"No one gets through." Some military guy yelled at me as he saw me approaching.

"I need to get through I have to get back to the peninsula." I yelled back.

"No one is able to get across the National Harbor Bridge. Head back home. You should not be out."

"I am trying to get home. I have to go that way.Please I am hurt and need medical attention" I kept creeping closer as I spoke to him.

"Turn around and head home. We will not tell you again." The soldier moved into a balanced shooting stance and raised his weapon toward me.

I stopped but I was close enough to see that the guy was in a low-level hazmat suit. There were several other military personnel along the barricade that were also in hazmat suits. I decided that it would be prudent to turn around and find another way. This would have been a good time for GPS.

When I got back to the intersection I decided to head north toward the city. It did not seem to be barricaded off yet, so I might be able to find a way around the city and across to the bay bridge from the north side. I tried to remember how everything was laid out, but I was having a lot of trouble focusing and remembering where the roads went. Hopefully, there would be signs to follow. The Delaware beaches were a huge travel destination for the people on this side of the bridge.

The next thing I knew I was crossing the bridge over the Potomac River, which lead directly to downtown D.C. As I crossed the bridge all I could see were waves of people. There were so many people that it seemed that no one in the tri-state area was listening to the stay-at-home orders.

As I slowly drove through the crowds I could see barriers between groups of people. All of them were protesting something. Most were at odds with each other. One side of the road was wearing homemade hazmat suits and masks and screaming for protection, while the other side was running shirtless, mask-less and asking for freedom. Some for the lifting of the stay-at-home order and others ranting about too much government control in general.

I guess people had lost faith in the government in general if they ever really had any to begin with. Their handling of the pandemic was covered by the news media with reckless abandon. Every media outlet had been second-guessing every decision politicians made. Each side liking or disliking a decision depending on their beliefs. Then you had the trolls and hotbed groups on social media stirring the pot even more. I had been mostly ignoring all of the debates, but when you're on social media some of it is bound to leak through.

I felt that people just needed to let the politicians act like the elected officials that they were and let them make the decisions that needed to be made. We elected them and they had to have more knowledge of worldwide events than we did. There were reasons they did what they did.

Although there were a lot of people in the area, the roads were mostly clear. The military was using the roads as barriers between groups. I got off the main road and tried to remember how to cut through the city. Once off the main roads, there were fewer people trying to be seen. I did however see a massive beatdown of one individual. He happened to be wearing a mask, as per the order, and a group of people seemed to take a dislike to that. I did not stay to help, I did not want to get involved in negative situations of others. I felt bad, but there was nothing I could really do.

Two times after that, I had groups of people rush into the road to try and stop me from driving through. I have no idea what they were yelling at me. I was not able to focus well. I was barely able to see the next group when they had a large biker-looking fellow rush me and try to knock me off my bike. I decided that I needed to get out of this town quickly. I think that they either wanted me off the streets or wanted my bike. I knew that if I stopped or was knocked down, I would never get back up or possibly even survive the altercation. I decided that the speed limit meant nothing any longer. I was getting worse, I felt my strength waning and my focus disappearing.

After what felt like forever, really only about a mile, I was in front of the Capitol building. What I saw there was even worse than anything I had seen before. The area in front of and the grounds around the building were barricaded off and covered in blood stains. There seemed to have been some kind of massacre. Bodies lay in the streets and the grounds. Obviously, there had been some kind of fight that the first responders tried to quell. I saw cops, firefighters, EMTs and civilians in different levels of dismemberment.

Somehow there were a few that were still moving. One lady, in particular, was missing the lower half of her body but continued to drag herself across the street toward me. Her eyes had a blue glow to them. There was no way any drug could keep a person moving after that much damage. I had heard that LSD and other hard drugs when combined with adrenalin could keep people from feeling any pain and let them keep moving long after they should be dead. I always thought they were urban myths. Even then this is a whole new level of messed up. Maybe there were some truths to the pod-casts of reanimated corpses. This lady sure looked like she should be dead.

I lost track of time as I watched her drag herself towards me. The only thing that I remembered seeing in the next moments was an odd expression that worked across her face. It looked like she was listening to something I could not hear. She stopped moving, which broke my concentration on her and allowed me to see another guy attacking me from the right side. All I could do was lean over to the left, which put all my weight on my left calf. This caused searing pain to drop me to the ground under the weight of the bike.

I tried to lift it, but could not get enough strength to move it. The bike was not that heavy but the pain in my leg was taking away all of my strength. I was trapped, but the move allowed the attacker to fly over the top of me. He looked confused for a second as he got up off of the ground until his eyes focused on me again. His eyes were also glowing blue, they seemed to have no pupil or color. They looked almost like a seer in my fantasy comics. One thing I could tell was that they were filled with nothing but anger. That was the only word that could describe the look that this man gave me. He looked at the half-woman lying on the road, still inching towards me and something passed between them.

A terrifying scream then broke the air. Both of the people stopped looking at me and looked off into the area of the scream. From behind an overturned ambulance came a large hulking man. He would have made Arnold's terminator look small. As his eyes looked in my direction, I could tell this was the man in charge. He walked slowly over to me, while the other two watched him, picked up my bike and tossed it to the side like a toy. I knew that I was going to die. There were three of them, I was barely holding onto consciousness and was way too weak to put up even the smallest of fights. I basically lay on the ground while this bchcmoth towered over me and waited to die. No life flashing before my eyes, no real fear, just acceptance.

The large man with glowing blue eyes slowly knelt on the ground before me and put a hand, almost lovingly, on my face. I felt nothing at first but could see he was enjoying the touch. A little weird, but hey whatever man, just finish this quickly I did not want to suffer.

Just as something felt weird and I was starting to blackout, a shot rang out and hot liquid splashed over my face and chest. That was just seconds before the now headless body of the behemoth landed next to me. Time stopped and seconds seemed to slowly tick by before all hell broke loose.

The half-woman and the would-be tackler suddenly screamed and lost their minds. More shots rang out for a couple of seconds before another set of screams came from the other side of the street. I watched two or three different rounds rip into the tackler's chest with very little effect. In truth, it only seemed to make him madder. I watched him almost smile as the shots stopped and the other screams started. It was like he was looking for a fight.

Five people in ragged and bloodstained fatigues ran out from a building across the street, weapons drawn and fierce looks upon their faces. The tackler and the half-woman seemed to sense their intentions and called out in a high-pitched scream that hurt my ears.

As the fighters were fifty to sixty yards away from me, I saw four other people run from behind the overturned ambulance. Then five more. The fighters slowed a little as fear crept upon them. Then a shot rang out again. It seemed that they had left one person in a sniper position. In quick succession, two more of the tackler's friends went down into heaps on the ground. Both missing their heads.

This emboldened the fighters again and they quickly closed the gap and stood between me and my attackers. The fighters looked like they had been through hell already. They must have been there when the initial attacks happened. They looked tired but determined. I could tell that they were military of some sort by their gear and their formations. They worked together as a unit. You can only do that if you train and fight together a lot.

I was trying to get up and find my bike. My head was swimming more than it was before, but I knew that these fighters, although brave, would not be able to hold off the attackers forever. They would eventually fall or run like most people due when the odds are against them. I had trouble standing and my focus was completely gone. I only found my bike because I tripped over it and fell to the ground. The only thoughts in my head were to get away from this fight and ask the question. Why had these people stood up for me? I was nothing to them.

The attackers would win and come after me again. I was hurt, my mind was filled with cotton and I could not think. I needed to leave while all of the others were distracted. As I got the bike up and sat down I could tell that one handlebar was slightly bent from where it had hit the ground. There was nothing I could do about it now. I had to take a second to gather myself again before I was able to push myself to try to start it.

As I did I looked at the chaos all around me. One of the fighters was a tall black female. She lead the team, it seemed. She was ordering others on movements and where to help each other out, all while fighting tooth and nail herself. She carried a metal bat with her that she wielded like a samurai sword. Smooth effortless motions from one attack to the next. It was like I was watching her dance in the middle of the battlefield. She looked at me quizzically as I sat on my bike. Then when I started my bike it became a look of disappointment. She knew that I was not going to help her and her fighters. I was leaving them to their own destiny and fates. I do not know why they risked their lives to help me, but I was not going to make the mistake of returning the favor. I was not a fighter. If I joined them to help, I would not only die myself and I would most likely get some of them killed in the process.

I could almost feel the anger and resentment pouring off of her into my back as I put the bike into gear and rode away. I do not know why, but I felt bad disappointing this woman. I had never met her before and would probably never see her again, but I felt bad for leaving her and her team as I did. There was nothing that could have been done at that point though, so I pointed my bike east and drove as fast as I could away from the chaos.

I did not make it far, however, only about half a mile before tiredness came over me that I had never felt before. I guess the adrenalin was wearing off and I was crashing hard. Now, when I say that I did not mean figuratively crashing from the sudden drop in blood pressure. I mean that I literally crashed hard into a copse of trees. I do not remember ever seeing a forest in the middle of downtown Washington D.C. But, there it was and I did not have enough sense to brake or turn. All I could do was lay the bike down on my right side to protect the hurt leg and hope I did not die.

I do not remember any impact. I just remember seeing fallen leaves and branches all around me as I passed out again.

Days

The next thing I knew I was waking up beside my poor bike. I was sore everywhere and very very thirsty. I looked at my watch. It was an old analog watch that my father had given me, it showed the date along with the time. Well, it did before, but the battery must have died because it was not working. Because of this, I did not know how long I had laid there, unconscious. With the way things had been progressing throughout the D.C. downtown area, I hoped that it had not been that long.

The facts told me otherwise though. For one, my head was clearer than it had been in the last couple of days. Especially clearer since the behemoth had touched me. Then there was the fact that my leg did not hurt as much, it seemed to be in the process of healing. I landed with my left leg above me and on top of the bike, elevating it. When I moved I was stiff like I had been in one position too long, but when I went to stand I could put more pressure on my leg. The thirst that I was feeling also made me believe that I had been laying here for days. I was thirstier than when I walked for almost two days without water.

I assessed my condition and the condition of my bike as I pulled a water bottle out of my bag and drained it. For me, the helmet and the rider's jacket protected me from most of the damage. My right leg was scraped up, but not too bad. The bike had some small damage. One handle was bent, the side that I had hit on. It was unfortunately the same side it had landed on when the behemoth threw it off of me so the bend was a bit worse. But besides a few scratches to the tank and body, everything else seemed to be in working order.

As I put the empty water bottle back in my bag, I thought about drinking another. I was still very thirsty, but I figured that I needed to moderate my drinking for two reasons. One, so I did not get sick, I needed my body to adjust to the new intake of water. Then two, I needed to assess the situation outside of my safe zone. I may need to make the water stretch.

Since I had assessed my bike and my body I now had to assess my situation. I was down under a large set of trees. I was still on the road so my guess would be that the tree had fallen for some reason and covered most of the road. The branches and leaves were thick, especially for fall. This is most likely what kept me hidden from the view of anyone passing by. I would need to see what the rest of D.C. was like before I ran off toward home.Before I pulled my bike out of the brush, I decided to take a look around on foot first. I slowly poked my head out of the bush and looked around. The first thing I noticed was the quiet. It seemed to be around midday but I could not hear the protesters or military personnel yelling. No bullhorns, no military vehicles driving around. Nothing.

It was only about a half mile back to the area where I was attacked. Maybe I could find someone there to help me again. Although, they probably would not be really happy to see me. If not maybe there would be some clue as to how long I was out.

I tested my leg out with a slow walk at first. It was tight but seemed to hold my weight just fine. I pumped it up to a regular walk and then a fast-paced walk. My leg seemed to be ok, but I was getting out of breath. It was just a couple of weeks ago that I was running 5ks and now I couldn't keep up with Grandma walking the mall. The half a mile might take longer than expected.

Once there I stayed out of sight and assessed the scene as I caught my breath. I would really need to get back to training once I got home. Once I could hear over my own breathing again, I found the same situation as before, yet perfectly quiet. The scene had only changed slightly in the days that I was gone. Some bodies still lay along the grounds. Thankfully none of them were moving this time. I also did not see bodies wearing ripped and worn fatigues. This could mean that they all survived, or that their bodies were taken with the survivors. I would probably never know for sure. I hoped it was the former.

As I stood there thinking about this, I started thinking about the creatures that had attacked me. They had communicated in some way with each other. A way outside of the screams that they made. They did not act like any human I had ever seen. They definitely did not die like a normal human. What could have caused these behaviors? I had seen Blue Lightning do some weird things, but I was beginning to think that that was not the correct answer. There had to be more to it. The people were too animalistic for just drug use. They also seemed to be thinking clearly.

Maybe some of the rumors about the undead were true, although they did not look like the zombies from movies. The answer had to be something that I was not thinking about. I would talk it over with my parents when I got home. If I got home.

Since there did not seem to be anyone here, saviors or attackers. I decided to go back to the bike and get back on the road. I took a slower pace than before so I did not get myself so out of breath. When I got there I leaned over to pick the bike back up and get it on the kickstand. I could barely lift it. I accomplished this feat by brute will and basic strength and took a break for a couple of minutes after. I must still be hurt worse than I thought, I really needed to get home.

I ate some food and had a little more water before I started my journey. D.C. was only two hours away from home on a good day. Barring anything out of the ordinary I should make it home at some point today. I put my bag on my back and mounted the bike. I kicked the starter. Nothing. I pulled the choke on and hit the starter pedal again. Nothing. I checked the gas, half tank. The clutch was working, the throttle was moving. I had no idea how to get this thing started. I was at the end of my knowledge of these things. I got off the bike and sat down with my back against it, defeated.

After all that I had been through, I was now sitting against a bike that would not start. Only a couple hours away from home and hopefully, safety. I could not give up and walk the rest of the way because I would be out of breath in less than half a mile. It would take forever to get home in half-mile increments. Let alone not having enough food or water to make that trip.

I stood up to try to walk off some of my anger. I was so close and this stupid bike wouldn't just start and make my life a little easier. I took two steps turned and kicked the engine block. The first thing that happened was that the bike fell back over, so now I would have to lift it back up again. Something that I could barely do five minutes ago. Second, the pain that radiated through my good leg was excruciating. That was probably one of the dumbest things I could have done at that moment. Shot in one leg and break the foot on the other. Not rather brilliant if I do say so myself.

All I could do at that point was yell at the top of my lungs in anger. Yell at the fact that all of my troubles along the way have just piled on top of one another. I should have been driving my Liberty home days ago. I should be sitting in my room or my parents living room talking to someone while drinking ice water. Not sitting on the side of the road with a bum, broken bike, one hurt foot and one leg with a bullet hole in it. Life just wasn't cutting me any breaks. All I needed was one thing to go right. One thing to get me back on the road so I could get home. I thought all of this as I threw myself back onto the ground with my arms crossed.

I allowed myself a couple of more minutes to wallow in my own self-pity before getting back on my feet and looking for a solution. My Dad always said that there is a solution, you just have to be open-minded enough to see it. As I calmed down I thought about the fact that I was winded from my short walk a while ago. Then lifting the bike took a lot from me. Maybe the problem was that I was not getting enough kick when I hit the starter. Usually, I was stronger than I was right then, so the issue may just lie with me.

I fought to right the bike again and set the kickstand. After a minute or two of rest, I stood up on the bike with it still resting on the kickstand so I could use the full force of my body weight on the starter. As I dropped down I hit the gas. The bike hiccupped, sputtered then died. Anger started to flood me, but I calmed myself and thought it through. The choke was still set on full. Maybe I flooded the engine. I turned the choke down and tried it again. It flared to life and stayed started. I revved the engine a couple of times to be sure. It sounded good. It was the best sound that I had heard in a while, to be honest.

I dropped the bike down off its kickstand and pushed it out of the fallen trees. The tree had fallen completely over the road. I had to push the bike onto the sidewalk on the other side of the street. Once on the bike, I had to steady myself and get comfortable before I started. Just as I felt like I was comfortable, I saw a large form rounding a corner onto the road that I was on. It stopped at the corner and looked in my direction. I could not see any details, but I would guess that it smiled before turning towards me and taking off at a full gallop.

I had to head directly toward him. There was no time to turn the bike around on the sidewalk and The street was blocked by the tree. I threw the bike in gear and ran at him in a deadly game of chicken. 10 feet from him I swerved hard to the left, then to the right. I narrowly avoided the building, but I had gotten past him and his long reach. He hadn't known which direction I was going to swerve, so he did not lunge at me. I only took one second to look back at him as he turned before I was back full throttle and leaving him behind.

I took a couple of turns from road to road so my line would not be straight from where I just was. I did not know the intelligence of these people and I was not going to underestimate it. It took a couple of blocks before I felt like I had lost him where I could relax and figure out where I was.

It turned out that I must have traveled farther than I had thought. I ended up just outside of the old RFK stadium, which used to be home to the Washington Redskins or whatever they changed their name to. It had to be several miles from where I had woken up. The great thing was that I knew where the stadium was in reference to Rt.50 and the Bay Bridge. It would be an easy thirty-minute drive and then I would be back on the peninsula and almost home. My dad was a big football fan. We would visit stadiums in every state that we traveled to. Of course, we passed this stadium and the new FedEx field multiple times a year, just leaving the peninsula for vacation.

I wondered if we would be able to see another football game. Everything seemed to be falling apart around us. People were acting strange and attacking people. It seemed the biblical apocalypse may indeed have been upon us.

More important matters were at hand though. Getting onto Rt 50, crossing the bridge and getting home. The trek was coming to an end. The last major hurdle seemed to have been crossed. There was no way these things could stop me from crossing the bridge. It would take a military blockade or them blowing up the bridge to stop me from getting home at that point. I wondered what Mom was making for dinner tonight.

Home

I really needed to address a few things before I got to the bridge. First was that I needed to stop and try to straighten out my handlebar. It was only slightly bent, but enough that I was struggling to keep the bike straight. The second was that I needed to see if any of the gas stations on this side of the bridge had gas and were working.

The first one was not too hard. I stopped the bike and set the kickstand. I then sat back on the seat with my feet on the handlebars and pushed with everything I had. The bar moved slightly at first, then on my second attempt, it moved a bit more. It was not perfect by any stretch, but it was better and doable. With the way this bar moved, I had to make sure I did not hit it again or it might break off completely.

The second was a little more in question. I had some gas, probably enough to get over the bridge, but I had no idea what condition the other side was in. I wanted to be sure I had enough to get home. There were plenty of gas stations along the 295 and even Rt 50. I just had to keep my eye out and see if any of them were open. Unfortunately, not many of the stations were visible enough from the interstate to see if they were working before exiting. There were a lot of cars on the road, but none of them were occupied or moving. I am not sure what happened in the day or days that I was out, but it seemed that people left the D.C. area in a hurry.

I took a couple of different exits over the next 30 minutes. None of the gas stations were open or operating. The power was on, but the pumps were turned off. Just before the Bay Bridge, I pulled off again in an area with multiple gas stations. Two of the three in this area were dark and seemed abandoned. The third had the lights on and people walking around. I pulled up cautiously to make sure I wasn't going to be run off, like before. The people stopped and looked at me as I approached.

"Can we help you son?" An older gentleman asked

"Just looking to top off before I head over the bridge." I stated

"You going over the Bay bridge?"

"Yeah I live in Delaware, just trying to make it home."

"You might want to rethink that. The military has the bridge walled off from this side. Only letting people off the Peninsula for two days. Then that even stopped earlier today. You're the first traveler we have seen since."

"What do you mean the bridge is walled off?" I stopped the bike and shut the engine off.

"They got them jersey walls up and are stopping anyone from this side from going across. Not sure why but they don't seem to be playing around. But as for your gas, we can allow you to top your bike off. We still got a little gas left. We ain't taking money though, doesn't seem to be worth anything during the end of the world. You got anything to trade?"

"Not really. I have some food and water, nothing special though."

"Well, that bike won't take much. How about a couple cans of food and we will call it even?"

"OK. I'm heading home anyway. Probably won't need it." I took my bag off my back and rifled through the contents. I did not have any cans, but I showed them the protein bars and they nodded their agreement.

"You most likely will, but if you're trying to get home you probably need the gas more right now. Should have come through two days ago, you would have been fine." Then he turned to one of the others. " Jesse go ahead and get the pump running and get him fixed up."

"Thank you again. Everyone else seems to be out of gas or closed down. Also a couple of days ago there were a lot of protesters around, now it seems like a ghost town. "

"Lots of people ran out of the city when the lock downs started. Headed to family in the rural areas or their beach homes I guess. Them protesters left two days ago. The military got sick of the creatures attacking everyone and forced everyone out of the area. No one to protest to anyway, all the politicians got sent out in helicopters and suburbans the day before that for their safety." The guy was chewing on a toothpick. He was working it around his mouth as he talked. It was very distracting.

"What creatures are you talking about?" I asked.

"You ain't seen them? They look human but will kill you with their touch.Nasty things, people say they are like zombies or the undead or something. I don't know I haven't been close to one myself and don't plan to be. You're all filled up. Good luck with the rest of your trip." With the last word he turned and walked inside the building, closed and locked the door behind him.

I stood looking after them for a minute trying to process the things I was just told. First I was knocked out for at least two days, the protesters were moved out at least that long ago. Then what were these human-like creatures he spoke about? Was that what attacked me before? They did seem off and unhuman-like, more animalistic. Then more importantly the bridge was walled off. They were trying to stop people from getting across the bridge? Why? I would have to try my luck and talk to the military at the bridge and plead my case if it came to that. With that thought, I got back on the bike and got back on the road. I still wanted to get back home tonight if at all possible. Seemed like the longer I waited the more obstacles were in my way. Better to get it done and get home now.

I hit the interstate at full speed and poured more on as I got onto it and headed east. I was really glad that I straightened the handlebars the best I could, but it was still a little difficult to control at 90. I backed it off to about 80 and left it there until I could see the lights of the military at the bridge entrance. The guy at the gas station was not kidding about everything being blocked. There were lights out front, barriers and vehicles blocking the eastbound roads. The westbound side was open and only blocked by a few military vehicles and personnel. I slowed as I approached the barriers and the first checkpoint. The lights were blinding, so I could not see the people in front of me.

"Where do you think you are going son?" Boomed a voice from behind the barricade. He did not seem to have a bull horn just a demanding presence and voice to go with it.

"I need to cross the bridge and get home. I live in Millsboro. I've had a little trouble on the roads to get home and have been delayed a lot."

"Sorry to tell you son, but you aren't getting home without a boat. All the bridges in and out have been closed."

"I thought it was just the bridges in. I was told they were letting people out. Not that it really helps me." I was trying to speak loud enough for him to hear me, but not seem like I was yelling at him.

"We were letting people off the peninsula until two days ago. Stopped all travel now. This outbreak is getting worse and we have been told to not let anyone travel in or out. The people there need to shelter in place and the people here need to do the same. We figure about two weeks of full lock-down and we can get everything back moving again. Let this sickness kill itself out. The scientists will figure something out by then." He stated.

At this point, I was not sure if he was delusional and believed what he was saying, or if he was just playing a part in all of this. He was in the military he could have been just following orders. Either way, I did not care about the scientists or about them finding a cure. I needed to get across the bridge.

"I am just one person, I won't even meet with anyone but my family. Can't you just let me across?" I pleaded.

"Sorry son, no can do. Orders are orders." He turned his back to walk away.

Just then a vehicle crested the top of the bridge heading west coming towards the barricades in the eastbound lanes. I thought this was odd as the other side was supposed to be blocking their side as this guy was blocking his. I assumed anyway. The military guy thought it was odd too because he broke off from me immediately and jumped on his men and the radio to find out who was on the bridge. He took one more stern look at me and disappeared around the back of a truck.

The next thing that I did was probably not the smartest thing that I had ever done, but it seemed like the only option left to me at the time. As soon as he disappeared and the soldier's eyes were off of me, I put the bike in gear and gunned it up the westbound ramp to the bridge. I was through the barriers and past them before they knew what was happening. I wasn't sure what I would do when I got to the other side, but I figured it was better to ask forgiveness than permission at this point. Especially since asking permission hadn't worked. Or I might end up in some military jail, it was a toss-up.

As I ran past the truck that the guy was behind all I heard was "Goddammit!" and then wind in my ears. I then had 5 miles to figure out what I would say to stay out of jail and get myself home. I knew that they would radio ahead and have the east side of the bridge ready for me when I got there. I couldn't hope for another distraction to help me out.

I ran slower than usual to buy myself a little bit of time. The weather was nice and I had always enjoyed the drives across the bridge. As I was reminiscing about past times with my family, I started to notice odd boxes and packages on the bridge in certain places. I figured they must just be supplies. I also remembered the truck on the other side of the bridge and started to look to see if they could be seen from there.

If you do not know the Chesapeake Bay Bridge is actually two separate bridges. One is three lanes that usually holds the westbound traffic. Then you have a two-lane that houses the eastbound traffic. So with me being on the westbound bridge heading east, I was looking across the divide to the other bridge looking for a truck that had been heading west. Guess we were both in the wrong lanes.

After I got about halfway across I finally saw them, but they were heading east the way that they had come. The truck was driving recklessly fast too. I decided it would be prudent for me to pick up my pace too. If they were not supposed to be on the bridge maybe I could use them as a distraction again and get past the second set of barriers and soldiers. When I saw the truck it had been about a mile behind me and catching up quickly. I picked up my pace and was running about 80 again with them still outpacing me. Because of that, they hit the end of the bridge before me. Just as I was heading down the slope.

The scene was chaos.

The barricades were everywhere and blocking every entry of the road from the east. The soldiers were set up facing the bridge expecting me to come across. A bunch had gotten up and started to run to the other entrance of the bridge to stop the truck as it came across too. Split forces would make it easier for me to squeeze through and I was a much smaller target than the truck.

I watched as the truck slowed down as it neared the soldiers. There seemed to be some confusion amongst them as it approached.

I watched two soldiers get forced to the ground by their compatriots. The other five allowed the truck to approach, then jumped in the back. The truck sped off leaving the two soldiers on the ground. They got up quickly and fired their rifles at the truck.

I decided that it would not be best to try and speed through at this point. There seemed to be a lot of tension and I did not want to be shot again. I slowed as I approached. When they told me to stop I complied and put my hands in the air to show them that I did not have any weapons on me. A couple of the soldiers started to approach me.

"Hey aren't you that guy we saved back in D.C.?"

I had no idea what they were talking about. There was no way this was the same crew.

"Sarge, wasn't this the guy that was being drained by that creature by the capitol? The one that got scared and sped off?" said a second soldier

"Wasn't that like three days ago? How is he just getting here? It does look like that chicken shit though." This was the first guy again.

"Yeah that bike is pretty recognizable. He ran off as we were putting our asses on the line to save him. Now he shows up as part of our squad jumps in an runs off?" Both of the soldiers had closed in on me and were standing pretty close looking very menacing.

"Get him off his bike and we can have a chat with him about tonight and that night three days ago. I gotta call in and let the LT know what just happened. Who in the hell did those National Guard guys run off with. All of this has to be reported. Just hold him...."

I will never know what would come next or what questions they wanted answers to. At that exact second the world around us blew up. I mean literally blew up. There was a length of explosives that went off on the eastbound bridge. The level of sights and sounds was astonishing. It was like nothing I had ever seen or heard before. The soldiers and I were all knocked to the ground. Dust and debris went flying in every direction. Water was splashing up into a mist in the air and waves started crashing at our feet.

When I was able to regain my feet the soldiers were already in motion. They moved behind the cover of their vehicles and were looking for the two that were nearest that bridge. There was still so much dust in the air that they could not see them. I took this as my opportunity, much like before, to make my getaway. I hopped back on the bike and sped off through the debris.

The soldiers were so distracted that they did not even try to stop me. A few seconds later I was very glad that I decided to run when I did because there was a second explosion. This one rocked the westbound bridge and dropped it into the bay too. Luckily my forward motion was going with the shock wave and I was able to keep my balance. I stopped and turned to see if the soldiers were alright. It seemed that most were protected by the barricades and vehicles they were behind. There was nothing more that I could do, so I turned back and sped off, again.

A little over an hour later I was pulling into my parent's driveway. I was covered in dust and in massive need of a good night's sleep. I knew my parents and sister would have a lot of questions, I just hoped they could wait until tomorrow. I parked the bike and put the kickstand down. As I took my helmet off I heard a noise and turned to my right.

I was then looking down the barrel of a Remington 870 pump action 12 gauge shotgun. I knew this gun well. There was also a big brown dog growling at me from beside the gun-wielder. I think it took a second for my Dad and Andromeda to realize who I was, but he soon dropped the gun and picked me up off the bike in a huge hug. He called for the girls to come out and join us as I knelt down to pet my sister's dog.

After a lot of hugs and quick questions, I finally made it inside to sit down. The level of relaxation that hit me in that living room was so intense that I didn't really know what it was. I started to pet Andromeda as I laid my head back into the chair. The room got dark and my eyelids got heavy. I could still hear everyone talking to me, and asking me questions, but I had lost all of my energy to answer them. In the midst of all the questions, I fell asleep in that chair and slept soundly until the morning.

Questions

When I woke up the next morning, I was covered in one of my old blankets with Andromeda curled up at my feet. Everyone else seemed to still be asleep, so I just snuggled back into the blanket and enjoyed the calm feeling of being safe. I did not know how much I had missed this place. I guess fleeing and fighting for my life over the last weeks with only this destination in mind spoke volumes. But that was intellectual, this was emotional. I had been drained physically and emotionally on this trip. It was nice to finally relax.

That was of course until my sister ran out of her room and dropped herself into my lap.

"Where did you come from?" She asked. "You were so tired last night that you hardly said a single word. Where did you get the motorcycle? Where did you learn to drive one? Daddy never taught you that. You never knew how to ride one before. How come you are so dirty? Couldn't you take a shower on the road? Why didn't you call us to tell us you were coming home?"

I think there were a lot more questions asked in a span of about thirty seconds. This girl could talk a mile a minute. I just smiled and let her talk. Although she was asking questions I learned a long time ago that trying to answer any of them before she was done would only be met with more questions. I just needed to let her burn herself out. My smile was wearing off and my patience was wearing a little thin when my dad walked in and told her to stop.

"Your brother just woke up. It looks like he had a hard couple of days. There is no reason to berate him with your diarrhea of the mouth first thing. Matt, you said something quickly last night about being hurt, maybe shot? Let me see the injury." Dad said as he walked over to the chair I had been sleeping in.

I showed my dad my leg. The calf was red and irritated. It seemed like it should have hurt a lot more than it did. Well, that was what I thought until my dad pushed on the wound. The first thing that happened was some disgusting puss poured out. Then a smell hit me like nothing I had ever smelled before. I think I heard

Ava gag at the same time I heard a scream. Turns out that scream was from me.

As my vision started to clear, my dad stood up and yelled for my mother.

"Hey, I'm going to go get the neighbor. What's her name? She is a nurse. I think they sent her home the other day. I think her Jeep is still in the driveway."

"Laura is her name. What was all that noise?" Mom asked from the bedroom.

"That was your son screaming like a girl when I touched the wound on his leg. It is definitely infected. We need to see if she can do anything or if we should risk taking him to the hospital. I am not sure that is too safe." Dad was talking as he put his jacket on.

"Why wouldn't the hospitals be safe?" I asked.

"This infection or virus or whatever has gone crazy around here. You have to wear a mask to go outside, then if you have a fever or any symptoms, you have to quarantine. Which basically meant they put you in a room and ignore the reason you're there until they are sure you don't have whatever this thing is. With all of that people are irate and there have been fights, stabbings and shootings in the emergency room. I am not really sure it is safe anywhere right now. You may not have seen any of that while you were on the road but it has been downright crazy here." Dad said as he walked out of the door.

Crazy on the peninsula huh? I may not have seen any while on the road. I was not sure how much of my story I was willing to share with my family. In the past, I was prone to exaggeration. It was a type of storytelling to me when I was young. I was not sure how much they would believe if I told them. I hadn't said much the night before, I was exhausted and just happy to be home. I knew the questions were going to come, so I figured I would just generalize. It would worry my mother and sister more if I told the complete truth anyway.

Dad was back in a couple of minutes with the neighbor, Laura. I never knew her and only knew she was a nurse because she had a sticker on her Jeep that stated as much. She was a small-framed woman about 5'3". She probably only weighed 115 lbs soaking wet. But she walked with an authority that told people that she was in charge. After she introduced herself to me she bent down to examine my leg. She was a little more gentle than my father at this point.

"It is definitely infected. How long have you had this wound?" She asked as she moved her hands around my leg and up to my hip.

"A couple of days. I am not really sure. I lost some time sleeping and I am not sure how long I slept." I generalized.

"You said it was a bullet wound?"

"Yes, a ricochet off the pavement."

She started pressing harder around the wound. It seemed like she was trying to see if the bullet was still in the leg. She couldn't tell and did not want to be wrong and let the bullet stay.

"Go to Bebee hospital in Lewes. They still have some good staff doctors. Most of the doctors in the area left when they heard about the evacuation and shutting down the bridges, but you should be good. You need an x-ray and some antibiotics." She said

"Is it safe? I have heard a lot of rumors." Mom worriedly asked.

"Relatively. Most of the residents of Lewes evacuated so they are not as crazy as the western hospitals in Delaware. When you get to the intake tell them that I sent you. My last name is Reeder. I work there or used to before I left last week. They will help you out. Let me know when you get back if you need anything." Laura explained as she stood up.

"Thanks again for coming over. In these times it is hard to find people to help." Mom said.

She waved to me and I thought she smiled, but it was hard to tell under her mask. Dad walked out with her most likely to make sure she got home ok. While mom went to go get dressed. Throughout all of this Andromeda sat at my feet and never moved. She had a weird look on her face, like fierce determination to safeguard me. It seemed odd, but I liked the comfort it gave me to have her close.

While looking down at Andromeda I breathed in a long satisfying breath. While it was relaxing, I got a whiff of myself. I needed a shower badly. While Mom was getting dressed, I got myself up and got in the shower. The hot water felt good, so I just let it run over me as I lost all sense of time.

The next thing I realized someone was knocking on the bathroom door. Ava was asking if I would be done soon as Mom and Dad wanted to get going. They wanted to be home before dark. I replied in the affirmative and decided to wash up and get out.

I walked into the living room while Mom and Dad were arguing. Mom wanted to go with me to the hospital. Dad was adamantly refusing. He stated that it was not safe. Besides the fact that they would not let anyone in the ER with me anyway. He would just be dropping me off and waiting in the parking lot. Eventually, Mom relented and Dad and I walked to the truck.

I will say that the shower and the prodding from Dad and Laura made my leg start to hurt a little more. I really hoped they would do something for me at the hospital. Otherwise, I was not sure how we were going to deal with the infection.

Dad was usually quiet while driving. Never feeling the need to fill comfortable silence with noise for the sake of noise. Ava did that enough for all of us. Today though he seemed preoccupied and nervous as we drove into town. It was about a 20-minute drive total, but it somehow felt longer. I noticed that my dad carried his pistol on his hip today. He also had a shotgun in the truck with us, just behind the seats. It also seemed like he was carrying his hunting knife on his leg.

None of this was overly odd at different times. The shotgun and hunting knife were usually there when he was going hunting. Sometimes he carried his pistol with him, but it was not a natural habit. He was nervous, he did not know what was happening around us and felt he needed to be prepared for anything coming our way. I am not sure if I had ever seen him like this. My dad was a large man. Over 6'3" and 230 lbs. A little overweight but not much. He was not one to fight if he did not have to but was not scared of them either. There was not much that scared him. Most people were nervous around him, not the other way around.

To see him like this made what was happening in the world a little more real. I knew that I had been through a couple of close calls in the past weeks. Somehow though I felt it would all be alright when I came home. It would be like it always had been. In a word, safe. But seeing my dad nervous and carrying weapons like this on a quick ride to the hospital made me even more nervous.

"Dad, we can just take care of this at home if the hospital is too bad."

"What?.. Oh sorry, I was not paying attention. No, we will get you the care you need. The hospital will be fine. Nothing will go wrong today. You just got home. Now we need to get you feeling better. Make sure your leg will be ok." he said the words. They just didn't sound right, it felt like he was reassuring himself more than me.

"What has been going on around here?" I asked trying to keep myself preoccupied.

"Same things as everywhere else, I guess. I have been watching the news and it looks like things are going to go wrong long before they get right again."

"Is that why you are so nervous?"

"Nervous? I am not nervous. Everything is fine. How about you? What happened on your trip home? You lost your truck and got shot? Not a good time bud."

I laughed a little at that. Not a good time? Yeah, that was the understatement of the year. I was still not sure how much I should share with him. I decided to just dumb down the story to its most basic and go from there. I told him about how Daytona was going crazy with people trying to leave and that they were hoarding gas and toilet paper. Then I told him about heading out and how my truck got stolen. I watched him chuckle and shake his head at that, but he didn't say anything. I followed that by finding the bike, yet I told him the farm had been abandoned. I never mentioned the bodies or massacre in the kitchen. I skimmed over how I found my truck and the sniper lunatic. I told him that I was coming up the highway when a shot rang out. I happened to catch the stray shot off a ricochet from the pavement.

"Must have been an errant shot from someone hunting too close to the highway. With people not traveling on those roads, people probably thought they would be good hunting grounds." He commented.

Sure. It was someone hunting near the road alright. Just hunting for the apex predator, humans. Next, I told him about the protesters and the military presence in D.C. Just nothing about the war that seemed to be raging there.

"Oh yeah! The Bay Bridge got blown up. Some military guys were there and blew up both bridges just after I came across."

"What! Oh shit! Did you see the explosion?"

"Yeah but from a ways away." I lied.

"That's good. They should have blown up that bridge years ago. Keep those tourists out of here, right?" He laughed at that. A quick laugh with no real humor in it. I reciprocated in a similar manner. "Well, at least you made it home. The hard part should be over. We still have power here in the U.S. of A. anyways. The other countries can figure it out on their own. We can get through today and figure out the rest after you're back on your feet 100%."

We pulled up to the hospital about then. He pulled up near the emergency room and stopped the truck. As I went to get out he grabbed my arm gently.

"I know you didn't tell me the whole story. I get it, sometimes it is to protect those around you. Keep to this story with your mom and Ava. Maybe someday you will feel like telling me the complete story. In your own time though." He was gentle when he said this. There was something in his eyes I had never seen before. I am still not sure what it was. All I could do was nod and turn to go inside. I would have to think about it and tell him the whole story later. It may help him protect our family better.

Hospital

As I walked into the emergency room everything seemed to be in chaos. There were people, security and nurses everywhere. I slowly walked my way to the check-in station. There was a tired-looking woman in scrubs sitting behind the desk. She looked like she had been there for 6 days straight.

As I approached the desk she slowly looked up and asked " What are your symptoms?"

"Symptoms for what? I got shot in the leg, so I guess my symptoms would be pain and infection?" I stated quizzically.

"Oh, sorry almost everyone that comes in here says they have the virus that the CDC is talking about. The reason we are indoors and have the mask order. The funny thing is though, there are no symptoms for this thing. So I do not know what these people are making up. Here fill this form out. Do you have insurance?" She looked up for the first time.

"I do have insurance. But, is that why there are so many people here? And all of the security?" I asked while looking around at the chaos.

"Yes, the people do not like it when we tell them that there is nothing we can do for the virus. It does not cause any ill effects or death that we can tell. We have gotten an order from the CDC to send these people away if they do not have any real emergency. But they refuse to leave. Hence the security." She added a flourish of a wave indicating the people in the waiting room.

" Will I be waiting long? Laura Reeder looked at my leg and told me it may still have the bullet in it and it is definitely infected."

"You know Laura huh? Yeah, she retired at just the right time. Time enough to miss all of this chaos. To be honest honey, you're the first person today that came in with a real injury. I'll get you right back to the doctor."

"His name isn't Stephen Strange is it? Or Bruce Banner?"

"No Hon, why?" She kind of looked at me when I asked that question.

"No reason, just asking. Thanks" I handed her the papers she asked for and walked away to find a seat.

She was right. I was called back about five minutes later. As I walked to the locked door I felt like a celebrity that had pissed off the world on the red carpet. People were everywhere trying to get in front of me to see the doctor. Security had to escort me to the door and stand guard with their backs to me as I went through and closed it. The other side of the door was the opposite of chaos. A nice younger nurse met me just beyond the door and escorted me to the bed. There were only a few other beds with people in them.

She asked me the standard questions and asked me to raise my pant leg for her to see the wound. I had intentionally worn baggy sweats to make it as easy as possible. She turned around to put on a set of gloves as I pulled the pant leg up. When she turned back around, her eyes got really wide and she inhaled deeply.

"How long has it been like this? When were you wounded?" She quickly slid her chair close and grabbed my leg to look at it closer.

"A couple of days I think. I did not really pay much attention to it. I am not really sure how long ago it was. Maybe a week. Time kind of ran away from me for a while."

She nodded and left the room at a quick pace. It didn't seem like she was even waiting for me to answer her question. I guess it was rhetorical. A short time later a guy entered the bed area with a wheelchair. He took me to the x-ray area for a couple of pictures. He was a man of few words, no words really. After the pictures were done he took me back.

A little while later the nurse came back with a doctor in tow. He did not resemble any of the aforementioned doctors, nor Doom or Richards either. It seemed to be a good sign. He did introduce himself as Doctor Bebee, related to the hospital somehow I was guessing. He informed me that the bullet fragment was no longer in my leg, but it was badly infected. He was going to start me on an IV drip with some high-level antibiotics, they would take about an hour to run through. Then he would send me home with a prescription for a week's worth of pills.

"Typically I would write a script for the local pharmacy, but seeing how the world is falling apart and we have to have security in the hospital to keep people out, I will just give them to you here." He informed me.

I figured the hour would seem like forever. I had no phone, no social media, no games or computer. I did not even think to bring a book to read. Life in this new world had other ideas though. Minutes after they put the IV in my arm and administered the medication I needed, there was a loud ruckus outside of the locking doors. People were yelling and screaming. All of a sudden the doors sounded like they were being kicked by a mule. More yelling, and orders being given by men with very deep voices. Then a loud pop and a hissing noise. The kicking stopped and the screams rose to new levels. I could see smoke coming from under the door. A nurse ran over and stuffed a towel behind it to stop the smoke.

"Is everything OK?" I asked her.

"Yes, it happens once or twice a day. People get past security and try to kick the door open. The guards usually have to use a smoke bomb or pepper spray to get them to back off. Luckily this time was just a smoke grenade."

"Jeez, really. Why are you still here doing this?"

"I am here to help people who need it like you. Sorry though I have to go. Hey all! Smoke went off, get ready for the injuries coming in!" She walked off to grab a cart.

She was right too. Minutes after the sounds stopped outside three people were brought into the ER. One had a big gash over his eyes, one was holding his ribs and the other could barely walk. I heard the nurse call for a doctor. I wasn't really eavesdropping, but I did hear a few things about these people. One had been trampled and had some broken ribs, and the other had no apparent injuries but possibly had gotten smoke in their lungs. They were close to the grenade when it went off and then got pushed to the ground as everyone tried to get away. I did not hear what happened to the one with the gash, but I am guessing he got hit in the face with something.

A few minutes after that, one of the guards came in and had a nurse tend to his hands and forearm. I guess he got bit by one of the people and almost broke his hand punching the girl to get her to release his arm. Just about the time the security guard got fixed up and headed back out to the lobby, my nurse came over and unhooked my IV and handed me a bag with a pill bottle in it.

"Elevate and ice that leg as often as you can. Take these as prescribed. Don't stop taking them if it clears up take them all. You hear me?" She asked sternly.

"Yes, Ma'am." I said as she wrinkled her nose at me calling her ma'am.

She then escorted me to the door and opened it with a key card. The lobby was almost empty as I entered it this time. The doors were barred from the inside and several security guards were standing outside. As I walked up one of the guards lifted the bar and let me out of the door. As I walked outside I could see my dad's truck. I could also see people lingering near the hospital, some in their cars and others just sitting in odd places. I was surprised that there were not any cops outside to help security.

I walked to my dad's truck and got in. He looked at me as I got in, but didn't say anything. He started the truck and put it in gear. As we drove out of the parking lot I noticed that he was driving with his right hand only. Now for most people, this would not be odd as it is his dominant hand. My dad though this was different, he always drove with his left hand on the wheel.

After we got on the main road heading out of town I found out why he was driving different. He lifted his left hand from next to his leg and put his pistol back in the holster on the dash. He had been holding the gun at the ready the entire time we were in town. As he put the gun away I looked at him quizzically. All he said was Be Prepared. That was obviously the scout motto and had become a sort of family motto too.

He asked me about the doctor's visit and I told him what happened. After I told him about the almost riot and the smoke grenade, he just told me to leave that out when I talked to the girls. He was trying to protect them from knowing just how bad the world was becoming. I got that, wasn't I doing the same thing for him too?

When we got home, Mom was asking questions about the visit and how my leg was. I told her the story too, minus the riot and smoke. After I was done, Ava and Mom asked about my trip home. I told them a similar version to Dad. Stolen truck, found a nice farm and the bike. I told them that the farmer let me take the bike to get home, not a lie really, they weren't going to be using it. Then I told them I broke my phone and computer on the trip, and that's why I did not call and let them know. Mom had been worried because she had tried to call me and it went straight to voicemail.

Ava asked how I got across the bridge. She said that her socials were going nuts about the bridges being blown up by the military to keep the virus on or off the peninsula. There was some discussion back and forth about that. I told her that the bridges were blown up, I was not sure by whom, but that I had crossed it before that happened. I heard it after I got across. Just lucky timing I guess.

"Why did you even come that way, we didn't go that way when we visited you in Florida, or when we went to Disney World. We only go that way when we go to Baltimore. Even when we go to Busch Gardens in Williamsburg we use the tunnels. Did you know the tunnels were going to be blown up? Were they already destroyed when you went there, is that why you took so long and went the wrong way? Or are you just dumb and went the long way around? You know you do that a lot around here. You don't pay attention a lot when you are driving and miss turns." Ava rambled.

" I missed the turns I needed. I lost my phone and GPS before then and the light on the bike is not good. So I missed the sign that I needed OK. And shut up you don't even drive yet." I snarked back. Starting to wonder about missing home.

"I will be learning soon. Well, next year if we go back to school. Dad said he may teach me sooner if the world keeps falling apart though."

Ava then told me that she had heard that the tunnels were blown and several bridges at the C&D canal were blown up too. Delmarva was truly an island now and not a peninsula since there was no way off of it. I wondered if it was the same group of people that did all of the destruction or if different groups just had similar ideas. I still did not understand stranding all of us on the peninsula with no way to get off. With a virus that does not cause sickness or death, according to the nurse, what are they trying to stop? Or did they know about the creatures and what they really were? Was the virus the CDC was warning us about the cause of these odd beings?

I thought about these things as Ava talked on and on about people we knew in school and what was happening around the area. She told me that her school was shut down and since she and Momma worked retail at the outlets, they were out of work too. My

Dad worked for a construction company so they were still working when they could find jobs and crews to do them, but he ran things remotely as much as he could.

The good thing about all of that information was that everyone was staying home and able to stay safe. We lived in a small community outside of town. Half of the homes were part-timers. My Mom said that about another 10% left when everything started going bad. That only left about 20 families in our neighborhood. All of us had at least an acre of land, so our homes were not close together at all. The community was safe, with only one way in and the same way out. If we hunkered down here the world could fall apart a little over the next few weeks, we would be fine. Nothing really happened in our community anyway.

As we were talking my dad had turned the television on and had the local news station playing. It seemed that they were pulling in live feeds from some of the cities near us. Chaos seemed to rule the streets. People running and shooting at other people. Riots, protests, fires and more were shown in the span of 2-3 minutes, from all across the area.

"What is it like out here?' My mom asked us while she was watching the feed.

"Nothing like that. Pretty quiet from here to Lewes and back." My dad told her, as he looked sideways at me.

"Yeah, I did not see anything but a couple of protesters when I came through D.C." I lied.

Food

The following couple of days passed easily. My family fell into an old routine that had been years in the making. Dad was not working much, most of the crews had been part of companies across the bridge. With the bridges down, they were not sure of the money coming in. Mail was not running as it should and banks were not trusted by most of the construction workers before any of this happened, let alone now. Mom and Ava were already out of work, so the only part we had to get used to was the whole family being home at once.

Before I left for college, Ava and I were busy every day. Mom and Dad worked 8-9 hours each day. We had dinner together and maybe watched a show at night. Now though, we were all home all the time. I had gotten used to having a place to myself, or at least with people my age. My injury sidelined me most of the time, so I sat around with my leg up, either under ice or just elevated. The infection was going away and each day I had more mobility and less pain. Even the virus and apocalypse did not stop everyone from being a little annoyed with everyone else in our house.

The days passed though and we got used to the new normal. Dad watched the news out in the garage when he wanted to see what was happening. I would go watch it with him sometimes but tried to avoid it the best I could. Ava and Mom kept themselves busy with crafts and scrapbooks. About a week and a half after I returned home Mom wanted to go to the grocery store for a few odds and ends. Mostly I think just to get out of the house. Dad adamantly refused to let her go and told her that he and I would go. She wasn't happy about it but relented. Ava put up a fight about going to, but Dad squashed that even easier. So Mom put together a list and sent us to the store. The store parking lot was eerily vacant. When I had left Florida there had been a run at the grocery stores for everyday items. They were madhouses. Now, weeks later, it seemed that everyone was avoiding the one in Millsboro.

Dad and I walked into the store. He still had his pistol and his knife. He had me carry another pistol that he owned too. I think that we surprised the cashier when we walked in, it seemed like we woke him up with a start.

"H-Hello, welcome. Can we help you with anything?" The kid asked as he stood up.

"No, just here to pick up a few things." Dad answered. "You guys seem a little slow, sorry if we startled you."

"Well, a few things is all we have. The store hasn't gotten any shipments in over a week. The news says that the bridges in and out are all blown up. Can't stock a store when we aren't getting supplies." The cashier informed us. "We had a run on items just after they said the bridges were gone. People picked up anything they could think of. We don't have much left. Get what you can, rumor has it that we won't be open past this weekend if nothing else comes in." He then sat back down and rested his head in his hand.

Dad and I perused the store for a few minutes. We found a few odd items that we could use. Ava's almond milk was available, but we did have to resort to turkey bacon and a few veggie meat items. We figured they would be in case of emergency only, or we could feed them to Andromeda if her food ran out.

We took the items to the cashier, who was sleeping in his chair again. There did not seem to be anyone else working. I called his name to wake him up and asked him where everyone else was. He told me that people just stopped showing up for their shifts, as he started ringing up our measly items. Today he seemed to be the only person that came in. Didn't matter though, he said, because we were the first customers of the day. As the total came up, Dad pulled out a debit card.

"You can't use that. Our system went down when Europe went dark, guess our server was over there."

"I don't have enough cash for this. I guess we will have to come back, or just leave it."

"Don't worry about it. Most of this stuff is close to expiration. If we close we are just going to throw it away. No one is doing inventory anyhow."

"I don't like not paying. Is there anything I can do for you?"

"How about we call it a tab or an IOU? I'll keep the receipt and tape it here in customer service with your name on it. If we are open in two weeks and things start running again, you can pay it then. I know you are local, you used to coach my brother's tee ball team. I went to a few games a couple of years back. You'll pay if you're able." The kid smiled trying to be helpful.

"I will. Thanks. Hope to see you in a couple of weeks. Tell your brother I said hi."

We then walked out of the store with our IOU groceries. Most of the stuff we would not want to pay for anyhow. Which is probably why it was still on the shelves. We got in the truck and turned towards home. I was a little surprised when Dad missed the turn for home.

"Gonna check out a few of the farms around the area. If the stores aren't getting trucks they might not be able to get rid of their vegetables to the big manufacturers. We have a lot of big farms, little farms and chicken farms around here. They might have some of the items we need." Dad explained.

We drove around for a while. There were a lot of stands that had popped up in front of the farmhouses. It was just after the fall harvest, so they had root vegetables, like potatoes, radishes and beets. They also had cauliflower, broccoli, lettuce and cabbage. Most of the smaller farms had lost the contracts with local grocery stores so they were trying to sell what they could before they spoiled. Dad was able to bargain for some, but as he said in the store he hadn't had a lot of cash on him. He did make a deal with a few of the farmers where he would provide some wood or some help building things for them in place of cash. Seemed like the barter system was making a quick comeback.

In a few hours, we had accumulated a healthy amount of vegetables and some seeds for growing our own things. Dad would be busy for the next few days helping out the farmers to pay off the debt, but they also promised more if he kept his end of the deal. As we drove home I asked him about the fields that still seemed to be full of corn and soybeans.

"I guess they had no one to help plow and harvest, or they had nowhere to send them because of the factory shutdowns and the lack of truck drivers. It seems to be a big loss to some of the biggest farmers on the shore. I wonder what the chicken farmers are going to do when they can't get rid of the birds." He explained looking thoughtful.

It all seemed like a waste to me, but they were dead and brown by this point. They would only be good for feed or burning. Nothing we could use or harvest, so we headed back home. When we arrived, Mom was standing outside looking angry. She started yelling at us as soon as Dad turned off the truck. She was worried something had happened. Dad had left his phone at home. She had been calling and could not get through, it seemed like the system was down or overloaded. She had expected us home hours before. Dad had to calm her down and explain what happened. After he showed her the load of vegetables that we had gotten, she lightened up and walked back into the house. I guess our punishment was to unload everything ourselves. It was an easy punishment if that was all she wanted from us. Dad even said that he should have stopped by home after the store to explain. It was not good to worry people unnecessarily.

Once all the stuff was unloaded we went into the house to face the wrath a little more. Unexpectedly, there was no wrath to face. Mom was just happy we were safe and home. She was thrilled about the haul of vegetables we had gotten and was looking up the best ways to can or store them all. Lunchtime had come and gone, so I went to the pantry to grab a quick snack before dinner.

Ava came out of her room screaming like she had been shot, or had seen a spider in her room. Either way would have been the same. All of us asked her what was happening, but she just held up her phone and started rambling. After a few minutes, she calmed down and slowed her speech down to normal levels. We found out that all of her social media platforms had gone down. She had tried to get on them and the pages would not load. She tried our WiFi and cellular to no avail. The apps were dark.

Now for me, this was a minor inconvenience. For my sister, the world just ended. Everything else going on and this is what had sent her off the deep end? Dad and I had been keeping most of the worst parts of the world falling apart from her. As much as we could since it was all over social media too. With her out of work and not going to school her socials had been her only way to connect to the world. Yet, it was still a little dramatic to scream over it for as long as she did.

Dad told her to stop crying about it. He told her it was probably just a glitch and that everything would be back up in a few days. Some of the servers were probably backed up overseas. With Europe and other countries turning off their power supplies, the apps probably went down for basic maintenance. This seemed to calm her down a bit, but she still looked like a lost puppy.

I still had not gotten my snack at this point, so I grabbed a bag of chips and sat down to watch television. I then found out that that too was out. The tv turned on but the cable box was blank. Another sign that society was falling down around us. I decided to pick up a book and read instead. It was a real book, not an e-book so nothing could cause that to stop working.

Life went on for a couple more days like this. The social sites and cable did not come back on. The longer it went the more concerned everyone in the house became. These were small things, but they were part of our entertainment. We all read books, except Ava, regularly, but escaping into electronics and movies was a good way to pass the vacant hours. We did not know that this was just the beginning.

On November 1st the lights went out.

Dark

When I say that the lights went out. It was not like flicking a switch and everything went dark. It was more like the time when a car hit the telephone pole on one of the main streets near our house. There was a flicker then dark. Then the lights came back on and then flickered again. This caused a couple of the breakers in the electrical box to pop. The power then came back on again fully and stayed for a minute. About the time, my dad went to get up and fix the breakers it dimmed. Then it went out completely.

The lights stayed off for a day. There were not that many line workers still in the area or at least coming to work. My dad had an old battery-powered radio for camping, so we listened to it to see if anyone knew what was going on. There were people killing themselves at the power substations. The fences had been knocked down or left open and people were wandering in. No one was sure if this was a suicide thing, or if they were unaware of what they were doing. Several bodies had been found burned to death. The flickering was when one or more of these people would overload the system so badly that the transformers would blow.

Once the transformers were replaced the power would come back on, for a day or so then go out again. This went on for about a week before we lost power completely. Nothing was ever said as to why they stopped fixing the local power or if it was becoming too widespread to contain. The local radio stations that had generators to run on kept broadcasting. There were news reports from all around the country. It seemed that the power was out everywhere. Life without electricity was something I never thought would happen. But you can never predict the future.

With the bridges blown, media and electrical services down and the local emergency services undermanned and overtaxed everyone was at a loss for what to do. For the first few days, everyone was trying to carry on as normal. We had lost power before, we knew how to camp it was just an adjustment. My dad was always listening to the radio. There was no music on it anymore, just new feeds. There were more and more people telling stories about the dead being reanimated, calling them Deaders.

These dead rising would attack people and kill them. No one knew how you died if you were attacked. Several sources said they ate your brains and guts like zombies in the movies. Some sources said that they just touched you once and took your soul. Others suggested that you died of fright and natural causes. Then there were a few that stated the reason for death stemmed from psychic powers including telepathy and telekinesis.

In the end no one knew anything. They did not know what these things were, how they were made, or how they killed you. The biggest problem was that no one knew how to kill them either. A lot of people told stories of others trying to stab them in the brain or shoot them in the head, all the zombie tricks we always "knew" would work. None of them did.

With the loss of power, the human element in the world went off the rails further too. I could attest to incidents of people losing their minds before, but the total loss of power had people lose everything that had made our society. Societal norms were no longer the glue holding people together. It was like the book Lord of the Flies. People reverted to cavemen. If you were stronger you took what you wanted. Areas were taken over by new gangs and new gang leaders all trying to get their day. It was being called the Fall of Society.

These times were when we veered the farthest from what our world had become before we tried turning the corner to get back to a semblance of what we had. My dad saw all of this happening and set to work on the house. He left a few times to go to his job sites and get material. We all pitched in and secured the doors and windows better. We did not board them up but made it difficult for someone to gain entry through them. While out he also stopped by a few gun shops and other places that sold ammo to stock up. He went on forays into town for food a few times too, just to keep our supply up. Each and every time he went alone. He refused to take either of the girls and wanted me to stay behind to protect them while he was gone. He always left others behind to do things his own way. It was one of the things that I never understood about him.

Mom restricted our food a bit. She knew that food would be scarce in the winter, we had a decent stock, but nowhere near enough to get us through. Mom and Dad would stay up at night and talk about ways to stretch the food we had or look for more in the area. They did not think Ava or I were awake when they talked about these things, but I heard them a few times. I wanted to tell them that I was an adult and could help out with the problems we were facing. I knew more about what these things were than they did, even if I did not understand a lot of it myself. I had lived through attacks, but I could not use that argument without telling them the true and complete version of my trip home. In the end, I would just close my door and lay back down to try and sleep the night away.

Our community was small but not very close-knit. A couple of times since I had been home, the neighbors would come by and talk to my parents about different things. This increased exponentially after the power went out. Most of them were older and did not know how to live in a world with no rules and no power. A couple of them were worried about the medications that they were on, food and water running out and what would happen then. They were not self-sufficient people. They did not know how to farm, hunt, fish, or even make basic house repairs. They knew that my dad could do all of these things. He became someone that they looked at to help out in this time of crisis.

The HOA had become an impromptu council. They tried to make decisions for the community for the benefit of all. My dad disagreed with most of the policies that they tried to enact, calling them socialist at best and communist at worst. Then there were the ones that he called just plain stupid. He refused to take a leadership role in the community or to even lend a hand to most if it took his time away from his preparations. I was not sure he was right in a lot of those instances. This group was trying to do the best they could with the skills and knowledge they had. If someone had more food than they could eat they should share it with others? If they had supplies someone else needed, why not share them? If someone like him had the knowledge to help others survive, why not share it? My dad's mentality was obviously not the same and we had a few arguments about it.

I decided to help out where I could in the community. I did not have anywhere near the same knowledge as my dad, but I had lived with him and helped him most of my life. I tried my best and most of the others valued what I imparted to them. I did this mostly while my dad was out on his solo forays so it did not inconvenience him, and I didn't want him to know that I was doing it at all, to be honest.

One thing my dad did agree to was a neighborhood watch and wellness checks on the remaining families. My dad had brought this up as something for others to do, to keep an eye on each other even before the power went out. We had always been a neighborhood plagued with basic unlocked car burglaries. Being a higher-end neighborhood in an area that was lower-end tended to bring these kinds of problems. With the riots and other noise going on my dad feared these would increase in amount and intensity. They had not seemed to by that point, but you never knew what was around the corner.

One of the people on the council was a retired police officer. He recruited a couple of us teenagers and a few of the men to walk the community and keep an eye out for things. He did a quick training on things and requested that no one carry firearms while on patrol. Untrained people tended to cause more problems when they were armed than when they were not. He did go over homes in the neighborhood where weapons were kept and the owners who knew how to use them well. If anything happened we were to notify these individuals and they would do what they felt was needed.

My dad was not keen on me joining the group that he had solicited for. He felt it was necessary for others, but not for our family. My mom on the other hand was happy about me helping out, with the watch and the other neighborhood problems. Ava was oblivious to most. She helped more around the house and played with Andromeda as much as she could. I think boredom was killing her. She was always very active on her social media and in real life. I asked Dad about Ava helping out with the watch, it would give us another body and it would help with her boredom. He adamantly refused. No reason just a hard no. Ava for her part wanted to help but she would never go against Dad's wishes.

The days went on in this way for about two weeks. Around the middle of November, my dad started coming home from his trips with large fuel cans and windows. Lot and lots of windows.

Greenhouse

The windows ended up being for a greenhouse. My dad had the brilliant idea to build it in the backyard of our house to have the ability to grow vegetables year-round. He recruited me to help every chance I had. With this, there was little downtime. I picked up as many watches as they needed, then helped Dad during the day.

The greenhouse went up well. The windows were all similar sizes, so it made making the frame pretty easy. I guess the builder, nor the new homeowners, will miss the windows since the houses will never be built and there is most likely no one to pay for the material anymore. The only problem that we had was air leaks. We could not seem to get the frame to stop leaking air into the greenhouse. It was not too bad in November, even though the weather turned colder than it had in years. But an air leak like this when the wind is whipping and the temperature drops to the teens at night will kill any plant near the leak.

We used water to find the leaks, then tried to seal them with silicone. After the third or fourth leak and failure, I spoke to Dad and asked him to give up on the greenhouse for a little while. Get the plants in the dirt and then work on them later. He looked at me and seemed confused for a second, then irritated, then finally a little angry.

"You never walk away from a job that isn't finished. Is this job finished?" he asked.

"No."

"Then we don't walk away."

"But the plants need to get in the ground and other things need to get done. It's not quitting, it's finding a new task until the old task has a solution."

"I get what you're saying, son. I do. But this task needs to get completed before the other tasks can get started. Fixing this after the other things are done makes this one harder than it is and may double the work. We'll finish this job and then move on to the next step."

With that, he walked away and I just watched him go. There was no anger in his voice when he said those words. The last words didn't even seem to have an air of irritation. He almost seemed sad. I thought about it a little more and felt that he needed this to work. He needed to provide for our family and make sure that we would all be OK. No matter how frustrating it may be. I had to admire the sentiment.

A couple of days later I was on a night watch when I noticed one of the elderly neighbors up and walking in their house around 3 am. While I knew older people had to get up multiple times a night to relieve themselves his movements seemed odd to me. There were no lights on, which again was not super odd. It was just the pattern of the walking that seemed odd. I walked to the head of the watch and woke him up. He always told us that if something seemed odd, to wake him up no matter the time. When he came to the door he looked tired but alert.

"I don't sleep much anyway. What is it Matthew?" he stated as he rubbed his eyes.

I informed him of what I saw and my thoughts on the whole thing. He agreed that it may be odd, especially since this neighbor, in particular, had been ill as of late and did not look to recover. He had been bedridden for three weeks. When the nurse, Laura, had gone to check on him and feed him earlier in the day, he had still been unable to stand.

The watch captain went back inside and got dressed. We walked to the home. He went up and knocked on the door. No answer. The odd walking pattern did not even seem to change. After knocking three more times the watch captain decided to try the door. It was locked but the spare had been left hidden on the porch for Laura to enter.

Once we found the key the captain entered the home. He had me stay outside so we did not spook the neighbor. He had been trained while on the force to deal with similar situations, or so he thought. Once he entered the home I went to a window to see what was happening inside. The captain was speaking to the neighbor, who did not seem to notice. As the captain entered the same room as him though, the neighbor seemed to come alive. His head came up, and he turned and looked at the captain for the first time.

The captain seemed to see something that did not seem right. His face contorted in what looked like fear. The neighbor moved across the room with unnerving speed for someone that had supposedly been on bed rest for the last three weeks. He reached out and took the captain to the floor. I ran towards the door to help. The captain must have gotten up and away because by the time I got to there the captain was yelling for me to stay away and locked it. Locked himself inside.

I beat on the door for a few seconds then ran back to the nearest window. The captain and the neighbor were no longer in that room. I looked and listened, but could not hear anything. I decided that I needed more help. I ran home and woke up my dad.

"What?" He said groggily.

I informed him of what I had seen and what had happened. He jumped up, all sleep gone from his eyes. He grabbed the pistol that he kept next to the bed and threw on a pair of pants. He did not even grab a shirt or shoes even though the weather was close to 40 degrees.

Once we got to the home Dad tried the door and found it locked. He checked each window as he worked his way around the back of the home. He did not say anything if he saw them. He told me to stay around the front and keep an eye out through the small window. As I stood on my tiptoes and looked through the small half-moon window at the top of the door I thought I could see the captain's foot but I was unsure.

I heard glass break as Dad broke a small window in the rear door to enter the home. Then I heard my dad yell, though I could not tell what he had said. Then there seemed like a scuffle and then a gunshot. I heard my dad yell then nothing. I waited for a few more seconds, then tried the front door again. When it did not open I ran for the back. As I rounded the corner, I ran directly into my dad. He had been coming to the front.

"We need to go! Now!" he yelled.

"What? What happened? Where is the captain?"

"He is gone."

"Did you shoot him?"

"No, I did not shoot him." He said while he screwed up his face in utter confusion. Basically asking how I could even ask that question. "He was already dead when I got there. He was leaning against the front door. I think he made it that far to save you."

"Then why did you shoot?"

"The neighbor was dead. He was dead and walking around. That is why he was acting weird. He attacked me and caught me by surprise. I shot at him to get him away. It barely slowed him. I then high-tailed it out here. We need to go now. Go wake up the rest of your watch. I have a plan."

I did as asked and was back in front of the house with most of the watch within 30 minutes. By that time my dad, now with a shirt and shoes, had brought and piled up different pieces of plywood. We all looked at him oddly as he handed out a few gloves and drills.

"So there is a deader inside this house. I don't know about you but I do not know how to kill these things. The best thing to do is avoid. We can't risk letting this thing out, it has already killed the watch captain. What we are going to do is board up the windows and doors of this home. If anyone asks there is a dead body inside, which is not a lie, and we had no way to get rid of the body so we boarded it up to keep others out. Does anyone have a problem with that?"

"Is that going to keep it in? Are we sure it can't get out?" Asked one of the watch.

"I am reasonably sure. When I left I shut the door behind me, even with a broken window it stayed inside at the door. I don't think it will be able to get out. So if there are not any more questions?" Dad asked while looking around."We need to get to work."

Everyone nodded and started putting on gloves and grabbing the wood. The house was closed up tight within the hour, well before any of the others would wake up to question the decision. After the work was done, we looked to my dad to run the watch. There was no one left with any experience in the military or law enforcement. My dad had some time in the Navy and a few years working at Delaware prisons, before leaving and going into construction. He adamantly refused. He looked at me and nominated me in his stead. Although others were older I had shown knowledge and I had also spent the most time on my own in this new chaotic world. I looked around at the others and no one seemed to disagree. I took this new responsibility on my shoulders and set the watch for the remainder of the morning.

The rest of us headed off to bed for what was left of the morning. After I logged some sleep I would have to reset some things on the watch and get other things back on track. It would not be a good day. After I woke up I looked around and could not find my dad inside the house. I groggily walked outside and saw him breaking up the dirt in the greenhouse to get ready for planting. I looked at him and he just pointed to the glass roof and gave a thumbs up, meaning the air leaks were all taken care of. I nodded my head and went back inside to grab my shoes and a sweatshirt.

When I showed up outside and grabbed a rake my dad looked at me quizzically.

"The job isn't finished." Was all I said. He just nodded and got back to work. The watch could wait another hour. It felt good to finish the last project before starting a new one. As usual, my dad was right.

Watch

The first day as watch captain was not fun. I had one member from each household pulled to my house so I could address the new issue all at once. I knew that most of these people had heard about the deaders through the television and radio when they still worked, but they had never seen one with their own eyes. They had also lived in constant denial that it would happen to them. It would not happen here. But, as usual, they were wrong.

I explained the night before to everyone. When they heard about the loss of the captain sadness took over the crowd. There was also an air of need, the need to survive. Deaders were real. They had become part of reality for us and now we needed to understand how to deal with them. I asked if anyone had been outside of our area after the lockdown but before losing power. No one had, I was the only one who had any experience with these things. That experience was mostly running and almost dying before being saved. Great!

I told everyone to gather their loved ones and tell them about the incident from the previous night. I also told them to be on the lookout for anything strange, anyone acting outside of their normal. If they saw anything they needed to tell someone on the watch so they could inform me. I left the crowd with that information and sent them back to their homes. I had a few ideas for changes in the coming days, but I needed time to iron them out and I also needed to speak to my dad about them as a few involved him.

After everyone left I went out to find my father. He was in the new greenhouse, checking his watering lines and new plants. I talked to him about my plans for the watch. I told him I would like to turn it into more of a security patrol than a watch. We talked about how so many people lived alone. I felt that they were susceptible to greater danger than the others. The danger of dying alone and becoming a deader and becoming a target to vagabonds that may pass through. It had been a couple of weeks since we had lost power, people were getting desperate for food and I had seen more people moving around during my forays into town. I suggested that people that were living alone, especially if they lived in the front or outside of the community, should move closer to the interior with someone else that was alone. This would allow companionship and security for both. It would also pool our resources into a smaller area, which would help with my next idea.

That idea was to gather the remaining food and put it in one central location. To pull all of the community into one unit. We would take turns cooking and farming. Anyone with the know-how to fix, make or do things would all be put together to get the best use out of them all. Instead of everyone looking out for themselves we needed to look out for everyone. The winter was coming and with that would come hardships, food shortages, freezing temperatures and broken homes. Human beings, I explained, are social animals. We need companionship and camaraderie to survive as much as food and water. We need to live not just survive. With everyone helping and pitching in when they could we would grow as a group instead of pulling away. If we did not change how we were working we would fall apart.

My dad did not like the idea of relying on others or others relying on him. He felt that some would have to take larger burdens and some would just reap the benefits. I explained that we would have to keep a watch for that to make sure that everyone pulled their weight, even the kids. He reluctantly told me that he would back the decision and do what I was asking him. He just hoped that others would do the same. With this blessing, I figured I would push my luck just a bit farther. I asked him to help train the security force. I was not the one and there were not many others that had the knowledge that he did.

"Didn't I just say something about a larger burden placed on some?" He said then walked away. I could tell that he was only slightly serious. He would help because it would make everything safer for everyone, including our family.

It felt odd making these types of changes. Most of the people in this community were older than my parents. They had watched me grow up in the same house where we were living. Telling them what I felt needed to be done a day or so after the old watch captain was killed seemed like too much. These people would not listen to me. They would want someone else, someone older with more experience to make these types of decisions. Not some snot-nosed 20-something that barely had any college education. These thoughts ran through my head on an endless loop for hours while I made the new watch list. I figured we would keep everything the same for now and implement the changes gradually. There was no reason to rush everything on people all at once.

While these thoughts were pervasive, I had also seen these same people follow what the watch captain and my dad had said without thought or argument. Still, they were older and people respected them. Round and round these thoughts went until dinner time that night.

I spoke to my mom and Ava for the first time that day over the dinner table. They had been at the briefing about the event and the watch captain, but I had then only spoken to dad and sequestered myself in my room afterward. Ava looked scared. She had not believed the stories and had never known someone who was killed. She was in a little bit of shock, as I assume a lot of people were in the community. As I explained what I had talked to Dad about, my mom seemed to be completely on board with the ideas. Ava listened but not much seemed to be affecting her. I felt that she and the kids her age needed something to do to keep their minds occupied. The imagination of kids can go wild. That could manifest itself in many different ways, none of them good. My grandmother used to say that bad things came from idle hands.

The next day I went in to talk to the watch. I informed them of the changes and how we would need to become a security force. We would need to keep the peace from inside and outside threats. A couple of them walked off and did not want any part of being a "police force willing to take freedoms away from individuals". The ones that stayed seemed to be on board so I worked out a training schedule with them based on my dad's recommendations. This put the first part of my plan into action.

Later that day I decided to work on the second part. I went to the people that were living alone and spoke to them about their safety and the ways that I felt they could be safer. Some escorted me out of the door seconds after I entered, which was to be expected by some. Others were willing to listen and be part of the conversation. Some had been worried about the same problems, while others were just lonely. We set up a time in the coming days to get everyone together, talk about it and work out the details.

Life went on and got back to our new normal for a couple of days until the day we were supposed to have that meeting. Mother nature decided that she had her plans and hit us with an early winter storm. There was wind, driving rain and a massive drop in temperature. We had thought that our house was ready for the cold, but we found out that the cold driven by massive winds was different. It found every crack and crevice in the home and drove its icy nails into them. That day was rough but the night was even worse. It was not safe for the watch to be out, so everyone just hunkered down in their own homes and hoped for the best.

The storm blew itself out early the following morning. As we ventured outside we could see that it had done damage to everything around us. Trees had blown down in the woods behind the community, trees had also blown down in some of the neighbor's yards. One looked to have fallen on part of a house. As we started to venture towards it we could see that others were already there, helping the neighbor who had the damage.

I informed my dad that I was going to walk the neighborhood and check for other damage and get the watch to check on others. This turned out to be a good thing and a bad thing all at once. I had not made it halfway around the development when one of the younger members came running up and told me that we had a problem at the front of the community. The look on his face was pure fear so I sent him to fetch my dad and I ran to the home that he had told me about. It felt good to get some running in. I had worked so much and ridden on the bike for so long that I had neglected to run since I had left Florida. My muscles remembered their job though and I was running full pace the whole way. When I got to the scene though, my legs and the rest of my body almost gave up on me. I had to steady myself and brace for the scene that had unfolded.

The first part of the scene that got me was the amount of blood. It seemed that someone had a 5-gallon bucket of it and just flung it everywhere in the house. It looked as if someone or multiple someones had been drug out the front door and into the street. This is where the trail ended due to being washed away in the rain from the previous night. This house had a family of three living there. It was two parents and an adult boy. With all of the blood, there were no bodies around. There were, however, weapons laying everywhere in the house. Guns, bats, knives and even a machete. Whoever was here and whatever had happened, they had left in such a hurry that they left the weapons behind.

When my dad arrived he surveyed the scene and was just as lost as I was. I went and talked to the closest neighbor but they had not seen or heard anything. The storm had been so loud and fierce that they had curled up in their bedroom, which was on the far side of the house from the scene. We were lost, so we just gathered up the weapons and any food that was left in the house and took them back to my house for storage.

The people that had lived in that home had kept to themselves. The amount of blood and weapons suggested a fight of some sort, but where had the bodies gone? Unfortunately, later that night we found out. One of the neighbors about four doors down from this house had a generator stored in his shed. When the storm hit he decided that he wanted to heat his house. So while we were looking at the bloodbath down the street he got his generator out and set it up to his HVAC system outside of the house and a few of the inside circuits. When the sun went down that night he went outside and started it up so he could have heat and a few lights running.

Since the weather had cleared we put our watch back out. Around 10 o'clock that night I was alerted to a problem in the front of the community. I responded and found the house with the generator was being attacked. There were six people outside of the house. Three were leaned over the generator, one was by the electrical panel and two seemed to be trying to enter the house at the front door. We shut off our flashlights and moved closer for a better look. When we got there we could see that three of the people were the family from the blood-bath house. It was dark, but you could see that something was not right in their movements.

The owner suddenly turned on a couple of outside lights and charged out of the back door. When the lights came on you could see that the people had been cut and slashed in different places. The dad looked to have been shot in the face but was still walking around. Deaders! The other three were unknowns. They must have broken into the house during the storm, either looking for food or shelter, but the family put up a bigger fight than they had expected. In the end, they were all killed. Only to rise again as deaders. Now they were being drawn to the generator or the lights.

As the guy rushed out of the house and started blasting at the intruders with a shotgun. Seconds later the generator went out and all of the lights went off. He was taken off guard as one of the deaders came from around the front of the house. He went down under the attack. Three of the other deaders then joined in the festivities. Seconds later the deaders wandered off, back out of the community and the guy laid still.

It had all happened so quickly that I had not had any time to react. I stood there and watched this man get killed while I did nothing. I wasn't sure what I could have done, but the inaction caused me some concern. Even if I hadn't been able to save this guy, I should have been able to run and warn the others in the community. Was I the man to be watch captain, the guy to run the security of our home? Luckily the threat did not move further in. They just turned around and left.

When I knew it was safe, I went up to the guy to check on him. I knew what I would find, but I needed to be sure. As I suspected, he was dead. There were no marks on his body and nothing to point to the cause, but he was dead all the same. I left to inform the nurse and my dad of what had happened. We took the body and buried it in a shallow grave behind the house. We then took the shotgun, ammo and any food he had left inside. He was surprisingly well-stocked in both. We took it all back and added it to the growing stockpile. It was hard taking these things knowing what had become of the previous owners, but it was the right thing to do for those of us that were still alive.

The next day we had our meeting. I informed everyone of the new incidents and what I thought had happened. It convinced those that were on the fence to jump down and comply. Over the next few days, we consolidated all of the people that were living alone and those that lived away from others into a smaller-knit unit. We now only took up fifteen of the thirty houses that we had only days before. Hopefully, we would all be safer for it.

Jobs

Over the coming weeks, our community came together better than it had before. Everyone liked my plan of sharing responsibilities and one of our neighbors had taken on the responsibility of speaking to everyone and assigning them jobs. The kids would be helpers or foragers depending on their ages. We would need a lot of wood over the next couple of months to keep warm and keep everyone fed. Adults would do the hunting, but there were a lot of good root vegetables and nut trees in the area. The rest of the community would rotate the cooking, cleaning and other chores.

There were a few houses that had outdoor firepits but none were quite as large as ours. They were mostly for small backyard fires. Our pit was all brick and was five feet by five feet. It was great for getting enough coals hot and cooking larger meals. This put my mom in charge of a lot of the dinners with help from others. She did not seem to mind. She liked staying home, especially now, and this allowed her to help and be social. A win all around.

Thanksgiving had come and gone without much muss or fuss from the community. A lot of people had either lost family or lost contact with them. There were no flights and no one driving long distances to come to dinner and a backyard football game. Christmas on the other hand was on its way and was the talk of the town.

We were running short on food already. The men had been hunting and they were able to take a few deer, rabbits and squirrels. The meat that was not used right away was smoked and salted to keep it as jerky. With no power, there were no refrigerators so we could not keep the meat very long. The weather was not consistent enough with the cold to make ice boxes outside to help out. We had to consistently have hunters out for fresh meat. This was getting harder as the woods around the community were not very big, so they had to rely on new prey wandering in. Dad's vegetables were growing and would help, but it took months for most vegetables to grow so they were not very helpful at this time, though they did help in a pinch.

People were also needing other items besides food. We had figured out a way to do without most modern conveniences but some things were just needed. I took my bike and worked the surrounding areas as best as I could. I stayed away from any area that seemed to be occupied either by the dead or the living. This made me take longer and longer rides each time. Lately, I had also started getting Christmas lists from the other members of our community. Small items that they would like to find for gifts or to be able to make gifts. I did what I could, but a lot of the lists went unfulfilled.

As Christmas approached more people moved into new homes with their neighbors to help save firewood and to have some companionship during the long nights. Most of the homes occupied had fireplaces or had added a brick fireplace off the main room. Dad had gotten some concrete blocks and helped people cut small holes in an exterior wall to add a type of fireplace to heat the home. The new security team was trained and working as a solid unit. Luckily there had been no real issues with deaders or bandits since the early weeks of November. Dad had been great with the team and trained them to shoot and how to be a little more security minded. Unfortunately, not all of the team members could be armed at all times because we only had a few pistols. Those community members that had their own were not willing to give them up.

Christmas Eve came and we had a meal together, which was not unusual. But the meal was a little bigger and a few people had brought out some specialty items that they had not been willing to share previously. One such item was lime Jello. It would have seemed small back before the fall but it was very special that night. Some of the trees in the community were decorated and one of the kids had brought a small douglas fir in from the woods while gathering firewood. We set it up near the cooking fire and decorated it as the meal was being made.

The atmosphere was joyful yet reserved as most people were thinking of the family lost and Christmas that had passed. Nothing would ever be like it was before. We would have to learn to remember but move forward in the coming years. Everyone was fine with letting the others be a little solemn that night and reminisce on the loss of family and our former lives.

A few presents were exchanged and it made everyone perk up just a little. The kids had fun with a few toys that I found in my travels. After the kids were put down a few of the adults left to keep watch over them, and a bottle of Southern Comfort was brought out. It had been kept by one of the neighbors for a special occasion. He felt that that night was special enough. This lets the other adults let their guard down for a little bit that night, though no one got drunk enough to lose their sense of self. It was too dangerous of a time to let that happen.

My Dad let my sister and I try a glass of it ourselves.

"There are no laws anymore. There is no guarantee to our life anymore. One glass of whiskey will not hurt them." He said when mom gave him a cross look.

Mom shouldn't have worried though. When my sister tried hers she gagged and almost threw the rest of the glass out. I had a similar feeling when I tried it too, but made myself sip it and try to learn to enjoy it. My dad seemed to get a good chuckle out of our reactions, which is probably why he let us try it.

The next morning was nothing like it was before the fall, we all got up and got back to work. Nothing stopped anymore. There were no days off or vacations. It did not matter what the calendar showed each day was about survival, especially in the winter. Unfortunately, our luck also ran out that day. I am not sure if the roving band saw our decorations or just happened upon us, but we were under siege from a large group of bandits by 11 am.

The first alarm went out as a member of the security team saw the group walking down the main road outside of the community. The forewarning allowed us to get the kids and non-combatants to a safe hiding place in a couple of different homes. The security team and community members had drilled this a couple of times over the last months and it went smoothly. Everyone was doing their job and we were ready by the time the group entered the community.

We watched from a few different vantage points as they entered. The 20 members of their group spread out as the street forked just past the entrance of the development. All of them seemed to be well-armed and confident. When they reached a house they would enter, eight of the members would enter, while two members stayed outside to keep watch. This kept us from being able to trap them in a house to get some control. We also broke into two groups to stay with them as they went through the homes.

It did not seem prudent to run out from hiding and stand in front of them and ask them to leave. Dad had split to lead the group of security watching the other bandits. He had told me to stay hidden and watch from the shadows. We were not trained or armed enough for a full frontal assault on a group this large. We needed to let them check the homes that had been cleared and hope they felt that going too far into the community was dangerous. If not then we would have to try to take them out of hiding.

At first, they were just checking the empty homes. Ones that we had cleared for this particular reason, but they were quickly approaching the occupied homes. We were not sure what this group would do when the doors were locked and barricaded. It did not look as though this group would just give up and move on. The group that my team was tailing came up to the first house that we had secured. After they tried the door and found it locked one of their members stepped back and shot the locks and hinges off the door with a shotgun. The other group must have had the same idea because we could also hear shots from that side of the community. Luckily this house was empty. It was just locked to put a barrier up for intruders. After they cleared the house they moved on to the first home that was occupied.

Before they could try the door I fired my rifle into their midst. I did not try to hit anyone, in particular, I was just trying to get their attention. I succeeded better than I thought. One of their members fell to the ground and did not seem to move after. I could not stop and think about the fact that I had just killed a man for the first time in my life, mostly by accident. The day may end with me killing more than just that, I would have to deal with it after this situation was handled, or maybe if things went wrong I wouldn't have to deal with it at all because I would be dead. That was not a thought that I wanted to have but being realistic in these types of situations was always the best bet.

As their team member dropped their group dropped into shooting stances and fell behind cover if they could. I almost expected them to start shooting in our general direction, but it seemed they were better trained than that.

"Who is out there?" One of their members yelled.

"I am, what's it to you." I yelled.

"You just killed one of my guys without even a warning. I would like to know why."

"Because you walked into our territory without asking and started kicking in doors." I tried to keep moving as I was talking so he could not get a bead on where I was.

"We had no idea this area was occupied. We are with the military. We are looking for survivors. We are just trying to help."

"Bullshit! There is no military. There is no government. Plus you are not even dressed like the military. You are just thugs moving around and taking what they can. You didn't knock, you tried the door then shot out the hinges and locks. You need to just move along. We have you surrounded."

"Believe what you want. We are militia, we broke off from the military before the fall. The government was weak. We are trying to start our government and help people in their time of need. Plus if we were surrounded you would not have let us get this far. You are out-manned and outgunned. Come out and we can talk."

"You are just gonna let me come out and talk after I killed your man. I don't think so. We let you get this far so we can control the area. If you couldn't tell all the homes we let you in were abandoned. You don't find that odd? Let's skip the talk and get to the part when you leave."

As this went back and forth I watch the man on the ground start to move. Relief hit me harder than I thought it would when I realized I did not kill him. They were so focused on looking for me that they did not notice.

"We are not looking for trouble, but as you say you shot one of mine and I would like to look at the man that could pull the trigger like that."

"Just go and don't come back."

"That is not going to happen."

He started to say more but was cut off when shots rang out from the other side. I am guessing our guys were engaging the other group. At least that's what I was hoping. As I watched the leader of this group made a few hand motions to his team and they spread out around him. They were adding distance between them and trying to get a better bead on where we were. As they did this a couple of shots went off from different positions. It was our guys shooting to keep them behind cover and hemmed in. This was a tactic that we had worked out to try to keep them grouped together. This was the first time we had put it into action. We would have to see if it worked.

Their team stopped moving and took cover again. This time though they lost a little bit of bearing and a few of them shot blind into the areas of our shots. Their leader did not seem happy about this and let them know it. I could not make out the words, but the idea was there. The downed guy was moving more and was trying to sit up. As I watched the guy went from prone to standing. Dread filled my soul. The movements were like the dead guy in the house that had killed the captain. This guy was not alive, I had killed him. He was now rising from the dead to live again as a deader. I had never seen the dead rise before, it was simple yet unnerving. It also did not take as long as I suspected it would. Not good.

As the guy started looking around the members of the raiders finally became aware of their teammate moving around again. They quickly turned away from us and concentrated their attention on him. It quickly moved to the nearest man and tried to attack him. Shots rang out from a couple of the raiders as the deader approached. It for the most part ignored the bullets and concentrated on its target. The amount of abuse this thing took was amazing. As it came closer, the raiders backed up keeping it at a minimum five-foot distance. My team let them move from cover. None of us could shoot at them to keep them hemmed in just to watch them die at the hands of a deader. One of the guys tripped on a plant and fell backward. As his teammates tried to help him up the deader leaped towards them. He landed on the downed guy. Instead of trying to save him the others jumped back and one shot the downed teammate in the head killing him instantly.

I was amazed and awed that these people could turn against their own so fast. He had not been bitten or scratched. The guy just shot him to put him out of his misery. This did not help though, as soon as the life left the downed raider, the deader lost interest and ran towards the next. That guy dodged but backed into another teammate and they both went down in a heap. The deader turned faster than should have been possible and jumped on the downed two. One was not lucky (unlucky) enough to be killed before the deader grabbed him.

I could not see what happened but the deader grabbed the guy, he went rigid and then limp in a matter of 30 seconds. The deader moved on to attack again and that raider never moved again. As this was happening the first downed raider sat up and joined his deader brethren in the attack. I guess shooting him in the head did not stop him from rising again. I watched as the leader of the raiders looked confused too. This seemed to break their resolve. The group broke ranks and started running out of the community. Their leader tried to keep them together at first but then threw up his hands and joined them. I sent a scout after them to make sure they left and stayed gone while the rest of us kept an eye on our two deaders.

A couple of minutes later the scout reported back. Not only had our group left but so had the other group. I guessed that they had some type of communication between them to stay together so closely. That being the case I sent another scout off to find the rest of our security team and have them join us. We needed a plan to deal with these deaders.

Once the other team joined us we talked and came up with a bad plan, but the only one we could come up with. We would have one of us play decoy and lead them into an empty house. Once in the house, the decoy would run out of the back door and then someone else would close the front door. We would board this house up so everyone stayed away. Since we did not know how to kill them, it was the best we could do.

I volunteered to be the decoy and shed my gear so I could move faster. Running was my thing, I just did not enjoy running for my life. A couple of minutes later we were all set up and it was time to get started. The deaders had moved after the raiders for a bit, but then just started milling about in front of one of the homes towards the front of the development. We picked a house just away from them and made our move.

I ran towards the deaders waving my arms and screaming like an idiot. I did not know what attracted these things so I tried it all. Whichever it was, I got their attention a little faster than I had hoped. As they approached me I turned on the speed and ran towards the house we had picked. I reached the house with about

10 feet of clear space behind me. That was until I tripped up the stairs and face-planted just inside the door.

Stupid! I got to my feet but I had lost almost half of my lead. I couldn't dwell on it. I just got up and sprinted through the house. I had been in this house a lot as a kid which was part of the reason we picked it. The floor plan was pretty open, but it had a few walls to separate the rooms. This would allow me to keep the deaders close but still have some security. A few seconds after entering the house, the back door was in sight. I heard the front door slam shut. I was then clear of the back door and then it was shut behind me.

"Well, that was easier than I thought." I said this knowing that my heart was still beating out of my chest.

"Yeah well let's not do that again." My dad said as he drew me into a hug.

"Just another day in the new world. Just doing my job."

"Ok next time someone else can take that part though."

"We will see. I am just glad that is over. Let's get this thing boarded up and get some lunch. I'm hungry."

My dad just smiled and chuckled to himself. He knew how scared I was and I knew he was just as scared. Neither of us would admit it though. Not sure why we wouldn't, but with each other, this is how we expressed it. Just our way I guess.

Broken

The following days went by without anything bringing so much adrenalin. All the decorations were taken down and the days droned on. We lost two people to illness in the month of January. With everyone living close by and knowing that they were ill we were able to move them to an empty house and board it up before they rose again.

This is how we decided to deal with any deaths. Within minutes of the death, we had to have the body in an empty house. There were plenty of houses that were not being used so we did not have any problems doing it. We never opened the homes that we boarded up to see if the deaders were still moving around. I think that none of us wanted to know.

Another side of putting the dead in these houses was security. Not only did this keep them from attacking us, but if another group of raiders decided to go house to house, they would have a big surprise. Hopefully enough to keep them away.

All in all the winter that started cold early had stayed pretty temperate in January. I took longer rides and stay out a little longer than I probably should have because the weather was nice. I was the head of security, I helped my dad work on the other's homes and our own. I liked the rides as a way to get away. I was not shirking responsibilities, I was one of the only ones that would go out into town. When I was gone my second in command, also an Eagle Scout was filling in just fine. He had as much training and knowledge as I did. I just had more real-world experience since the Fall.

Ava had started getting more responsibility. She was taking a group of older kids into the woods to gather wood and look for anything useful. She wanted to learn how to ride my bike and start going on forays with me. I had spoken to Dad about this and he was almost on board. I think in the spring he would relent and let her go. Eventually, maybe she could do the run on her own. The only part that may hold it all up was if she was going to go out we needed to tell her about the deaders. She had been sheltered about them for the most part. We had not even told her about the roaming dead-locked in the boarded-up homes in our community. I hated keeping things from her. We used to be close and talked quite a bit. With the things that I had been through and the things that I have had to do and keep from her and Mom, I felt like a distance was building between us. I did not like it but it was Dad's wish to keep certain things to myself.

Before I knew it January was at an end. Dad's vegetable garden was producing a few carrots and broccoli, we were still waiting on the squash and other veggies. It was nice getting fresh vegetables in the meat stew that we ate more nights than not. It was easy to keep the pot warm and add new things to it each day to keep things fresh. It was what they did back in the day, or at least that's what I was told.

I went out on a foray into Lewes on the first day of February. A day that would live in infamy for me and my family. The day started normally. Mom and Dad had the dinner shift for the community tonight. Mom had asked for some kind of sweets if I could find them. I decided that Lewes would be the best bet because there were some confectionery shops and candy stores in the area. I kissed Mom, petted Andromeda and waved to Ava and Dad on my way out for the day. My bike had been acting a little weird over the last couple of trips. I thought that maybe the gas was starting to go bad and gum up the engine but I hoped it was just a fouled spark plug. While on my trip to Lewes I was also going to stop by a few of the auto parts stores to look for parts.

As I got into town I found a few things for Mom and the parts I needed for my bike pretty quickly. I found more than I could carry, so I decided to take a few things and hide them in the stores to pick up later. I kept a mental inventory of what was there. Hopefully, no one would look too hard when they came into the stores. With the day going so well I felt like I had time to kill before having to get back so I headed down to an old stomping ground, Lewes Bay beach. There used to be a Dairy Queen there and we would watch the Cape May-Lewes Ferry come and go throughout the summer with our great-grandmother.

I shut the bike off and walked to the water. -Yes I made sure I took the key with me- I walked up and down the beach for a while just lost in the past and feeling the need to relax. The pressure of having to be responsible for the security and safety of others were getting to me. I had never wanted any type of management role, especially one where the results were counted in lives saved and lost. I guess I got lost a little longer than I had expected, the next thing I knew the sun was on its lower arc. Damn, too much time had gone by.

I ran back to the bike. A little lost time would not be life or death. I did have other responsibilities to attend to. Dad wanted me to help Mom cut the veggies for the dinner tonight. As I got on the bike I kicked the starter and got it running. It immediately chugged and conked out. Frustrated, I kicked it again and again. Nothing. Anger started taking over and I kicked the bike one good time.

Pain brought me back into reality and I stopped ranting and decided to think. If the bike was struggling it may very well be the spark plug. I had a new one and the tools to replace it. The time taken would be minimal and then I would be back on the road. If that was the issue. One problem at a time. I grabbed my bag and went to work swapping out the plug. Minutes later everything was back together and I got back on the bike. Hoping and praying, I kicked it and it chugged. The second time it fired up and ran smoothly. I got lucky. I picked up my bag and got it set on my shoulders. I put the bike in gear and headed towards home.

As I was leaving Lewes I saw a large group of people on the road ahead of me. It was either deaders or raiders. Either way, I needed to be far away from them. I turned the bike down a side road. There were only two roads in and out of the town heading west. The group was on one so I headed to the other. As I turned down that road I saw cars blocking the path completely. It was odd but maybe people in the area did not want anyone on their road. Instead of going back out to the main road again and risking being seen, I decided to take the bike through the connecting backyards. This would keep me screened from anyone on the main road. It was a little slower going, but again there was no rush. The only urgency was trying to be home before sundown. Being the winter the sunset was early, but I still had plenty of time.

As I went through the third yard, I crested a small hill and came down looking at a very large pool of water. It looked like this homeowner decided his backyard should be a pond, foliage and all. I had very little time to adjust my course. As I did my bag threw my balance off a little and I came down hard on my left ankle before I was able to correct and get straight. My ankle hurt a bit but it was nothing that would hinder my riding. I headed out to the main road. I looked west and saw that the group had not moved much in the intervening minutes. I was well out and safe from prying eyes. I got back to Dewey Ave., My great-grandmother had lived on this street. The street was clear so I opened up the bike and shot toward home again.

The other road was clear and I had gotten very comfortable on the bike over the last few months so I was able to pour the speed on and make up a little time. The bike was running better so I was able to make good time. I finally made it home with no other distractions.

As I came up to the community something did not seem right. I slowed to a stop and removed my helmet to hear better. As soon as I did I heard shots ring out followed by a deader scream. My blood ran cold, the community was under attack and I had not been there to help. I quickly put my helmet back on and grabbed a gear. I shot into the community and pulled up to the very first house on the right. I stashed the bike on the side of the home and removed my helmet again. Multiple shots rang out followed by human yelling and screams. These all came from the rear part of the community. I pulled the pistol from my holster and ran around the back of the homes towards the fight.

I walked past one of the homes that we had boarded up. As I came up to the corner and looked around. My foot seemed to stick to the ground as I tried to move. Fear went through me until I realized that my boot was stuck on a nail. I calmed down and pulled my foot straight up to clear it. Then fear struck me again. I was standing on one of the plywood boards that we had used to close up the house and keep the deaders in. I was confused at first then realized the deaders attacking the community must be the ones that we kept locked away. I took a quick look at the other homes that we had locked down. All of them had the boards removed from the doors. My first thought was; How did they get out? That was quickly followed up by the fact that the doors were open and not broken. The deaders could not have broken their way out, they were let out. But, by whom? Answers to these questions had to wait. I would talk to my dad after this was over and we were safe. He would help me figure it all out. I decided that sneaking around the back was going to take too long. I needed to be safe, but quick. I decided that straight down the middle was the right way to go. There were houses to cover me, but it was a straight line to my house. There was no time to lose, I didn't know how long this attack had already been happening.

I reached the house across the street from my own. I could see a couple of bodies in the yards and street. Some of the bodies were bloody while others were not. In the driveway, I saw one of my friend's mom. She was bloody but still alive. I glanced across at my house and everything seemed to be clear and calm. I needed to help her first. I checked the area again and took off at a fast crouch to her. As soon as I got close I realized the mistake that I made. I looked at her eyes and they were glowing blue. She was a deader! There was so much blood that I did not see the injury to her chest and hips. She was barely moving because of the damage to her body, not because she was hurt. I quickly moved away from her and crossed the street.

There was no movement in my front yard, I moved around the left side of the house just as I did I heard a shotgun blast go off in the neighbor's yard. It was screened by large trees and an 8-foot fence. I quickly ran to the back of the fence line to see what was happening. As I reached the end of the fence I pulled my pistol up in the ready position and slowly peaked around. There was a mass of bodies at the neighbor's back door. It seemed like they were trying to get into the house but something was keeping them out. As I watched, that was something that was someone, the husband. As I watched the door gave and he was pulled out of the doorway and pounced upon by three deaders. His scream was short but piercing. Shaking my head for not being able to do anything for my elderly neighbor, I gathered myself and ran back to the street. I hid in the trees while I looked up and down the street for the source of the shooting. As I was looking, my dad ran around from the right side of our house and headed straight for me.

Just behind him were three deaders. They were fast and gaining on my dad quickly. He seemed injured and had blood all over the front of him down to his boots. I called out to him, which was a mistake. He slowed as he looked up towards my call. This half-step was all it took for the deaders to overtake him. As the first one grabbed his shoulder Dad turned and pulled the trigger on his shotgun. The blast at that close range took half of the face-off the deader. It fell, releasing its grip on his shoulder, but that was quickly replaced with another deader grabbing his shirt. My dad was able to pull them along until he got to the driveway. As he did the third deader tackled Dad at his legs and they all went down in a heap. Amazingly the deader missing half of his face was back in the fight too.

What did it take to kill these things? As this thought passed through my head it dropped on top of my dad. I ran from my cover and raised the pistol and aim at the creatures trying to kill my dad. I hesitated as I lined up the first shot worried that I would hit Dad. This hesitation allowed one of the deaders to look up and see me. His face was pure electric. The look of satisfaction as it tried to kill my father was pure evil. Its head was up so I took my shot. I missed wide right but got its attention on me. If I could draw this one off maybe Dad could fight off the other two. The deader rose to come after me. Suddenly, the deader was back on the ground.

"Matthew! Run. Run for your life and save the girls. They are your responsibility now."

"What? No! Let him go. I'll draw him off."

"It's too late. I can already feel it. I will hold them here as long as I can. You go. Get the girls. Take care of them."

I took a step towards my dad. There was no way I was leaving him there. Tears had started to blur my vision. I knew that I could not save him. I knew there was nothing that I could do, but I had to try. I had to do something to get these creatures off of him, even if it meant them taking me instead.

"Matthew. Go. Get the girls. My job is finished. I have protected everyone as long as I could. It's your job now. I am passing the responsibility to you. Your job is not done."

"Where? Where are they? I'll get them and come back for you."

"No use coming back. Just go. They're safe. Hiding..." As he spoke his head lulled to the side. The deaders stopped looking at him and started to rise as they looked back at me.

"Dad?! Dad! Where are they hiding?" I called out one last time.

I never heard anything more from him. He died there on the pavement more worried about Mom, Ava and me than himself. I could not shake the feeling that my call out to him and my lack of action caused his death in some way. I stood there for a few more seconds then took off towards the back of the house. The fire and the cooking pot had been knocked around and had spilled its contents across the patio.

I got to the back door and pulled it open. I shut the door softly behind me. I did not call out to draw any attention to myself. I did not know if anyone was about that shouldn't be. I quickly checked Ava's room. I then went to my room and grabbed my go bag. I went through the house in under 30 seconds. I had not heard from the girls or seen any signs of Andromeda. I let out a very low whistle to get her attention. If Andromeda was not in the house neither was Ava. This then led to the idea that Mom was not here either. They must have been hiding somewhere else.

As quietly as I entered, I left. I decided to circle back to the front of the community, checking the homes as I went until I found the girls. I refused to walk to the front of our house, there was no way I could stand seeing Dad dead on the ground. Part of me hoped that he would be ok. But I knew he was not, that our family would never be the same again and that it was all my fault.

Red

As soon as I rounded the back of the neighbor's fence I saw a new enemy entering the fray. There was a group of bandits working their way through the other backyards checking homes as they went. It looked like the same guys that we had run off a couple of weeks ago. They must have been the ones that opened the boarded-up homes and released the deaders. We gave them a weapon against us.

The group was leaving the house two doors down as I rounded the fence. I was angry and these people were the ones that caused all of the chaos and death in my community. Anger blacked out all thought. These people were the ones responsible for Dad's death. They were responsible for the fact that I could not find my mother and sister.

I hid in a couple of trees and waited for them to enter the next house. As they entered they left one member outside of the door front door and one outside the backdoor to keep watch. Good, they kept the same pattern. As he turned his back I ran and covered the distance between us in seconds. The ground was soft so there was no sound to carry to his ears. I was on him and tackled him to the ground before he knew what hit him.

We wrestled on the ground for a few seconds until I pulled my gun and shot him in the temple point blank. Red mist filled the air as the red in my vision consumed all. The gunshot drew the attention of the other members and I could hear boots running through the home to the back door. I waited until they stopped and the knob started to turn, then emptied my pistol into the door. The gun had enough punch to go through the door and into anyone that was behind it.

With my gun empty, I reached down and grabbed the M4 that the bandit had carried. I pointed it toward the house and pulled the trigger. The weapon was set to fully automatic. After a short burst to the left of the door, I fired another to the right. More boots were hitting the floor as they ran towards the front but also cries of pain from inside. The weapon jammed open, meaning it was empty. I did not have time to look for another clip on the body in front of me, assuming he even had one. I dropped the M4 and reloaded my pistol. All the training that Dad had put me through made it all muscle memory, no thought. As I sent the slide home on the pistol the front door guard rounded the corner of the home. He slowed as he came around the corner. I dropped to one knee and sighted him up. As he lifted his weapon towards me I pumped one round into his chest and one into his neck. He quickly dropped. The others would be coming around the house soon too. I did not know how many were left so I decided to run. I had to draw these killers away from the community. I did not know where the girls were so I could not let these guys search for any more homes. I could only hope that they had not been found before I had run into the bandits.

As I ran into the next yard I heard the bandits yelling. A couple of them fired their weapons in my direction. As I rounded the side of the house a bullet hit my bag and my shoulder. The impact and the turn threw me to the ground. I rolled and came out of my backpack. I did not have the time to fix it, so I left it and continued to run. My shoulder hurt but worked. I would have to worry about it later. A couple of more yards to go and I would reach my bike. I seemed to be pulling away from my pursuers. I would need the lead to increase a little bit more so I dug deep and poured more anger and pain into my stride. I would only need a few seconds to get the bike started and get moving.

I could see the house hiding my bike as more shots rang out. Distance helped as the shots went wide. I took a glance back and could see that there were only 5 guys following me. Hopefully, these were the only ones left to be able to move quickly. I decided to slow down just a bit and raised the pistol. I flung a couple of rounds back in their direction to get them to slow further. It was a gamble, but it worked as they dove for cover.

I reached for the bike and jumped on. I kicked the starter and it fired up quickly. I was really glad I had replaced the spark plug earlier. -Wow, had all of that happened on the same day?- I pushed the thought away and put the bike in gear. If I tried to run away from them they would have a couple of seconds of good shots at me. I decided to play chicken with them. Something that they would hopefully not expect. I quickly reloaded the pistol and put it in my weaker left hand. I turned the bike towards them and poured on the speed.

I tore off from around the house and directly into the group of bandits. They were closer than I thought they would be, or I took longer than I thought. They quickly scattered as I ran into their group. They had surprised me so I was not able to get any shots off. Luckily, they weren't either. After I passed them, I dug in my heel and spun the bike in a 180-degree turn to go right back at them. This time I was ready and aimed the gun, firing off as I went through them again. Between the bike playing chicken with them and the shots thrown in their direction, they all threw themselves out of the way and to the ground.

Seconds later I was past them and headed to the open road. I bent over the handlebars as far as I could go, leaving them the smallest target I could. A few shots rang out but nothing hit me. I was not sure about the bike. Then I was clear and turning down the main road. I was hoping that I had just made their lives difficult enough to have them leave and follow me instead of staying in the community. It was all I could do to make up for getting my father killed.

A few miles down the road I stopped on the side of the road. I had not heard any type of pursuit. I thought that the bandits were on foot so they would not have been able to keep up even if they had pursued. As I sat on the side of the road the anger left my body in a rush. The day and events caught up with me and I broke down. Five minutes later I pulled myself together. My father had died and I had killed an unknown number of people in cold blood. The men had been killers and thieves, but that did not change the fact that I had lost myself and killed those men in anger. I told myself that it was necessary. That it was needed to protect the others in the community. That it was to protect what was left of my family. But I also knew it was the anger. It took over and I needed to focus it. I honed it to a point and found the easiest and closest target.

I had to take stock of my situation. I lost my bag and only had one clip of ammunition left. The day was warm so I only had a light sweatshirt, which was covered in blood and had a hole in the shoulder. Thinking about that I pulled the material back and checked the wound. It was just a graze. It would scar and it bled like hell, but no real damage done.

What I needed to do was get back around the bandits and check the community again for Mom and Ava. If I headed east a little further I could take a side road that would take me along the field that ran up to the back of the community. I could go in on foot and see what was happening.

As I decided on this course of action I heard an engine rumble from the direction of the community. I turned to look and saw a large military-type vehicle speeding toward me. How much do you wanna bet that truck was not coming to help? I jumped back on the bike and got it started. I looked back one more time to see what this truck was doing. As I did, a guy leaned out of the passenger side window with a rifle pointed in my direction. I did not wait any longer. I grabbed a gear and jetted off to the west. The truck accelerated after me.

I was able to stay in front of them pretty easily. Their military truck was big and scary, but not very fast. I played with them for a little while making sure I led them farther and farther from the community. After I felt we were far enough away and the night was setting in, I put the throttle down and pulled away from them quickly. I had been trying so hard to lead them away that I was a little lost. No matter. Sussex County was pretty easy, just head in one direction until you hit one of 6 major roads. I decided to just keep heading what seemed to be west until I found a road I knew. It was a bit harder nowadays with no lights keeping the roads lit up the road signs were harder to see. It also did not help that it was cloudy so the moon was no help.

Before I was able to find a road I knew, the bike decided to sputter and die. There should be no way that it was out of gas. I glided as far as it would let me, then got off and pushed it off the road. There was a house next to the road that seemed abandoned. I pushed the bike behind the house and then headed to the front door. The house had an enclosed porch on the front. The storm door was broken and hanging off at an odd angle. No worries, a lot of these homes had these doors broken. As I stepped on the porch though a sudden sense of dread came over me. The front door to the home was broken too. My initial thought was to leave and try another house. But this area was not that populated before The Fall so there were not many houses around. I tightened the grip on my pistol and headed in to clear the house. As I walked through the house nothing seemed out of place. It was a single-story house with no basement so I cleared it quickly.

Since the house was clear I decided to go ahead and stay. I went back out to check the bike and found that the gas tank was empty. There was no light so I could not diagnose the issue at that time. I went back into the house and decided to figure the issue out in the morning. I pushed the front door as closed as I could then sat down on the couch to figure out my next steps. The day and emotions must have caught up with me because the next thing I knew it was morning. I came awake instantly and jumped off the couch. Something had woken me up. I looked towards the front door and could see bodies walking up the stairs onto the front porch. Last night I had pushed the door closed as much as possible, but it still hung off at an odd angle. A small push and it would fall inward allowing entry. The couch I had laid on last night was pushed up against the far wall that housed a bookcase. With the little time that I had left I dove behind the couch and hid there. I had nothing with me to grab. My pistol was still on my hip and I had nothing else with me. There should be nothing to show that I had been there.

The people pushed the door open and walked into the room. I could hear them moving about, but no one was talking or making any other noise. I decided to take a quick peek around the couch to see what I was dealing with. I saw six bodies. Five adults and one child. All of them were moving oddly. One seemed to sense that I was watching. As it turned its head towards me I could see glowing blue eyes. It was a deader. They were all deaders!

I did not wait for anything else. I bolted from my hiding spot and ran out of the open front door. Luckily I did not have any gear with me because the couch and the door were tight fits as was. As I hit the front yard more deaders were heading for the house. I was running and looking for pursuit so I was not able to adjust quickly enough. I ran into one, bounced off and into another. I couldn't think. I didn't have time to think. I just ran. I hit my pace and kept running in a straight line. These creatures were out all night. I was rested. They were dead and relied on something supernatural to feed their muscles. I was lean, and mean and had been well-fed over the last couple of months. This meant I should be able to outrun them.

A couple of minutes later, I started to flag. I looked behind me and did not see any deaders following. Either I outran them or they did not pursue. I could not tell you, I had not looked behind me since I broke through the outer door of the porch. During the mad dash to safety. I had not had any thought other than to get away. I had not thought through surviving. I had lost my bag and my gear during the run-in with the bandits at the community, now I lost my bike running from the deader den. The light sweatshirt I was wearing would not help long in the February cold.

I lacked a plan of any sort. Running from the bandits stopped me from staying in the community and searching for the girls. I had started yesterday relaxed, belly full and with a full set of supplies in Lewes. I was now lost somewhere between Millsboro and Laurel, with no bike, no supplies, hungry and stressed. I had also started yesterday with a full family, now I was alone.

Cold

The day was cold. Starting the morning with an all-out run and breaking a sweat did not help. I was thirsty, hungry and tired before the day was two hours old. The mad dash from the deader den had taken a lot of my energy from me too. That on top of depressive thoughts running around my head flagged me more than a hot day running for Coach in Florida.

Thinking of Florida only seemed to make me colder. The days than had been happy and I had a lot of my life ahead of me. Now I was sure that I had blown my family apart and that we would never be together again. I could not stop these thoughts from rolling around my head. It felt like they were creating a black hole in my mind pulling in everything that would give me hope or make me happy and destroying it with the black of nothingness.

It was in this state that I wandered throughout the day. I had no direction. By the time the sun started to set I found that I had walked west instead of east and ended up in Seaford instead of heading back to Millsboro. It had gotten too late in the day to do anything about it. Not like I would have made the correct choice anyway. Everything that I had been doing turned out wrong. Including running the security team in the community. When they needed me most, I was out sunning on the beach. The idea to keep the deaders locked in their homes instead of finding a way to kill them was a bright idea too. It let the bandits use them against us and kill the people I was supposed to be protecting. With these thoughts, I found a house that I could crash in for the night. Maybe it would have food and water too. But, the last house I entered was a deader den. I did not feel that a decision to enter the house would end well. I decided instead to enter the woods near the home and stay there for the night.

I found a clearing that was well surrounded by holly trees and old briers. It should keep me cloaked and safe for the night. It only got colder as the sun went down. I decided that I had to risk a fire for the night to survive. I gathered enough wood and started the process of lighting a fire without a lighter or flint and steel. I had done it a couple of times before in the Scouts for wilderness survival. It took a while and had to be done correctly. I most likely would screw it up and freeze to death overnight.

Surprisingly, I got the fire going and was able to warm up a bit. About an hour later I heard talking and footsteps in the woods. I quickly banked the fire to keep the light from escaping my burrow. I must have been too late because a couple of minutes later five guys entered my little hideout. They looked rough. A few bloodstains on their clothes and open wounds on their faces. These guys had been through a lot. They looked a bit rough too.

"Well, who do we have here?" said a tall guy with a long bushy beard.

"It looks like a guy that is struggling a bit. He is out here with a banked fire and no coat on." The second guy was shorter but his beard was just as long, but straggly instead of bushy.

"It seems to be mighty cold out here for no fire and no jacket. Are you doing alright son?" Bushy beard said.

The other three guys kept a lookout on the area but did not seem threatening or overly dangerous. Really what did I have to steal? The clothes on my back were well-worn and not something that most people would desire. Plus all of the guys were stockier than I was so they wouldn't fit anyway.

"I am just trying to get by until I can get back home." I told them.

"Well, where are you trying to get? Not much out this way." straggly beard said as he kneeled a few feet from me.

"Lewes-Millsboro area. I got turned around today and headed the wrong way. I was kinda out of it. I haven't eaten in a while." I was trying to be nondescript. There was something about these guys that I didn't like.

"Yeah, well why didn't you say so? Jacob get that fire back to burning. Let's give this guy some food. Mike give him your extra sweatshirt for a bit so he can warm up. We got some venison jerky, it ain't much but it should help. Here take my canteen you look thirsty." Bushy beard approached me with a canteen.

"What is all this gonna cost me? Not too many just handing stuff out anymore." I asked hesitantly.

"Nothing mate. Maybe just let us sit by your fire tonight. Then the lot of us can be on our way early tomorrow. Not good to be out here alone." He sat near me on an old log.

Jacob got the fire back burning pretty quickly as Mike lent me his sweatshirt. It was big and smelled a bit, but it was good to be warm. I opened the canteen and was so thirsty that I gulped a mouthful before realizing what it was. If you want to call it water it would be referred to as firewater. I pulled it down with a cough trying to get my breath as it burned all the way into my stomach. The guys had a good time laughing at me.

"Forgot to tell you that is lightning in a bottle. Found some homemade moonshine in a still a month back. It is pretty awful but it will warm you up. Take another shot while we warm up a small soup for us all." Bushy told me while he was laughing to himself.

I decided that a good buzz would do wonders for my depressive state. Food would help too. That was on its way so I took another gulp. That one was not as rough because I was expecting it. I had to make sure I did not keep gulping it down though. I hadn't eaten all day something that strong would hit fast and hard.

The guys and I started talking a bit as the soup started to steep. Turns out Bushy beard's name was Craig. I already knew Jacob and Mike. The other two were Andrew and William, though I was not sure which one was which. I would probably forget them all by morning anyway. They had been scavenging out near Millsboro a few days ago and were heading back to Harrington. They had been on the move for a couple of months. It had gotten cold in Delaware so they took what they had and decided to get to a house they knew they could keep warm. There was no one at home waiting for them, all they had was each other. The familiarity would be nice.

They talked about traveling together while passing around the soup and the lightning. The more they talked about their connection the more I drank and thought about my lost family. As the night went on things got a bit blurry. I do remember talking about a bunch of bandits that had attacked my community by letting the deaders out of the houses and setting them on my friends and family. I didn't pick up on it at the time, but Craig seemed to pass a peculiar look onto his friends.

They asked questions about it and I told them that I had shot a guy point blank then shot into a house and hurt a couple of guys. I wasn't proud but I had just lost my family and needed to make others hurt too. I kept rambling about getting to my bike and running the guys down before heading out and getting lost on the way.

"Where is this bike of yours bud?" Craig asked.

"Lost it. Ran out of gas and then decided to sleep in a deader den for the night. Real bright huh?" I drunkenly blurted. I am not even sure my sentences were coherent by this point. The lighting was doing a number on my brain. I was finally warm, but I could not seem to stop talking. The guys seemed interested in my story and everything I had done since. Any time I had a break in my story they would pass the lightning to me and ask another question.

The rest of the night disappeared.

The morning came with my head and stomach aching. I rolled over to puke up last night's libations and found that my hands were tied behind me. My legs were tied together too. I looked around and found Craig sitting on a log across the long-dead, fire from me.

"Well good morning sunshine. Did you have a good night last night? You certainly put a hurting on my shine supply. It's alright though. It got you talking and kept you doing that all night long." As he was talking he reached behind his back and pulled out a backpack. "Look familiar Matthew?"

My eyes and head were in so much pain that the confusion was hard to shake off. He lifted it up again and showed me a hole in the bag.

"Let me help. You look confused. It's your bag. See this is where you got shot and rolled out of it to run away like a coward after bull-rushing and killing a guy trying to get food for his family." Craig was snarling by this point.

Slowly my brain started to catch up. Only until my stomach finally gave up and I puked all over myself. It took three solid minutes to get my stomach to stop rejecting its contents. I could then look and found that it was my bag. The certainty of that and who these guys were slammed into me like a Mack truck.

"I... I know who you are."

"Yeah, we figured out who you were last night." He looked up as two guys, William and Andrew I think, grabbed me and sat me in front of a tree. They took another rope and tied me to it so I could not lean forward or move at all. "You are the one who killed members of our family. You killed Todd outside. Then George and Michael when you shot through the door. Michael did not die right away. He died rather painfully over the next day." Craig glared at me and then stood up. "Now you are going to die in a rather painful way too."

The two guys behind me grabbed my head and mouth. They started pouring the moonshine down my throat. I tried not to drink but it was coming so fast that I felt like I was breathing it in. They did this four or five times. There was no food in my stomach left from last night and my hangover was already giving me a blazing headache and body aches. After I was able to catch my breath they did it again until the bottle was empty.

"Now, you drank quite a bit last night until you blacked out. You just took in that much and a little more. With the fact that you just chunked up all the contents of your stomach, I think this may hit you a little harder. You know it makes you feel warmer, but actually lowers your body temperature allowing you to catch hypothermia a lot easier?"

As he said that Jacob and Mike threw a large bucket of water all over me. I realized then that the sweatshirt was also missing. I was down to my t-shirt and jeans. They even took my shoes and socks. I couldn't tell before because the bindings were so tight I was losing feeling in my feet. The water was cold and I started to shiver as soon as it hit me.

"So you get to stay here and freeze to death. It doesn't look like a warm day coming. So you can think about the revenge you tried to take out on my family. Remember karma comes back tenfold there my boy." Craig turned with the last word and headed off into the woods.

The others fell into step behind him. I called out for them, but they never stopped to look back. A minute later Jacob came back and set a radio down near me. It was a bigger battery-operated type. He turned it on to a channel with static and maxed out the volume. The screeching was like ice to my brain. It was way too loud, I couldn't think. He stood up and spit in my direction then walked off. I never saw any of those five guys again.

I guess it was karma for them to find me. I deserved this death. I deserved it for killing the people they loved and letting the ones I loved die. Hours went by with brain-numbing cold and static. After a while, I forgot why I was sitting in the woods. I needed to get up and get home the sun would be going down soon. Dad would be mad if I was home late. As I thought about that, my dad walked out of the woods and told me to get up and get home. I tried to get up but found that my legs and arms weren't working. I tried to tell him something was wrong, but he didn't want to listen to excuses. He told me that I left before the job was done and that I had things to do.

I was really confused and tried to get up again. I noticed that I was no longer cold, it seemed odd but I thought that maybe this was a problem. I couldn't for the life of me figure out why though, I hated being cold. I was having a little trouble breathing and I was starting to get really tired. I somehow knew that I needed to stay awake, but I didn't want to. I looked for my dad, but he was gone. He could have at least turned the radio off. The music was bad, although I couldn't focus enough to tell the genre. I fought to stay awake for a little while longer, but as the sun went down I could not keep my eyes open any longer. It felt ok though because I would be able to see my dad again. Something kept telling me that if I went to sleep I would be with my dad again. That did not seem too bad. I just let it take over and I went to sleep. It was a sleep was deeper than anything that I had ever felt. My breathing problems stopped and my arms were able to relax. I sank deep into the tree behind me and deep into myself. Everything seemed to be working out ok. I would sleep, be warm and feel good.

Bright

There was nothing but calm at first. I remember wondering what had happened. I couldn't see my dad or the woods any longer. There was a distinct lack of light from all around. An indeterminable amount of time later though, the world that had surrounded me started glowing a pale blue. It started small then grew bit by bit. The light was never bright but it seemed to be pushing me. It was pushing me to move. I had a feeling that this place was being overrun by this light. It did not belong here. Just as fear started creeping in there was a flash of bright light. It was white and clean. It pushed the blue light back a little bit, though it seemed to be hiding in the shadows, lurking, waiting for its time to take control. I am not sure why I felt this way about the blue light, but not the white. It was just a feeling deep down in my soul.

Suddenly, there was chaos all around me. Bright lights in my face and hard ground beneath my back. I blinked and looked around as I took in a very long and hurtful breath. Something was pushing on my chest. I turned my head and saw several people surrounding me. I was lifted off the ground. Feeling returned to my body. All of the pain and cold seemed to fire all at once. I wanted to go back to the place where nothing hurt. To give in and rest. The only thing stopping me was the thought of my dad being ashamed of me for giving up when there was still work to be done.

The feeling of sleep tried to take me again. I fought so I could find out what was happening and where my dad was but the blackness won and I passed out again before I got any of those answers. As the white light receded and the world started to go black, the blue light seeped back in just as slowly. Oozing from the depths of somewhere to take control. The light was a dim blue.I felt that if I let it, and the other light did not return, the blue would get brighter. The brighter that blue light became, the harder I had to fight against it. The blue light pulsed dim then bright. Seconds seemed to go by and then it pulsed again. This time though it went even dimmer and seemed to recede completely.

The next thing I knew I was awake again riding along in a vehicle of some sort. I was strapped down to the cot that I was carried on before. Tubes and wires were strung across me and connected to me in various places. The road was jarring. I could hear others talking, but I could not seem to move or communicate with them.

"He is back. I've got a steady rhythm again. We keep losing him though." said a voice to my left.

"How many times have we lost him now? Three, four?" a second voice from behind me.

"Well if you count when we found him it would be four. But besides that time none of them have been for long. I don't think he should have any permanent brain damage."

"We don't know how long he was outside wet and freezing. We don't know how long he was gone the first time."

"We also don't know him. He may have been stupid before and we won't be able to tell." This one was the first male voice I had heard. It was to my right.

"We save who we find. That is the mission." From my left.

"Yet we don't cut the mission short to rush one guy back to the center. We are also out here to find supplies to keep us alive." The male stated quite loudly.

"Stand down private. It was my call." The voice to the left seemed to be in charge. Somehow this group was military or paramilitary.

That was all I could recall before it went black again. This time though the blue light was there, but did not creep in. It seemed at peace in its place for now. Like I had asserted some dominance and now it was ok to sit back and wait. It was foreboding, but it also seemed to lose the evil feel to its nature. It was hard to think and it is hard to describe. It just felt like it was ok being a passenger all of a sudden.

Later, I was shaken awake as the vehicle I was in reached a steep incline. I felt as if I was going to slide out of the front windshield. "I hate this incline. Isn't there something we can do to make this ride a bit better?" It was the woman behind me.

"No, anything we have added has been washed away at high tide. We are just lucky we hit a low tide and did not have to wait. I am not sure if I can keep this guy alive by myself for too much longer." The leader quietly stated.

Quickly after we leveled back out the road got very, very bumpy. It felt like we were riding on an old cobblestone road that had been heaved up from a volcanic eruption and an earthquake. I am not sure why that was so descriptive, it's just how it felt. We then had a second or two of the smooth road before I felt like I was going to fall out of the back. We were going up a steep incline this time. I found I was able to move a bit and gripped the sides of the bed to stop myself from falling.

"Whoa, we got you. It is not as bad as it feels. Nothing and no one is going to fall out. I promise. We got you." The woman to my left.

"Yeah plus, you're strapped in. It would be the rest of us that fell out first." Laughed the guy to my right.

Once we hit the level ground again I was able to relax. I fell into a deep, dreamless sleep. The blue glow was still ever present but did not feel menacing. When I woke up again I was being drug out of the vehicle and placed on a rolling gurney. I tried to raise my head and look around, but it was strapped into place. I fought a little to see my surroundings. A light and gentle hand rested on my chest. No words, but it seemed to convey calm. I took it in and felt the warmth in that touch. It was nice to feel again. To feel anything but the pain that I had gone through before. Before the dark and the blue.

I lay there relaxed and watching the fluorescent lights pass by overhead. I could hear the beeping of machines and monitors in other areas. I must have been in a hospital of some sort. No other place had the smell of antiseptic quite the same as a hospital. I remember being in places like this for surgery as a child. Then when my great-grandmother got sick she spent months in and out of hospitals with walls and smells just like this.

The lights just buzzed as we rolled by on our way to a place I knew nothing about. The heat kicked on while I was under a vent. I felt the hot forced air hit my face. It felt so good after the cold that I had endured. The truck had been warmer and I had been under blankets but it seemed that I was still cold down to my bones. Down to my soul. I shut my eyes to the light and was welcomed by the ever-present blue field of light. I wondered if I would ever close my eyes again and not see that dim blue glow.

As this thought passed through my head I had a sudden moment of clarity. How was I in a hospital with working heat and lights? Anything with power was attacked by the deaders.

Electricity was out across the world. No one can have power at this point. I must have conveyed my confusion without words because the calming hand came down on my chest again. It made it seem like this was all normal and everything would be ok.

I am not sure why I had this feeling with someone I could not even see, let alone had not met yet. I felt safe when they touched me. I would meet them eventually and I would ask them about the things that were bothering me. At that moment the only thing that seemed to be bothering me much at all was the need to sleep again. I closed my eyes and let the blue fade in. I let the worries slip away and concentrated on getting a deep healing sleep. When I awoke I would find out the answers to all of my questions. Of that I was sure.

The blue seeped in and was becoming a comfort to me now. It's funny how fast we can adapt to something new even if it is foreign and not understood. There was no such thing as normal and we adapted to new norms everyday.

Christiana

I woke up in a soft bed surrounded by soft sounds and the beeping of electrical machines. It was funny how not that long ago these sounds were everywhere and now they were out of place. I looked around the room that I was in. It was curtained off all around my bed so there was not much to see. I decided that I was just going to lay there a while longer until someone stopped by to check on me. I leaned back and closed my eyes. I was consciously trying to study the blue light that filled my vision when I closed my eyes. I sat there watching it come and go as I opened and closed my eyes. It was not bright, almost like light shining in your face when your eyes were closed. It was not enough to hurt or affect me falling asleep. As a matter of fact, I almost fell asleep again while waiting for someone to check on me.

That was until a thought pierced my mind and my soul at the same time. Deaders had glowing blue eyes. Is this what they saw? Was I undead? I had heard the others talking about losing me several times. Did they mean that I died several times? Had they used the electrical paddles to bring me back? Did it not work and I came back as a deader? Did deaders think about being dead? My mind was working overtime and in circles that would put Ava's questions per second to shame. I shot upright, the feeling of sleep completely lost in the panic that I had felt. As I tried to figure out the answers to these questions I heard an incessant beeping to my left. It was steadily beeping and increasing in pace every second. I could not take it anymore and thrashed my hand out and knocked the machine to the floor. I then got up and tore out the IV and tore off all of the sensor pads off my body. The beeping didn't stop it just became a high-pitched squeal.

As I got up to stomp the machine out of existence there was a commotion outside of the curtain. It was pulled back and three people in masks and scrubs stood still with their eyes wide. I realized that I was only wearing a hospital gown. My rear was hanging out in the breeze, though I am pretty sure that was not why they were staring. I slowly turned to them and pulled the gown closed in the back.

"Hello." I said as I waved nervously.

"What in the hell are you doing? First off, why are you out of bed, then why are you mauling our heart monitor?" The person that spoke was a tall woman with very intense eyes. She gave me a mom look that made me sit back on the bed.

"Sorry. It was loud." I sheepishly apologized.

"See that button? It is a call button. If it was too loud you call for us and we turn it down." She pointed to a white button strapped to the side of the bed. I looked at it and nodded.

"Wait, you said heart monitor?" I asked suddenly excited.

"Yes?"

"So I am not dead. I am not undead, not a deader?" I rambled as I sat up excitedly in bed.

"No, if you were a NLB you would be in a completely different area of the hospital. We only keep the living here." She came towards me and motioned for me to sit down.

An overwhelming sense of calm hit me so hard that I almost passed out. I felt like I had been holding my breath the whole time. The other two nurses came further into the room and started picking up the equipment that I had tried to destroy just seconds ago. The head nurse walked over and grabbed my arm to inspect the hole that the IV had been in.

"You did a number here. But we will just bandage it up. You can drink and eat now that you are awake. You know how close you were to becoming a NLB?" She looked at me quizzically as she cleaned the wound and bandaged it.

"You have said that twice now, I am assuming it is the same as a deader but what does it mean?"

"It means Non-Living Biological. It refers to the undead and is not so nonsensical as deader. It can also refer to other animals, not just humans." She explained. She had finished the bandage and the other two had reconnected my sensors. She then pushed me to lay back on the bed. "Now, no more tantrums. Please do not destroy any of my equipment. We do not have a lot of working pieces left. Are you hungry?"

I was ashamed of my actions and the fact that I was not thinking about anything when I was trying to destroy the heart monitor. I sheepishly nodded. The head nurse and one of the others left to finish their rounds or get me food, but they did not say. The third nurse paused as she was walking out. She was a small woman with bright blue eyes and dark brown hair.

"What happened to you out there? I heard a little from the soldiers but not a lot that made sense. They said they found you listening to a staticy radio while leaning on a tree in just a t-shirt."

"Well basically that is true, but none of it was my choice." I briefly explained the highlights of what had happened to her. "Can I ask you? Where are we?"

"You are at Christiana Hospital."

"Oh, I know that place, it's near Wilmington right?" I interrupted.

"Yes, we are underground and using generators to power all of the basement levels. We are working with a small division of soldiers that help get us supplies and bring us survivors." She slowly leaned again the wall, guessing that I had a few more questions.

"That is awesome. Have you been here long?" I sat up interested to learn what she knew.

"Yes, since the first death. My mom is one of the scientists that was studying the virus." She rolled her eyes like she didn't really want to be there. She stood up and turned to go.

"So you're not a nurse?"

"No I just help out. On the job training you could say. It was nice talking to you but I have to go get your food. I'll be back in a bit." She walked out and pulled the curtain.

I was alone again with the incessant beeping. I took it as a good sign this time as it meant my heart was beating. I sat back and thought about the little bit of information that I had gotten. I was still in Delaware and alive. That meant that once I was back on my feet I could get back home and make sure Mom and Ava were alright. I tried to stay positive and not think about them leaving the house or that anything had happened to them.

I was lost in thought when the nurse in training came back with my food. I was going to ask her some more questions but she handed me my plate, smiled at me and turned back around and left. The plate was small, but it smelled good. I ate slowly and let time pass. It was difficult to tell the time of day or how much time passed in a basement so I wasn't sure if I should sleep or try to stay awake. There was nothing worse than getting your circadian rhythm off. I was thinking about hitting the call button and asking when the curtain pulled back again. This time the woman entering was definitely not a nurse.

"Hello, I see you survived." She stood at the foot of the bed.

"Do I know you? Your voice sounds familiar."

"It should, I was on the team that found you and brought you back. Literally back to life and back to our base. I stopped in to see if you had lived or if my decision was the wrong one. I guess we won today." She hesitated. "Well, that is all I needed. See you around." She turned to walk back out of the curtain.

"Wait. I wanted to thank you. You know for saving my life. I heard someone saying that you shouldn't have done it."

"Yeah that was just Trey. He doesn't like when I make decisions he doesn't agree with. He always argues. He follows the orders but he complains a lot." She smiled as she said this.

"Well I appreciate you taking the chance."

"You would not happen to have any military experience, would you? Anything in security?" She asked slightly leaning forward.

"No military. I was a college student in Florida just before the lights went out and society fell." I wondered where her questions were going to lead.

"Florida? How the hell did you get back to Delaware then?" She seemed more interested.

"I drove my Liberty until it was stolen. Then I walked and found a motorcycle..."

"You have a motorcycle? What kind?"

"It was a small 250 cc dirt bike. But it is back in Millsboro or somewhere down there. I lost it. But it got me home and then I used it to do supply runs for my community."

"Crap, we could use a bike. But you mean you kept going out and getting supplies after the lights went out?" She seemed intrigued.

"Yeah. We needed stuff and I had the bike. I was also the only one to travel after the lockdowns. It just seemed like it should be me."

"You need a job?" She asked.

"No. I need to get back to Millsboro to check on my family as soon as possible." Hoping they would volunteer to take me back home.

"Millsboro, we found you near Seaford."

"Yeah, my community was attacked and I ran off trying to get the bandits to chase me. Afterwards I ended up in a deader den and got lost running from them." It seemed odd to sum it up so easily.

She looked at me with something I could not define. Was it curiosity or admiration? "We could use a guy like you. You sure you just need to get home?"

"I am not really a military type of guy." I started feeling uncomfortable. But then an idea hit me. "But if I join could we find my family and let them live here with me?"

"Technically we don't live here. We spend a lot of time on the road. Almost all of our time...."

"But my mom and sister could live here?" I interrupted.

"We could see. You have to get better first. Let me talk to the big guy." With that, she left. It was a very odd conversation. To offer me that type of position so easily did not seem to sit right. Did they need people that bad? I definitely did not want to join any odd military group. I had seen their type in all of the end-of-the-world comic books and movies. It was never good. I guess I would join though if it meant safety for the girls. That's always how they got you.

Offer

A couple of days went by and I did not see the female soldier again. I was starting to think that they would not let the girls live here. I knew if they didn't I would not stay here and help them at all. I had spoken to the nurses and found that I had lost two weeks. They said that I had woken up before yet I had no memory of it. It was already March. That meant the girls probably thought that I was dead. They had found dad and assumed that I was also gone. It pained me to think that they were alive and mourning me when I was alive. Of course, I was making the assumption that they were both still alive. This would always be my thought until I found their bodies. My family were survivors we would not go easy into the night. Regretfully, I almost had. It was a miracle that I was found at all. Let alone by a team that had the capability to save my life.

A couple of days later a soldier named Trey stopped by my bed. He wanted to see if I lived. "The only reason we found you was because of that static-producing radio. We had not seen any reason to go into that copse of trees, but the sound piqued our interest." he told me. He was very direct and didn't seem to care about how it sounded to me. It then got even better. "I also told Sarge not to save you. If you were tied up like that, obviously someone wanted you dead. You were either a thief, a rapist, or a murderer. We didn't need to worry about a person like that."

"That is not what it was at all. I was the victim because I ran across a couple of bandits." I explained.

"Well, that's your story and we have no one to corroborate it so i guess we have to believe it. Just know that I don't trust you because of how we found you. You will not be able to get the jump on anyone here. You got that?" He stared at me for a second too long then turned and left.

It was a disturbing realization that even though they saved me, people here may not trust me. Outsiders were always under suspicion in these types of situations. At least in comics. I did not have a lot of real-life situations to pull from on this subject. One morning, at least I assumed it was morning, Not too many days after that odd visit from Trey, the female soldier walked back into my room and handed me a cup of coffee. She looked like she had something to say. I just stayed quiet until she got to it.

"I have talked to you a couple of times and I don't even know your name." I broke the ice with an easy question.

"Huh? Oh. It's Veronica Hayes." She still seemed distant.

"Well, Veronica Hayes just say what you came here to say. You don't seem like the visit and sit idle type of person. I am really surprised you aren't back out in the field."

"Yeah." She laughed. "Not really. We are actually going back out tomorrow."

"Ok, so are you just here to say good bye and it's heartbreaking for you?" I laughed as I waggled my eyebrows at her.

"Ha!" A real laugh. "Not really there Romeo. Something has been bothering me. You look familiar but you said you came from Florida to Delaware. How did you get onto the peninsula? What route did you take?" This seemed to be the real reason for her hesitation.

"Well I was shot, I had lost my phone and my focus. I missed the bridge tunnel and came over the bay bridge from D.C."

As I said this she shot up so fast that the chair fell backward. "Are you kidding me!? You WERE the guy on the bike that we saved and then saw two days later coming across the bridge as they blew. I lost a team member in that explosion!"

"What? You were on the team that saved me in D.C.?" I stammcrcd.

"Yeah, the team that saved your ass that was on the ground and being drained by the NLB, only to run like a little bitch when we came to your aid. Trey was right. He thought it was you too. She had stopped talking to me and seemed to be working things out in her head as she stormed around my room. "Trey! Will! Get in here. Put this guy in a cell and lock him up. He should not be allowed to walk around here free. He was part of the crew that blew the bridge."

Trey and , I assume, Will stormed in and grabbed my arms and ripped the sensors off my chest. They were not nice about it either.

"Wait. No, I have no idea what that was. I wasn't part of it." I screamed at them as they dragged me out of the room.

Luckily I had changed into pants so my butt wasn't hanging out. "I just used it to get through the blockade. It was just bad timing."

No one seemed to be listening to me. They dragged me into another hallway with me screaming and pleading the whole way. I am not proud of it. I was saying everything I could to get them to let me leave. I needed them to let me go. I knew it had already been weeks and I needed to get back to the house to check on Mom and Ava. They needed my help.

The cell was empty and the door was strong and thick. It shut hard after they literally threw me in by my head. They turned and walked away. No one came to explain any further. I banged on the door for what seemed like an hour with no acknowledgment from anyone. I sat down with my back to the door and cried like a baby. Damn it, this sucked.

A couple of hours later a large older gentleman walked into the hallway and stopped in front of my door. By this time I had moved to the back of the cell sitting with my back to the wall and looking out of the small glass window in the door. All I could see was the ceiling and one of the fluorescent lights buzzing away with electricity. The guy looked through the small window and stared at me for a full minute before speaking. He seemed to be judging me or looking for something. He must not have found it. Or he did because he finally spoke.

"So you are the dangerous militia man that helped blow the bridges? You don't look like too much to me." he said as I tried to interrupt. He just held up his hand to stop me so he could continue. "I know what Sgt. Hayes believes. I know she thinks she knows what she saw. But I think she has some facts crossed or she doesn't have enough of the facts. I am going to ask you a few questions. I need you to stay seated there and answer honestly and without explanation unless I ask for it. . Can you do that?"

I nodded my affirmative.

"Good. Is your name Matthew Washington?"

"Yes."

"Did you travel from Florida to Delaware alone during the month of October?"

"Yes."

"Do you know who blew up the bridges here in Delaware?"

"I had nothing..." He held up a hand. So I changed my approach. "No."

"Do you know who blew up the tunnel in Virginia."

"I didn't even know the tunnel was blown up. No."

"Were you part of the militia that blew up the bay bridge ultimately killing one of my corporals?"

"No and I am sorry for your loss." I meant that too.

At this point, he had not moved a muscle. He had just fired off the questions in rapid succession. He must have gotten what he wanted because he then turned around and walked away with no further explanation. I was lost as to what I could do, I just sat there and tried to figure out how to get out and get back on the road.

I sat in the cell for another hour before I saw another soul. This soul was a small girl that brought me a tray of food. The door had a flap in it that she dropped to hand the tray to me. Once I took it she put the flap back up and walked away. She never looked at me or spoke a single word. After she walked away I realized it was the small nurse in training from before. We had some good conversations before. Now she seemed scared of me.

I sat down and ate the food I was given. Once I was done I sat the tray by the door and waited again. I tried to visualize my computer programs or my screen for the UAVs I flew in Florida. I could not remember what the screens looked like. I then tried to put a Dungeons and Dragons campaign together in my head for something to do, but I couldn't concentrate. Sitting there was a horrible feeling. All I could think about was Mom and Ava. How I was letting them down and failing my dad's last wish.

Later, dinner was brought to me in the same manner as lunch. It was a different person, but the demeanor was the same. All of these people thought I was a monster. I mean, if this was the same crew that saved me in D.C. I get them being mad that I left them. But putting me in with the militia group that killed their corporal and blew the bridges was just crazy. How could they think that I had anything to do with that. I told them I was coming from Florida and trying to get home. I always told them the truth. I had to make them believe me.

The lights went out a couple of hours later, or what I figured was a couple of hours since I had absolutely no way to tell time. They had left my watch with me, but it was still dead after the deader attack in D.C. I had never had the chance to replace the battery. I really just wore it out of habit.

The cell was pitch black. The odd blue glow crept into my vision and seemed to help me see in the dark. I could make out the walls, the door and the tray sitting on the floor. It wasn't as clear as I could see with the lights on, but I also wouldn't stumble if I had to traverse the cell in the dark. I decided that this was odd, yet compelling and needed to be understood. What caused this glow, and where did it come from? Did it have something to do with the deaders and what caused them to walk again after death? It had to be something similar because I had never heard of this phenomenon, even in my Sci-fi fiction books.

A couple of minutes after that the flap opened in the door and I heard an ear-splitting scream. The flap slammed shut and I heard feet running away from the cell. I had no idea what caused that commotion. I had bathed the day prior so the stink should have been minimal. A minute later I heard a group of boots stomping down the hallway. The door opened and the military guy that had asked the questions stood in the doorway surrounded by a group of fatigued soldiers, one of which was Veronica.

"Dear lord, what in the name of all that is holy are you?" He said this as he crossed his hands over his chest. "You need to come quietly with us. Do not fight. You will be restrained. Am I clear?" The soldiers seemed to be armed with batons and a riot shield.

"Yes." I was confused but figured I had to do what they said. "What is going on? What did I do?"

"It is not what you did, but what you are. Your eyes are glowing. The girls thought that you had died and risen again." He was hesitant to walk near me.

"What do you mean my eyes glow? Like a deaders? I am not dead. I am not one of those monsters. You can't treat me like one." I started to fight back, scared that they were going to have me killed. "I have to get back to my family. I have to make sure they are safe." I pleaded.

"We are not going to harm you. No matter what you may or may not have done prior, we need to see what you are now. We are going to take you to the scientists to see why your eyes glow like the dead." With that, he turned around and lead the group of soldiers down the hallway.

It was not a great change for me. I went from one cell to another. This one at least had a bed, yet the door was completely glass. There was not going to be any privacy here. As they closed the cell door a man wearing a torn and dirty lab coat walked into my view. He spoke with the soldier for a few minutes all the while looking at me. After they concluded their conversation he walked to the cell and introduced himself. The lead scientist, Dr. Testerman. He waited for a second for others to join him, then opened the cell door. He asked a lot of questions and I answered as honestly as I could, though he asked a lot of questions that I could not answer. He was not a very personable doctor, if he was graded on bedside manner he would most likely have never received his degree.

But he seemed to be a scientist doctor, not a medical one. He was very scientific in his questions and his tests. Blood and other fluid samples were taken and all three of them disappeared again. The whole process took about an hour. This happened regularly over the next couple of days. Blood and urine samples. Asking me simple and complex questions randomly to gauge my responses. It became cumbersome and annoying very quickly. One day Veronica entered the cell and I had enough.

"What are you here to say this time?" I snarked.

She opened the cell, and surprisingly she did not have any other soldiers with her. She held the door open, then stepped out of the way as if I was to exit the cell. All she said was "Come."

I hesitated then slowly got up and walked out of the cell. She closed the door behind me and then escorted me down the hall. Near the end of the hall was a men's locker room.

"Head in and take a shower. Take as long as you need. There is no way out and nothing in there that can be used to hurt yourself or anyone else. When you are done I or one of my men will be here to escort you back. They are currently adding bedding and some other amenities to your cell to make your stay a little more humane. Your cell is also being washed down so it doesn't stink anymore. The help was starting to gag as they gave you your food." Was that a joke that she just laid on me? Or did I smell that bad? I wasn't sure.

I guess whatever they got back from the tests couldn't have been that bad. Either that or the smell was so bad that they had to seem nice to get me to cooperate. It didn't matter much to me, I went into the locker room and went straight to the showers. I knew that I needed one badly. I had been able to wipe the hot spots when I was recovering but hadn't taken a real shower... I couldn't remember when. I turned on the water and let it run over me for so long that I felt it should have run out of hot water. After that, I felt better, so I washed up quickly, dried off and got dressed. When I walked out of the locker room Trey was standing at the door.

"Thought you were trying to drown yourself deader-man." He looked at me like I had a contagion. I also noticed he used my term for the undead, not theirs. "Let's go. The doctors want to see you."

With that, he walked down the hall expecting me to follow. I guess I was not being seen as a threat any longer. I was not much liked, it seemed, but it wasn't hostile. At the end of the hallway, I was taken to a sterile-looking room, Dr. Testerman and two others were there and looked my way as I walked in.

"Welcome, come in come in Matthew." Dr. Testerman seemed different. Personable? "Matthew we have a couple of quick tests we would like to do. Well, really they are just scans. No more blood or fluids today. Sorry, it took so long. Our generators were running low and we had to conserve power for two days so we couldn't put all of your tests through when we would have liked. Here, let's get started. The others here, George and Maria will take you through a few scans of your neck and head area. Just lay back on the table and I'll let you know what we have found."

I took a quick look back at Trey. It seemed he would be staying for everything. Maybe that was a good thing. If the doctor was to tell me there was nothing wrong, maybe he would lay off and tell the others too.

Now, I cannot remember all of the terms and words that Testerman used so I am just going to paraphrase. The tests that they ran showed that I was truly alive. I could have told them that. It showed normal levels in every way. One change was that there seemed to be some slowing in my fine motor skills, but not in my reactions to outside stimuli. The other change was obviously my glowing blue eyes. I still had iris color, which also happened to be blue, and normal-sized pupils. The glow only seemed to affect my sclera, the whites of the eyes, similar to that of an NLB.

Apparently, the meteor that crashed in Russia had alien plant life growing inside of it. Once cracked open, the plant life released some type of spore into the atmosphere. This was spread by local and worldwide weather patterns until it affected almost everything in the world. The spores ran through our systems without harming us, or at least not doing any harm that has been detected yet. Once we died, that changed. The reason for the NLB's rise from the dead was a coagulation of the spores in the host's cerebellum. The spores took in the electrical signals from the body and used them to activate parts of the brain and nervous system which allowed the body to move and function as if it were alive, but with very basic needs and desires.

One of the tells that the body is dead is the eyes. When the body dies the pupils dilate fully which makes the iris invisible. The spores in an NLB do nothing to change this feature, so all of them have large dilated pupils. Most glaze over with a white film similar to cataracts a short time after death. The sclera of the eye should not be affected by either the dilatation nor the cataract filming of the pupil yet they glow the same color as the spores. This phenomenon was not yet understood, but it was an alien species so some lack of understanding is to be expected.

He went on to say that while my body had spores in the blood and other fluids as most humans did, it also stored a larger amount of them in the brain stem. One of the tests they were running today was to see how much of a knot of the spores was there. Once they had a baseline they would conduct the scan several more times to see if it was growing or not. Testerman had no idea why my body started storing the spores in this way but he hypothesized that it was because I had died for a decent amount of time. This activated the spores and sent them to reactivate parts of my brain. He had not seen anyone with this affliction before and needed to study me further to come up with a better explanation.

At this point, I told him about the blue lights in my mind as I was dying. I told him how it would fade in and out. He seemed interested in this and wrote a few things down in a notebook. The scans were completed and he showed me on a computer screen how the spores were grouped and where in my head they were. He asked me if I had felt any different after coming back to life. I hadn't and I told him so. He wrote something down again and continued with his explanation.

The spores should not harm me, even though they were grouped in the basic function part of my brain. I had been speaking, eating, sleeping and operating like normal so far, and he did not see any reason why this would not continue. With that being said though, they told me that they would not be releasing me until they ran further cognitive and physical tests to see what the effects would be down the line.

"No! No way. I need to get back to my family yesterday. You have kept me here too long." I screamed as I jumped off the table.

Trey jumped towards me until Testerman held up his hand. "I understand your need to return to your family. But this is as much for you as it is for the rest of humanity. I am sure others have died and come back as you have. But none of them have the scientific team to study this anomaly. We have not seen this before and we need to know more. We hypothesize that there will be no harm from this, but we cannot be sure without further study. We need to see how you progress for the next few months..."

"Months!?" I screamed.

"Ok, not months locked here. But it will need to be an extended time-frame to make sure. These spores slow everything down in the body. That is how they keep the nlb bodies moving around so long. We need to be sure that you will not die and instantly turn and hurt someone. This is for your safety and those around you, specifically your family. We will treat you well, but you will have to be locked in a cell for the safety of those in our community. Do you understand?" Testerman had leaned towards me during the monologue he was giving. Up to the point that he had laid his hand on my knee when he asked if I understood. I just looked at him and his hand on my knee. I then punched him in the face.

"Screw you and your tests!" I stood up and faced Trey. I knew he was going to move toward me and Testerman would not stop him this time.

Trey had barely reacted by the time I turned to him. I had never been a fighter but this place was pissing me off and I was done with it. Trey was a trained fighter though and I did not fair well when he got me in his grip. Sooner than I would have liked he had me on the ground and completely neutralized. Several other soldiers entered the room and hauled me back to my cell. I guess my education and testing were over. I had a lot to think about though. The doc had used a lot of big words but I felt that I had a good understanding of what he had talked about. I wasn't dead, wasn't a deader but the spores were in my brain more than they should be. How would this affect me? Was it already doing it? The spores were supposed to activate the primal parts of the brain. Was this going to make me more primal, more violent? Maybe it already had. I had never punched anyone before, especially unprovoked.

Tests

The following day and for many days after, I was put through different tests. I did not know what half of them measured or showed. I just knew that I had no choice. They tried to ask me a lot of questions about how I felt and how things were going, I pretty much told them how they could screw themselves or how to screw off. Not my most shining moment but I was more pissed than I had ever been.

I felt a lot of guilt. My mom and sister most likely thought I was dead. They were mourning Dad and me still. I had failed Dad on the day of his death and was failing him every day after. I did not care about these tests or any of the results that these people were so interested in. I just needed to get home. I needed to make sure my family was safe. I hoped every second for a way out, along with the hope that what I had done that day had saved lives. Saved the lives of people in the community and more so the lives of my girls.

I lost track of time in the dungeon, days ran into one another. Half of the time I could only tell the time of day by the meal I was given. I was tested day and night at unknown intervals. But finally, Testerman told me that they had concluded the tests that they had been running. He explained that their original hypothesis seemed accurate and that there should be minimal effects on my mind and body from the group of spores in my brain. The mass had neither grown nor decreased in size over the time it had been monitored. Death was definitively off the table from this anomaly, as far as they could tell. He had sat me down in the same room as before to explain all of this to me. I did notice that his lip had completely healed from the punch to his face. It must have been weeks since then. Older people did not heal as fast. As he told me the new information I steamed with the thought of lost time. The time that I could have had with my family. The time I could have spent making sure they were safe and defending the house and community to make sure nothing like that incident happened again. I had to do everything to make sure Mom and Ava were safe. But here he was all healed from the punch I gave him weeks ago.

Weeks lost to determine the same thing I could have told him and he even thought was true before all of these wasted tests. He and his stupid scientific method used up time I did not have because he had to do an experiment. Not only did I lose time, but I hated being a lab rat.

All of this went through my head as Testerman kept talking. He said that the military would take me with them on a trip back to Sussex county. They would take me to the community and try to help me find my family. He was sorry for the lost time but they had to be sure. I told him that I understood why he did the things that he did. I understood the time he took away from me for the tests and hypotheses. He seemed to relax a little with that. So much so that he leaned forward to get up out of his chair. I stood up as he did and then punched him in the face again, it was not my proudest moment. I did understand, I just didn't appreciate it all.

Instead of trying to fight the guards I just fell to the ground and gave up waiting to go back to my cell. As I was taken out of the room I looked back and swore I saw a smile on the doctor's face or was it a grimace? I was taken back to my cell and told that Sgt Hayes would be by to talk about the trip to Sussex County. That could be in minutes or hours. It was hard to tell, so I got back to my new daily routine. While they kept me locked up I could not run, which was my favorite form of stress reduction and exercise. Locked in a 6x6 box did not give me a lot of options so I started with push-ups and crunches. I had added dips, planks and leg lift exercises since. I was probably in the best shape of my life. I would come in handy if I had to fight. I know my endurance had taken a hit but I knew how to work on that once I got back home.

It was the next day before Veronica came to my cell and told me the plan for getting back home. It would not be a straight trip. They had a mission in the Dover area and they still had to take their time and look for supplies and survivors. These missions took precedence even though they stole weeks from me for no reason at all. The sergeant was adamant on the matter though and told me that if it was not something I could deal with they would just open the door and let me walk back home. The problem there was that the bridges were out separating this part of New Castle County from the rest of Delaware. The hard angle driving was the embankments of the C&D Canal. When the bridges blew they blocked up the canal it was mostly dry but there was still water moving through. It was impossible to pass at high tide and dangerous even when the tide was low. I had to go along with their plan at least until we got past that.

We would be leaving early morning the following day to hit the tide right. There was not much for me to do while I waited for the day to pass, so I continued my workout regimen and tried not to think about the day to come. A set of black fatigues in my approximate size was brought to me when they brought my next meal. The uniform of the day I guessed. Dinner came and went and I barely touched it. My nerves were wound tighter than a clock spring. I tried to relax and then eventually tried to sleep. It took a while but I finally slept. The sleep was fitful and filled with dreams that I could not remember. What seemed like minutes after I fell asleep, I was rudely awoken by Trey telling me to get up and get ready.

After I got dressed, he walked me down the hallways to an area I had never been to before. He entered a code to open a set of double doors and walked through without waiting for me. The area behind the doors was bustling with activity. Most of our walk was completely quiet so this was a stark difference in noise and movement. Some people were pulling weapons while others were packing bags and taking them out of a door in the back. There was a lot more military personnel here than I had come close to suspecting. I thought it was just the one crew, I was very wrong. Veronica noticed that Trey and I had entered and walked over to us. She then pointed me to the back corner of the room. As we walked up to the crew there she introduced me to the rest of her team.

"Matt this is the team your going to be riding with. You know Trey and me." Trey nodded his head in my direction. "Then we have Will, Lyla and Chris. We have a couple of others riding with us today too. Of course we will also be riding with Drew our NCO. You met him before too. I am sure you remember. Drew is gathering members from another squad to run this trip with us. I am not sure who they will be yet. They will meet us at the truck before we leave." I did remember the big guy. I was not thrilled to be seeing him again.

After the introductions, Veronica threw a bag at me and told me how to pack it and what to pack it with. All of the stuff was on tables in the middle of the room. Once off campus, we were on our own and had to rely on what we took and what we could find. I made sure to follow her instructions very closely. Especially since she seemed to be watching me closely as I did.

We were ready quickly and loaded up. I asked for a gun but Trey and Veronica both laughed in my face. I guess I still wasn't to be trusted. I was given a small knife and what I figured was a baton. It was small but expandable. It would help in a close fight with a human, I guess. As we walked to the parking area Sgt. Hayes went over a few more rules. She really seemed to like her rules. I guessed that all members of the military did.

"You will listen to any of my regulars. Anything they say you do and do it quickly. When we are out of the truck you will keep your mouth shut. You will not speak at all. If you are spoken to you will speak only with body language. We will get to your little community when and if we can. We have a job to do. We are low on a few different supplies here and these people are more important to us than you are. Just like when we found you if we find a survivor that needs assistance we will help. If that help means bringing them back here for help we will do that." She paused and looked at Trey. I think that was as much for him as for me. "I do not want to hear anything about any of these decisions. Do you understand me?" She said this while looking me directly in the eyes. All I could do was nod.

The big man on campus walked up with four other soldiers. There were quick introductions all around. They were so quick that I instantly forgot their names. Now that everyone was there we loaded up. I was in the truck with Trey driving, Veronica and Drew, the NCO of the group. We would travel with two other vehicles, one SUV and one pickup. Drew looked at me when I loaded up and just asked if I was briefed. I nodded the affirmative and he turned back to the windshield. We drove out and headed south. I could barely contain my excitement for finally getting back on the road. This was slightly tempered by the glances from each of the team members in the truck with me. I was definitely not trusted.

The last time I crossed the C&D canal I was barely clinging to life and had thought the truck was falling as we crested each side of the banks. This time I was completely conscious and it felt the same. The banks were not made to be driven on, that was evident. At the bottom the view was surreal. I had driven over this bridge a lot of times in my life. Now the St. Georges bridge lay in rubble along the bottom of the canal. So did the old summit bridge and the railroad bridge a little further away. All of this rubble and steel was what blocked the canal enough at low tide for us to cross. Whoever the militia was that decided to cut the peninsula off from the rest of the country did their due diligence and made sure every way off the shore was taken care of. I mean who thinks about a railroad bridge?

Back when the world worked and society was still on the rise the drive to Dover would take about thirty minutes. Now that everything was broken and society had fallen it took us almost two hours. Our average speed was probably 30 mph. We slowed often to look at things and make sure there was nothing that the team was missing. We also took a very circuitous route to stay away from known hot spots. The drive did not make any of the other team members talkative. If anything they locked up and concentrated on the jobs at hand, look for survivors, supplies and potential threats. I did not know what to look for, but I mimicked those around me and tried to help. If I was going to be thrown in with these people I might as well make myself useful. My dad would be ashamed of me if I did not do at least that much. They didn't have to save my life before by rushing me a hundred miles to the only working hospital. They also didn't have to take their time and resources to take me back home. Sure the scientists kept me locked up like a lab experiment, but the soldiers I was riding with had nothing to do with that. They brought me along so I will do my best to help them when I could.

As we got to the outskirts of Dover the team stopped and everyone got out to game plan. I had assumed that the military would have radios in their vehicles and enough for each team member but as it turned out they didn't carry radios on their person, or in the trucks. Batteries were a source of power that drew the deaders. Because of this communication fell back over a hundred years. We had to speak to each other directly for anything to get accomplished. While it was good to connect, it really slowed down the process. Drew led the group and let us know that our intended targets were the mall, Delaware State University and the Dover Casino. All of these places would have potential food sources.

They all shut down prior to the fall which allowed for them to be boarded up and still be a source of supplies, But others knew this information too and they may attract survivors. They may also be hosts to NLBs, so we all had to be on the ball.

Will and Lyla were in the pickup. They would lead the group in and run point to the mall first. Each team would enter from a different entrance and work towards the center. With the plan in place, we loaded back up and took the ten-minute trip to the mall. We pulled up and exited the vehicle moving quickly to the entrance. I tried to mimic the movements of the military personnel around me. This got a nod from Drew but an eye roll from Trey. He was kind of a prick if you ask me. As we entered the mall I thought about a problem that I had not thought of before. I did not have a flashlight. The mall had skylights and windows in the doors, but there were a lot of areas that would not have this light available. I guess Drew had the same thought because he stopped and handed me a small light.

"Guessing you don't have one in your kit." He stated as he turned away. Man of few words.

As we continued on past the old storefronts all I noticed was the silence. Even with rubber-soled boots, my steps seemed to clump and echo through the entire place. The soldiers seemed to ease each step down with minimal sound. My dad had walked like that too. He was 250 pounds and could sneak up on a rabbit, he was so quict on his feet. The quiet was a little eerie. I remember the malls being loud and full of teenage angst and little kids running around as their parents shopped. Most of the stores had the cages pulled down and secured. The inventory behind them is still on display. I guess not too many people needed an AC/DC t-shirt these days. We only passed one store on our way where the cage had been broken, the shoe store. Shoes were strewn about. It made sense to me because a good pair of shoes was essential. Especially when you were cold and walking everywhere.

We checked the store quickly just to be sure and found nothing but empty boxes and shoes without mates. After continuing on we headed to the food court to meet the other teams. We were there first so Trey and Veronica started checking the restaurants for anything that may have been useful. They came up empty about the same time as the other two groups showed up from their respective areas. Nothing was found on any front. We worked our way back out quickly and headed over to the casino for our next check. The parking lots were all but connected so Trey made a beeline and crashed a fence instead of heading back out to the highway. It was efficient, but I also figured that he just wanted to break something, he seemed to be the type.

Discovery

Our entry to the casino was about the same as the mall. Each team entered from a different entrance and was to converge near the center of the casino floor. Our entry was chained and padlocked so it took an extra minute. We ended up entering the kitchen of one of the restaurants. There were still some non-perishable foods on the shelves and counters. It was exactly what we were looking for. We decided to take the time now to load them up in case we had to bug out quickly later. I helped Trey take them all out to the SUV as Drew and Veronica continued to keep watch inside.

After we got the food loaded in the truck we lined up and exited the kitchen. We had barely entered the main part of the restaurant before we heard gunfire from the casino floor. I thought that we would rush there to help. I stood up getting ready to go. It seems like almost every movie I ever watched would have the heroes run in and save the day. We did not do that. Drew looked at me and pointed for me to crouch down. He kept us in line, then shared a look with Veronica. She looked at me and then nodded reluctantly. I had no idea what they were doing until Drew turned and handed me a pistol. He asked if I knew how to use it, and I nodded yes. He seemed ok with that and turned back to lead the team further into the casino. I glanced over the gun quickly. Seeing where the safety was and then ejected the mag to see how many rounds I had. I may not have been keen on the military or hunting, but that didn't that I didn't know my way around a gun. I gripped the gun with two hands and held it with the barrel down and away. Veronica watched all of this and gave me a quick nod. I took up position behind Veronica and in front of Trey. As we stepped out of the restaurant Trey leaned in and said one thing to me.

"Don't shoot anyone on our team. You look like you played video games your whole life. So just think of it as friendly fire being on." After that, he just turned around and focused on protecting our rear.

The gunshots had stopped soon after they started. Hopefully, the other team had put down the threat and moved on. We kept moving slowly while looking for anything out of place. There seemed to be nothing but dead machines and dust hanging around. That was until we hit the main floor. Drew was there first and held us up. He called Trey and Veronica up to him while telling me to keep an eye out behind us. I could hear them talking but I was trying to concentrate on my surroundings. I actually jumped a little when Trey grabbed my shoulder telling me that we were moving on. That earned a chuckle and a head shake from him.

As I turned the corner I could see what caused all of the concern. Tables were turned over and there were bodies on the ground. Fortunately, they all seemed to be dead. They also looked like they had been there for a while. But if these bodies were dead and did not rise again to walk the earth then there had to have been deaders here to kill them. From what I knew that was the only way a body stayed that way. That is probably what elicited the gunshots. One of the other teams must have run into them somewhere. Another thing that I knew was that bullets did not stop a deader. If we ran into them shooting was just a deterrent for us to run the other way.

I started sweating and my heart was racing. I had never held a gun and gone into a real-life Call of Duty moment. I never wanted to join the military. I worked well behind a computer screen. The world around me seemed to shrink to what was directly in front of me. I had tunnel vision and my breathing was ragged. Veronica and Trey were busy doing their jobs and stopped paying attention to me. They were trusting me to do my part and help keep them safe. That ended quickly as I tripped and fell over a fallen trashcan. I truly never saw it. The sound reverberated off every single wall and the ceiling. If we were trying for stealth I had ruined that. Luckily there was no evidence that deaders were attracted to sound. Humans looking to kill us would be though. Drew looked back and shook his head as I got back to my feet. I started to say something but just closed my mouth and tried to focus again.

We had reached a bank of slot machines. They really hindered any sightlines that we may have had. Drew told us to spread out, two on each side of the machines. He sent Veronica and Trey to the far side and had me follow him up the middle. We worked our way further in. No sounds were heard from anywhere. Luckily the carpet hid even my heavy footsteps. When we came to the end of the slot machines we saw a car in the middle of the showroom floor. The car was riddled with bullet holes and there were bodies on the ground around it.

It seemed like this was just another set of gamblers caught by deaders. Until we noticed that these bodies were wearing familiar black fatigues. Veronica started to rush to their side to help but Drew caught her arm. We were all focused on the three bodies. The faces were turned away so it was hard to tell if they were part of our crew. Suddenly, we were attacked from behind. There was no noise, no warning just three deaders appearing out of nowhere and jumping at us. I pushed myself away and pulled up my gun to take a shot. I was confident in how to handle a pistol while on a range but this situation was nothing like that. My ragged breathing only came in gulps and gasps. My heart seemed to be skipping beats and my eyes refused to focus on the sights, only on what was happening around me. I could hear Trey yelling at me as he tried to push one deader off of himself. Drew had gotten the upper hand on his deader and was trying to secure it to a slot machine with a set of zip ties. Meanwhile, Veronica was screaming as her deader had its hand on her face.

My panic attack finally subsided. I could see clearly if I focused on Veronica and her attacker. My hand steadied and the sight came in crystal clear. I lined up the shot and hit the deader in the side of the head. It would not kill it, but it did break its concentration and hold on to Veronica. The deader turned towards me to see where the shot came from. As it did, Veronica moved quickly and secured its hand to a different machine. She then got up and staggered away. As she did I heard a couple of quick shots from Trey. The deader that had been attacking Veronica was still looking my way but couldn't seem to focus on me. It was a strange feeling. I must have lost myself in the look because the next thing I knew Drew was grabbing my shoulder and pulling me behind a bank of machines.

"Are you alright? Are you hurt?" He asked checking me for wounds.

"No, I am fine. Where is Veronica?"

"She is behind the machine over there. She is woozy but fine. That was a good shot. You saved her ass."

"I was so scared I would miss and hit her. Is Trey OK?" I asked suddenly looking around. I was really lost.

"We are all good. We got the three of them secured to different machines. Not sure how to kill them the docs haven't figured it out yet. But we can keep them from coming at us again." Drew stood up and turned back to the bodies on the ground. "I think that is our team. I need to go check on them."

He left my side and stopped to check on Veronica quickly. He approached the bodies with his weapon raised. He kneeled slowly and turned the first body over. I could tell as soon as he saw their face that it was part of our crew. He took a second and then yelled for Trey to help him with the bodies. When Trey reached his side they took everything they could from the corpses and carried it back to where I sat. It seemed cold to leave them there, but what else could we do. They were gone and we needed the equipment that they carried.

"You did OK with the pistol, but take this M1. It is set for a three-round burst. Be easy we don't have a lot of ammunition." With that, he turned and ordered everyone up.

Once Veronica and I were on our feet Drew led us past the car and further into the casino. We turned a corner and ran into Will, Lyla and Chris. They were at a full sprint heading in our direction.

"We gotta go! Where is the rest of the team?" Will asked on the verge of panic.

"Three are gone. We just found their bodies on the main floor. Cpl Smith where is your partner?" Drew responded. Chris just looked down and then at Will.

"This is a deader den. We ran into about 16 of them in one of the restaurants. Cpl Ngyuen went down under five of them sir. He bought us time to get out. But I think they are following us."

"Then we gotta go. Smith lead us. Oakley help Hayes she was partially drained. The rest of you stay at our backs and let us know what's coming." With that, the team moved out.

Chris sat with me for a second then moved and tapped me on the shoulder. He followed the others. I sat for another second then got up and walked backward slowly. I was just getting ready to turn and follow Chris when I saw movement at the end of the hall. I turned quickly to see if Chris was still close by but I couldn't see him. I looked back and didn't see anything again. Maybe my imagination was playing with me. Even with this thought, I decided to keep an eye out behind us as much as I could.

I turned and ran after the others to catch up. I thought I heard something from behind me so I turned to look. Again my timing was inopportune and I tripped. As I fell I saw a deader running towards our group. As I hit the floor I brought my gun up and fire a burst into the air. Even if they didn't know where I was they would hear the gunshots. I was not able to get to my feet before the first deader was on top of me. Well, he stood above me looking at me like the previous one did after it attacked Veronica. This deader was a small man, about 5 ft 6, built like an accountant. He looked at me for several seconds then lunged forward. All I could do was turn to the side and curl into a ball. It was a second or two before I realized that he did not attack me. He had just ran past me.

I turned back and got to my feet as a second and third deader ran past me too. It seemed that there was something about me that they didn't like? I took it as a good sign for now and ran after the rest of the crew. These deaders had been locked away in the casino for a while and were slower. I easily caught them and ran past them. I rounded the corner to the restaurant and saw two of the soldiers posted up outside of the doorway. Both of them had their weapons aimed at me so I slowed to a stop and put my hands up out of fear.

"What the Hell are you doing?" Screamed Lyla. "Put your hands down and get the Hell over here."

I took a second to realize that they had stopped to wait on me and protect my back if they could. It was not a normal situation. I hesitated too long though and the three deaders caught up to me I was getting my thoughts together. Apparently, a few of the other deaders were in better shape and able to move faster. Directly behind the initial three were four more new ones.

Lyla yelled and I hit the deck. She took a couple quick shots at the first deader as the other four ran past me. I could see Will had a confused look on his face as this happened, but it was just for a second before it cleared and he took a few shots too. I was on the wrong side of the barrels out in the open. I had no idea where any of the hallways or other doors went. If I decided to go another route I may not find the team again. I thought about that and decided it was good for my health to stay with them for now. This was not the time to be wandering around alone. I figured that if the deaders were ignoring me I would take that as an advantage. I got up and sprinted towards the doors. I hoped that I could get through before they shut out the deaders. As the deaders came within a couple feet of the doors Chris ran out and tackled the first two to the ground. He then got up and swung the accountant to throw him at the others running in. The accountant hit them about chest high and drove all four to the ground. As I ran by I tripped over a splayed-out arm. The deader's hand hit me just above my boot. At some point, my pant leg had pulled up and my shin was exposed. As I caught myself so I didn't fall again, I looked and saw the deader focus on me for the first time since all of this began. Ok so maybe I wasn't uninteresting to them. Weird. Something to unpack later I guess. I cleared the doors right behind Chris. Will and Lyla slammed the doors shut and barred them with a chair.

"What they hell was that?" Lyla asked.

"What me?" I asked.

"Yeah. How come they didn't attack you? They walked right by you without so much as a look." Will replied as Drew walked up to the group.

"What is going on here? Can this wait until we load up?" Drew asked.

"I don't think so. This guy just had seven deaders on his ass and they walked right by him without so much as a glance. It isn't normal." Lyla told him as she got up and walked away from me.

"Are you hurt? Did they drain you at all?" Drew asked me. I was bent over pulling my pant leg back down.

"No. They looked at me strange then just kind of ignored me. I can't explain it. At least until that last one when I tripped over him." I told him.

"Well, we need to get loaded up. We can figure out the rest then. Those doors won't hold forever." as if on cue the doors shook and one of the panes of glass cracked.

Everyone got the point and we all headed back to the truck. As we dropped the other three off at the other trucks Drew gave out the marching orders.

"With Hayes drained and Washington having this weird ability to not be seen by the deaders They are heading back. Smith will drive them back to the hospital and report to command there. Hayes will be tended to and Washington will have to be looked at by the doctors. We need to know why he was ignored by the dead."

"No! I need to get to my family. I need to get to Sussex county." I interrupted.

"No, you will do what I say. You were told that before. We need to see if your glowing blue eyes is causing something to be different with you after all. The rest of us will continue the Dover part of the mission then meet back at the hospital. Smith hopefully you can make the low tide again, but be careful and don't attempt a cross if it is not at dead low. Got me?"

"Yes Sir. I'll get them back safe."

I wanted to argue. I wanted to walk away. I knew that they would never let me. Whatever just caused these deaders to ignore me and go after the others was something the military and the scientists would need to study. It may be something that could help us against these creatures. I just hated that it would delay me from getting back to the girls, again.

More

When we got back on the road I could see that Veronica was passed out in the back seat. She was breathing heavily but steadily. It was getting late in the afternoon by now. It would not take us long to hit the C&D crossover. If I was right the tide would be in so we wouldn't be able to cross. This might be an opportunity for me to leave this group behind me and get to the people that were really important. It took hours for the tide to fall from fully high to fully low. If Veronica was out recovering from being drained and Chris decided to take a small nap, I might be able to sneak away. It will take a while to get back on foot, but it will be better than being stuck in that cell during more tests.

We pulled up to the embankment of the canal and the tide was still in. It was on the way out so I had missed the timing a bit, but it might still work for me. I looked at Veronica and she was still out cold. Chris looked beat from the long day on the road. As Chris put the SUV in park and walked out to check on the canal I made my mind up that as soon as he fell asleep I would make my run.

"Ok take it easy. I am going to check on Hayes and see if she needs anything. You stay in the truck. We will be here for another hour or so then we can be on our way." Chris told me as he opened the back door.

"Ok, I am just going to shut my eyes for a bit then. It has been a long day." I then faked a long drawn-out yawn. It worked as I wanted as Chris covered his mouth stifling a yawn too.

I laid back and closed my eyes to try and get Chris to do the same. It took about 10 minutes before he came back to sit in the driver's seat, but only about 10 more before he was lightly snoring beside me. I waited another five minutes before I eased my door open. I watched Chris intently the entire time. Once it was open enough, I lifted my pack off the floorboards and eased the door back shut.

During this time Chris never moved. I thought that I was home free and I threw my bag on my back and turned south. That was when the gun clicked.

"Get that bag off your back and get in the damn truck." Veronica must have recovered.

I turned back towards her and saw her pistol pointed at my face. As I looked at her I think the word recovered would have been a stretch. Her aim was true and her arm was steady even though her face was gaunt and she leaned against the truck for support. I slowly took my bag off and laid it on the ground.

"I am just trying.."

"Your just trying to leave with our supplies. I know what you're doing." She interrupted.

"OK, take the stuff." I kicked the bag towards her. "I'll leave without it."

"No, you are coming back as we were ordered. We need to see why those deaders ignored you. It may be the advantage we need. Get in the truck. Now." She waved her gun as she said this.

"I am not in your military. Drew has no authority over me." I argued.

"He does since you agreed to our terms to come on this mission. You agreed to follow all ordered. Remember? Or are you still that coward that is going to cut in run and let others fight and fall for you?"

I didn't understand the fall part. Did someone die in Washington when they rescued me? I almost asked but Chris had woken up and had gotten out of the truck too. As he rounded the back I figured I was screwed. I hung my head and complied. When I got in Chris got in beside me and handcuffed me to the center console with a flex cuff. I guess I wasn't going anywhere now.

Veronica fell back in the truck with a humpf. She was still hurt. Damn, I thought she would have been more out of it. As we all got set, Chris decided that the tide was low enough and he fired the engine to cross the canal. I could still see water above the rocks, but I guessed that he knew what he was doing. I grabbed the handle the best I could as we sped down the first embankment. As we hit the bottom and the SUV leveled out and water splashed over the windshield. The tires slipped and then grabbed as it slid sideways on the rocks. The water had to have been higher than Chris thought because it started leaking in from the floorboards. It wasn't much and the engine was still getting air so it was ok, I guessed.

A couple of more slips and heart stoppages and we were heading up the other side of the embankment. No issues with that, so we were on the way back to the hospital. As we pulled into the garage area, Chris jumped out to help Veronica. He left me tied to the console as he took her in and informed the team of the situation. It was a little while before two other soldiers came out and cut me free. They didn't cuff me or grab me but I could tell I had to head back inside and do what they said.

We walked back in and I went directly back to my cell. I slumped on the bunk and waited for the poking and prodding to begin again. The first thing that happened though was they brought me a meal. I didn't realize how hungry I was and how long it had been since I had eaten anything. There were protein bars in the bag, but on the way back I was sick to my stomach at the thought of failing my dad again so I hadn't eaten anything. I also figured that if I had been able to get away I would need all the food in the pack to get back home. That didn't work out so well.

After I ate, I laid back and rested my eyes. I must have dozed off because the next thing I knew there was a knock on the door and they were bringing me food again. I had slept through the night and then some. I was sore and it took me a second to figure out what was happening. As the tray was left for me I could see Dr. Testerman walking down the hallway toward me. Great.

Testerman walked into the cell and started talking to me about what happened and asking what I saw and what I felt. I did not answer his questions. I just concentrated on the food and ate very slowly. After a couple of minutes, he got the point and stood up.

"Well, I guess we do it the hard way young man. Lets grab him and get him to the other cell." Testerman spoke to someone outside of the cell.

As he stepped out the same two soldiers from yesterday stepped in and grabbed my arms. I thought this was a little much. They could take all the tests they wanted. The sooner it was all done the sooner we could go south. This was the idea until they took me to an area I had not seen before. This area had cells too but they were a bit different and had deaders roaming around inside of them.

I started to push back a bit as I had an idea of what the doc had in mind. We reached one cell in particular, Testerman stopped and opened the door. I freaked for a second. I knew there was a deader inside and he just opened the door and kept it open. It wasn't until I reached the door that I found out why. The deader was chained to the back wall. The chain ran from a collar around his neck to the wall about 5 feet up. The deader could only move about three feet from the wall.

"Keep him over there for a second. George you hold him while Tim enters the cell. I need to get a baseline." Testerman ordered.

Tim looked a little hesitant but did as he was asked. As soon as he crossed the threshold the deader snapped forward reaching as far as he could until the chain went tight. It continued to fight forward for a few more seconds then stepped back a half step and stared at him. Tim slowly backed out of the cell and stepped behind the door. We waited a minute then Testerman nodded to George who pushed me into the cell. He probably pushed me a little harder than he had to, but whatever. I slipped a bit and ended up just a scant few inches in front of the deader. The chain wasn't pulled tight so he could have lunged at me and probably grabbed me quickly. But again the deader looked at me quizzically and stood his ground. I stood there for a second and then slowly backed away. The deader only looked toward the door as Testerman walked into the doorway to ask me to walk out.

George and Tim then took me back to the research area for Testerman to run a couple of tests. The next couple of days we repeated this same test. Sometimes multiple times a day. We worked up from one chained deader to an unchained deader to multiple unchained deaders in the room. None of them gave me the time of day when I entered. Then they got creative and let multiple deaders into my cell while I was in eating or sleeping. Each time they caught me off guard, but the deaders never reacted to me. They never tried to attack me. A couple of them would look at me quizzically while others just straight ignored me.

One day they brought a big guy in. Testerman told me that this was what they called an NLB alpha. It seemed to lead the team of NLB's he was part of. I am not sure what that meant but I did think back to that day in D.C. A couple of deaders did seem to stop

and listen to the big guy when he entered the fray. Maybe they
were ruled by strength, like a pack of wolves. The strongest would
lead and get the spoils first. Seemed like an animal kingdom type
of scenario. When they let him in my cell he first spun on the
soldiers that brought him in and attacked the door. That was the
first time that had happened. Great, let's piss him off and then lock
him in the cell with the deader-boy. The alpha got frustrated that he
couldn't get out and turned to look at me. His gaze was intense for
a thing that had no irises. As he stared I felt a slight buzzing in the
back of my head. It was odd and very hard to describe. It only
lasted a second then the staring contest stopped and the buzzing
went away. He turned back to the door and started beating on the
glass. I hoped at that point that they would remove him from my
cell rather quickly.

  I told the doctor about the buzzing at the end of that session
and he seemed intrigued. The next couple of days I got a break.
Then a soldier I had not seen before came and got me and took me
to Testerman's office. Here he spoke to me about the tests and
more tests that he would be conducting.

  "This is bullshit. I have jumped through your hoops. It has
been over a week again. I need to get home." I screamed at him.

  "That is not going to happen. This new power that you
seem to have needs to be studied and we need to understand it. It
may be the best way for our soldiers to be safe in the field. It may
help my scientists too. If we could walk around here with no fear of
the NLB we could conduct tests and studies faster and with more
concentration. We may be able to develop a cure, or pathogen
faster. We will keep you here as long as it takes to understand."
Testerman really did not have a good bedside manner. He really
did not seem to care about me or anyone. Just his study of the
NLBs.

  "Then just kill a couple of your soldiers and revive them.
That seems to be how I got this ability. Then you could leave me
the Hell alone and let me go home." I was done with his bullshit.
At the time I was so irate that I didn't even comprehend the fact
that he said he was looking for a cure or a type of pathogen. But a
pathogen to do what? Wasn't the spore already causing a disease of
sorts?

"I am not sure it is as easy as that. We need to see if that is what actually caused it or if you have something special allowing you to do this."

"Oh Jesus H Christ. Whatever. I am done with this." I got up as I said this and tried to walk back to my cell. I had push-ups to do. I did notice Testerman flinch as I walked past him. Guess he thought I was going to punch him again. This made me a little happier.

The soldier had other ideas though and grabbed my shoulder to push me back into the seat. Testerman took out a few sticky pads and wires. He placed them on my head and chest. This had been done before, so I knew the drill. Once I was hooked up I was taken to a cell that had a machine in it. It was hidden behind a partition and wrapped in some type of foil. The wires were hooked up to the machine and it was then covered back over. I was told to sit in a chair and wait. Time passed and I had no idea what I was waiting for. Then the door opened and the alpha was brought into my cell. This time he took notice of me right away.

He walked over slowly and stared at me. I got that buzzing in my head. The fact that I never had this unless he was staring at me told me he was doing something to cause it. He reached a hand towards me and I jumped up away from him. I was a little slow because I was not expecting him to reach for me. But he missed my face by scant inches. He wasn't reaching for me, but the wires attachcd to mc. As he grabbed one I could feel an energy coming off of him. I could almost see his eyes glow brighter for a second. Suddenly the machine popped and smoked. The alpha lost interest in the wire he was holding and looked at the smoking machine then looked lost for a second. He definitely caused the machine to burn out by trying to absorb the energy from the wire. After that, he just stood around looking for something to do? I was just as lost and tried to keep a distance between him and me.

A couple of minutes later two soldiers came in and took the alpha out of the room. Testerman came in and took the foil off of the machine. It looked burnt and had definitely burned a fuse or something. Doc just shook his head and told me to take the pads off and place them with the machine. I guess it was the only one they had left. Testerman must have gotten some information though because he was looking at something on his pad attached to the machine. As he looked he became very intent on the information. So much so that I was able to walk out of the cell and down the hallway. I couldn't really go anywhere but it was nice to walk around free even for a short time.

As soon as I thought that, the lights flickered and went out. I heard a scream down the hall. The hall had the cells with all of the deaders in them. I thought about taking off and seeing if I could get out with the security system off, but I felt like I had to help. I ran down the hallway to see what happened. I got about halfway down and I could see the alpha in a cell with one of the soldiers that had escorted him back to his cell. The other guy was outside of the cell trying to hold the door shut. The soldier inside was not being attacked but he had no way out as long as the alpha was being held in. It seemed like the alpha knew he had a meal ready, but wanted the bird in the bush not the one in his hand. Sometimes my grandmother's old sayings spring up at the oddest times.

I grabbed the door and told the soldier to get into the hallway and close this area off. There didn't seem to be anyone else around so no one else was at risk. He looked at me for a second then shook his head and ran for the hallway door. As soon as he closed the door I released the door I was holding and let the alpha out. He ran out and whirled around looking for a target. Once he was clear of the door though I shut it again and locked the vulnerable soldier in. At least he was safe. I was betting I was reasonably safe too.

The alpha watched me shut the door and stared at me. The buzzing started again. It grew in intensity. More than it had before. It became so insistent that I dropped to my knees and put my hands over my ears as if that would help. My world spun and I couldn't get it to stop. I lost track of time. Suddenly, there was a loud bang and my head spun worse, so badly in fact that I fell onto my side with my hands trying to get my head to stop. The spinning got so bad that I lost my lunch, or was it dinner? Whatever it was that went off must have affected the alpha too because he fell and hit the wall and then the floor, and the buzzing stopped almost instantly. Soldiers ran in from the hallway and secured him. They threw him in another cell and slammed the lock home. This is when I noticed that the lights had come back on. I had lost my shot to get away, but at least I had saved the soldier. That made the sacrifice worth it, this time. I just hoped that it didn't cause me to lose my chance of finding the girls.

Newbies

When I got back to my cell I slept for what felt like a day. The alpha messing with my head, then whatever it was the soldiers used to drop him. My head had still been spinning so badly that I didn't remember much about getting back to my cell. When I woke up the door to my cell was open. This seemed odd and kind of like a setup, to be honest. I slowly got out of bed and got dressed. No one came to the door and I couldn't hear anything going on outside of the room. When it felt like I couldn't procrastinate any longer I walked to the door and looked out. There was no one in the hallway. I walked toward the area stations and there was no one there. Did everyone bug out and leave me here alone? Then I noticed that there was a note sitting on the desk with my name on it. I picked it up and read it.

Meet me in the cafeteria. We have a lot to discuss.

Sgt. Veronica Hayes

OK, odd but I was hungry. I decided the cloak and dagger would lure me in and I headed to the cafeteria. When I got there I immediately saw Veronica. Then Trey, Drew, Will and Lyla. Almost the whole team was there. I hesitated at the door until they all saw me.

"Come in. Sit down, we have breakfast. Don't worry about the lack of staff. Testerman gave them all the day off, which he has never done, and told them to stay out of the research area." Drew spoke first as he got up to get a plate for me. "First, we know what you did for that soldier yesterday. We all know you want to leave and that you tried to leave before Chris got you and Veronica back to the hospital a couple of weeks ago." Drew continued as he poured some coffee.

"What? A couple of weeks? That's how long I have been back?" I was dumbfounded. Time in this place took on a reality of its own.

"Yeah, but in that time you got with the program..."

"Yeah you didn't even punch Testerman this time." Trey piped up and laughed.

"Anyway, you got with the program and decided that a soldiers life was worth more than your freedom."

"That plus saving my life in the casino." Veronica piped up.

"With all of that, thank you all for the interruptions, we have decided to trust you to help us. To become part of the team. If you want to join. This time we will treat you as a full member. Yet you will still have to follow orders. One of those orders being that you must stay here on site until we train the new unit, with your help. Also taking the time to train you before we go on another mission. You came through last time, but you also locked up. If it was not for your new power you may not have made it."

"So, I save one dude and now all is forgiven. Just like that?"

"No. Not just like that. Why do you think none of us have been to see you over your time back?" Veronica asked.

"Figured you all didn't like me. I didn't really think about it."

"Well it was because we talked about how the failed mission went. How you acted and what went down. We also looked at your tests. Some of us were on watching the results. We have been tasked to take your new ability and see if it is trustworthy enough to use in the field."

"So your going to train me then see if I can operate in the field. If this ability to be unseen by the deaders is worth the time to what? Run more tests on?" I was lost in this conversation.

"No dummy. You are just the test dummy. We are going to test this ability on people that know what the Hell they are doing. Like me." Trey chimed in standing tall and pointing to himself like a nitwit.

"What?! How the Hell are you going to do that?"

"Its easier to show you. Lyla hit the lights."

Just like that the lights went out and the cafeteria was completely dark. I freaked out a bit thinking this was some kind of deader test. After the initial shock, I turned back to see what the others were doing and about lost my mind.

"What the actual Hell!?"I yelled. When I turned back to the team I saw 4 sets of dim blue eyes looking back at me. As I adjusted I could also see a lighter pair of eyes further in the back. It must have been Lyla at the light switches. "You guys are dead?"

"No. Lyla." the lights came back on. I had to blink at the sudden brightness. "We are alive, yet have the same ability you do.

Well hypothetically. It hasn't been tested yet." Drew finally sat down.

"How? Why?"

"Our unit was chosen. We are the most experienced in the field and we all volunteered."

"Yeah, I never want to be drained like that again. If dying real quick can stop that from happening. I was good with it." Veronica stated. She got up and walked over toward me. Once she reached me she grabbed my shoulder and sat me down. I hadn't even realized that I was still standing.

Once I was seated they explained to me what they did. During the testing that the doc had been running with me, the team talked about what they saw from me and the deader interactions in the field. They talked about all of the people they had lost and the times they or others had been drained to the brink of death. They spoke of a fallen teammate. The way they looked at me while they spoke about him I am guessing he was lost in D.C. while trying to save me. He was drained while away from the fight and on top of a building. No one knew what really happened they just knew the shots stopped and after the fight, they went looking. They found him dead while still laying in his position, sniper rifle in hand. They left him there in the same position to watch for others in the afterlife.

A lifetime in the military changes how your mind works, I guess, because they decided that this was a tactical advantage that they wanted to be able to utilize. During the last couple of days of testing with the alpha, Testerman had already set a plan in motion. He set a table up with the right drugs to stop their hearts, then restart them a couple of minutes later. Long enough to be truly dead, but not long enough to have long-lasting health effects, like brain damage. There had been a lot of studies on this and how the brain worked during death so he felt reasonably comfortable taking on the procedures.

The first one to volunteer was Veronica. She was already healed from the deader attack and was willing to try anything to not be in that situation again. It worked and she woke with a similar story about the blue light fading into her mind as mine. She only had it happen once, but then she woke up and her eyes glowed. The others quickly volunteered so that the unit would stay together and they could learn these new abilities as one unit. The only person I had not seen so far was Chris. He was absent. I almost asked where he was or if he decided not to go through with the procedure when I heard a commotion in the hall. The other five had their weapons and quickly armed themselves. I turned just in time to see a deader walking into the cafeteria. It was the alpha that they had used to test me.

"Holy shit. How did they get out?"

"They didn't get out. Chris let them out. That's where he has been. He also went though with the procedure yesterday. We wanted to explain this all to you then test how it worked when all of us were in one place." Drew explained as he watched the alpha walk around the first table and warily watch all of us.

Seconds later two more deaders walked in. Followed by three more. All of them walked in and looked around the room confused as to what they were seeing. Eventually, the alpha focused on me and my head started to buzz again. The buzzing was much more intense this time and I grabbed the sides of my head. Veronica reached over and grabbed my hand. As she did the buzzing sensation lessened and became bearable. At that point, I realized that the hand that had calmed me when I first entered this facility had been Veronica. This Veronica, not the Sgt. Hayes in the field. She was doing it again now. It was strange that she had this ability to help me calm down in chaotic situations.

I knew that I should not be focusing on this bit of information with six deaders circling the tables. But it seemed more interesting. I knew from the past weeks of testing that they were not going to mess with me too much. Then, just like that the buzzing stopped altogether. The alpha stopped looking at me and then just wandered to the back of the cafeteria.

"Ok, well I guess that answers that. Matt here isn't the only one that they can't see." Trey said with an air of arrogance.

"No, I disagree. Yes, it answers that question. What I disagree with is that they don't see us. They do see us. They look at us and can't figure out what they are looking at. We have the same electrical signal, but something in us has changed and they don't see us as food. I have been thinking about this for a while." I explained.

"Ok we are unseen to them. Either way it is really cool not having to be scared of them touching you."

"The Unseen. I like that. That will be our new unit name." Drew said as he snapped his fingers. Military people were really odd.

After all of the deaders filed past Chris walked in with a few of the dog catcher poles that they used to move the deaders around. I guess the test was over and it was time to round them all up again. I started to eat the food that had gone cold on my plate while all of this was happening. That was until Drew handed me one of the poles and told me the recruits have to do the dirty work. Damn was this what I was signing up for?

After all of the deaders were put back in their cages I went to go back to my cell. The food on the plate was all but forgotten about. I had all but agreed to stay on here and help these people learn their new abilities. I was going to learn how to be a soldier so I could be part of their Unseen unit. It would take time. The time that my mom and sister may not have if I was not there to protect them. But even when I was there I hadn't seemed to be of much use when it came right down to it. I mean my dad was drained right in front of me. There was nothing I could have done. Maybe if I used these new abilities and learned how to fight I could be of some use to others. Maybe in a couple weeks time we could head down and try the new training in the field and look for my family, or what was left of it. Wouldn't that be better than going there half-cocked? Half-trained and more of a liability than a savior. My track record on the savior part was not stellar.

In the end, staying on and being part of the greater good may be the work that I needed to finish. It would at least be work that my dad and I could both be proud of. The girls were strong I had to believe I would see them again.

Hazing

When I reached my cell I saw that it had been cleaned out. There was another note sitting on the desk. I guess in a new age without texting and Twitter we had to rely on the good old-fashioned handwritten notes. At least it wasn't folded into a triangle like old people used to do in school.

You don't live here anymore. You belong with your unit. Report to the bunk area to get your new assignment and uniforms.

SGM. Silver

I had no idea who that was or what the initials were. I guess I would go and find out. I walked down to the military area. It was separated from the research area by a set of double doors that have a key card and a code that had to be entered. As I reached the doors I was confused as to how I was going to get in without either. I decided that the best way would be to just knock. A couple seconds after I knocked the box where you enter the code buzzed.

"What?" Buzzed and electric heavy voice.

"It's Matt. Matt Washington. Umm I guess reporting for duty?" I stammered.

"What's the days password?" The electronic voice asked.

"Umm, I wasn't given a password."

"No password. OK, then you have to answer my questions three if the ere the other side he see."

"What? Three questions, is this a door or a troll bridge. I have heard that line before. Is that from Monty Python?"

"Nice, yeah, just messing with you. Try the door it should be open."

I heard the door buzz and I pulled it open. As I enter I saw Trey laughing with another soldier looking in my direction.

"Reporting for duty! Sir!" They joked.

What was I supposed to say? I decided to ignore them and move on to find the person that left the note. I figured they would be here waiting on me. They did tell me to go to the bunk area, so I needed to find that. I decided against trying to ask Trey so I looked around until I found Lyla.

"Hey Lyla, where is the bunk area?" I asked as I reached her.

She looked at me oddly and then at the soldier she was with. "Excuse me, private Washington. You should refer to me as Corporal Oakley. Always refer to others by their rank and surnames. Understand?"

"Yes ma'am."

"No, none of us are officers so no sir or ma'am. Plus I am not that much older than you. Just Corporal is fine."

"Yes, Corporal Oakley. Can you tell me where the bunk area is?" I was so confused. Was everyone going to haze me?

Corporal Lyla Oakley decided to relent and pointed me to a room near the back. I hung my head a bit and headed that way. I knocked as I entered the area. No one answered, but Drew was standing in front of the bunks. I did not know his rank or his last name so I just waved and waited for him to talk first.

"Hello, I can tell by your hesitant look that the others have gotten to you already. How bad was it?" Drew asked

"Ehh. Not too bad but I just don't know what to say." I replied as I looked around the room. It was a bigger room and had multiple rows of bunks. Most of them had sheets and blankets on them. All were nicely made. All but the one Drew stood in front of. The sheets and blanket were just sitting at the foot of the bed.

"This is your bunk. I knew you didn't have much, so I had new uniforms and some basic civilian clothes gathered for you. Not all are in the best shape but you don't want to wear the uniform all the time. A couple ground rules. When in uniform you will use surnames and ranks. If you don't know the rank just use the surname. Learn them quickly, even those not in your new squad. When not in uniform you can be informal as long as they are also not in uniform. You good with that?" Drew gave me this information as he waved me over to the bunk. He handed me the sheets and waved toward the bed. "You will make your bed every day. It will never be left sloppy. I know you have not been to boot camp so you will be behind. Almost all of the others here had been in the military before the fall. You need to learn and adjust quickly. You have already learned some of how we operate in the field. You will learn how to fight. With and without weapons. You will learn how the small military force we have here operates and how to operate inside of it. Are good with all of this?"

"Yes." I started then realized I did not know his last name or rank. "What is your name and rank?"

"Sergeant Major Silver."

"Oohh. That's what that meant on the note. I was so confused. Isn't Veronica a sergeant also?"

"She is a Sergeant. I am a Sergeant Major. It is vastly different. Don't confuse it and do not call me Sarge. Or Sergeant. It is always Sergeant Major." SGM Silver finished as he walked towards and out of the door. "Go ahead and make your bunk and get your stuff stowed. Training starts later today."

That is how I got started in the military. At least I got to keep my hair and wasn't yelled out nonstop for two or three months. I had heard boot camp was a pain in the ass. A couple of the guys I had trained with at school were ex-military. They had talked about boot camp a lot. I was glad I didn't need to go through it. I wasn't sure how people in the military made their beds. I looked at the others around and they had folds at the corners. I did not know how to do that but I did my best. As I finished up and got my clothes in the locker next to the bunk. Trey, or whatever his rank and name were, came into the area. I knew he was going to mess with me more than anything so I just set myself up for it. Just as I thought he came straight to my bunk and looked it over. He tsked and shook his head. He then ripped the blanket and sheets off and threw them on the ground.

"Not good enough. You need crisp corners and a tight bed. I should be able to bounce a quarter off of it." he screamed as he walked out. I heard him laughing as the door shut. I just took a deep breath and grabbed the sheets to do it again. Not sure how I was going to do it right with no direction. Just then Chris walked in.

"PFC Smith. Before you ask Washington. Smith is fine. You know how to do hospital corners?" Chris spoke as he walked towards my bunk and helped me grab the sheet.

I just shook my head and he nodded. He showed me how to do the corners and how to pull the sheets tight without pulling everything off again. I guess Chris, oops Smith, would be the one I go to when I need help. I guess he saw this in my face because he nodded and then followed up with another statement.

"Sgt. Hayes and Cpl Oakley will help as much as they can too. PFC Ragsdill is a jerk, but a great soldier. He is a guy you want in a fight. SGM Silver won't help much here. He will with your field operations though. Cpl Reid, Will, is good and he won't offer to help but if you ask he is the guy to go to for weapons. He really knows his shit. All of this will turn down after your first mission. We haven't had a new guy for a while so everyone is a bit amped about it. All of our squad will have your back when we leave here. Just get through the training and let us know how to work this new ability we have. It'll work out. You good?" Chris stood up to leave.

"Yeah, but Ragsdill? Seriously? You're not messing with me?" I asked hesitantly

PFC Smith just smiled and walked out. Great another game. I would have to make sure that was right before I used it talking to Trey.

I finished my bunk again and it looked better, closer to the others around it. Happy with it I walked out of the bunk room and tried to find SGM Silver. I needed to figure out what we were doing next. The faster we got my training started the faster I could get back home.

Training

SGM Silver had a training program in mind. I would train with Cpl Reid in all the weapons and tools we would use. He would walk me through some shooting drills. Unfortunately, we would not do much shooting as we needed all of the ammo we had. I would do hand-to-hand combat with, of all people, PFC Ragsdill. Yes, it was his real name. Then Sgt. Hayes and Pfc Smith would work with me on military regulations when we had time.

A lot of our time would be working on the new abilities that this dim blue-eye glow might have given us. I had been through a lot more testing with it than anyone else so I would actually be leading that training. The next two weeks would be inside this bunker, a hospital. Then maybe we would head out on a new mission. It sucked, but I had to rely on my gut instinct that the girls were ok and that we would be together again at some point. The others were not too keen on staying in one place for two weeks training the new guy either. I got the idea that they liked being on the move and out in the open.

The first week was rough. I came in each and every night bruised and sore from my fights with Trey. I know they were not supposed to be fights but he got under my skin and I lost my cool most times. I think he was trying to do that each and every time. He seemed to relish in the fact that he could beat me with no repercussions. He would show me a move or a style of fighting and then use it against me. All the while talking trash and getting me angry. I know he was trying to get me to focus and block out his taunts, but I really hated when he spoke.

Will was much better. The weapons were all pretty easy to get my head wrapped around, I had grown up with a lot of different guns in the house. I also played a lot of Call of Duty. We worked on breaking the weapons down and making sure they stayed in working order. As we did he told me about the weapon and all of its functions. It was tedious and monotonous, but it was good work that needed to be done. The coolest thing that Will showed me was the emp grenade. While there were also smoke, flash-bang and normal grenades, this one was completely new. The scientists figured out that the deaders saw electrical signals and fed off electricity so they designed a grenade that sent out a 25 kv electromagnetic pulse. This temporarily disrupted the electrical signals in the brain. It would frazzle a human, believe me, but would almost completely shut down a deader for a few minutes.

Once I gained the basics of how the squad would work and the hand-to-hand combat we started training for the field. This was difficult at first. The others worked well together and everything went smoothly. When I was thrown in I would gum up the works and cause us to be "killed" in a short amount of time. It was frustrating because I had seemed to work better with them when we were in the field. That could have been because everything had just fallen apart and we were all shooting from the hip, as they say. We trained this way for another two weeks or so before it all started clicking and we started working as a real unit. So much so that SGM Silver decided we were ready for some real-world work. I asked immediately if we could head to Millsboro to look for my family, but that was turned down. We were just doing a short training run in the Wilmington area. Somewhere that was well known and the area had already been mapped. I was disappointed for sure but saw the benefit of knowing the surroundings as we worked as a true squad for the first time. We also needed a better understanding of our new ability before venturing too far.

It was the last week of April when we rolled out of the hospital for our first mission as the Unseen squad. There had apparently been a few rumors of a wild animal stalking around the outskirts of Wilmington. It was said to have blue eyes like a deader. The bodies that were found were torn apart as you would expect from a large predator, but they did not rise again. With our new advantage over other squads, we were told to investigate. The area in question was just outside of Bellevue state park. It was a small wooded area surrounded by the city and suburbs. They figured that the animal was staying in the state park and venturing into the surrounding areas for kills. There were still a lot of people in these areas.

We left late in the morning. Since this animal most likely stalked its prey at night there was no reason to be out too early in the day. We took our time to get to the area and stake it out. Veronica, crap Sgt. Hayes was from Wilmington and knew a couple of the people in the area. After an hour or so of her talking to the few people that would answer their doors to soldiers, we found out that the animal usually only killed every couple of days. It was always at night and the local residents were scared to death of it.

Luckily, it had already been two days since the last known kill. That meant that night or the next it should show itself and look for a kill. PFC Ragsdill was a hunter and Cpl Oakley was a tracker. With them each leading a small group we fanned out around the park to see if there were any signs of the animal coming and going. Trey thought that if it was dead, like an NLB, it would have different patterns than live animals. Lyla countered with the idea that the NLBs were more reliant on the base and animalistic instincts than the average human. If this was true the animal should not change much and should keep to a normal pattern. Water and cover should be the main focus. This conversation went on and on as we got set up around the park.

Bellevue State Park had a nature preserve and was about 28 acres. That was a lot of ground to cover, yet most of it was pretty open. There were only a few areas of dense foliage. We knew it pretty much hunted towards the west side of the park, so we started there. A couple of hours later Lyla came up with a clue as to the type of animal we were tracking. It was a bobcat. The Brandywine Zoo had a Florida Bobcat on display when the world still worked. No one had checked to see if any of these animals had escaped. It made sense that this predator would be looking to feed. It also made sense that it came from the zoo as Delaware had very few native predatory animals.

Knowing that we were most likely looking for a bobcat made it a little easier for our trackers. I was completely lost out in the woods looking for an animal. Although my dad tried to teach me to hunt, I never really took to it. I rather kill things from my keyboard, virtually of course.

We entered the wooded area. We fanned out to cover more ground but stayed close enough to be within shouting distance. It was late April, so I understood the trees were in full bloom but to me, it seemed like the trees and the undergrowth was especially thick. I had not done a lot of hunting with my father but I did a lot of camping and hiking in the Scouts. I didn't remember it being like this. I did remember one of the scientists talking about how the spore had infected every living thing and had bumped the local fauna's growth into overdrive. That must be the answer to why everything was so thick.

Late afternoon came and went and it started to get dark, which meant that if this cat was going to hunt it was going to start soon. Lyla and Ragsdill were leading the group together since it had gotten dark. SGM Silver was deferring to their expertise. As the sun went down I thought I saw a small bit of blue glow in the grass around Will. He was off to my right and was walking through a particularly thick patch of weeds. It was there and gone so quickly that I thought I had imagined it. That was until I saw Chris walk through a copse of evergreens and the blue glow rained down on him.

"Chris! Stop!" I yelled.

He froze and dropped into a crouch pulling his weapon up and sweeping the area. The others dropped into their own crouches and did the same.

"Private Washington. What did you see?" SGM Silver asked as he made his way to my position.

"Unsure, Sergeant Major." I stated. Still unsure of my wording. "When Chris walked through that copse of trees I saw blue light rain down over him."

"PFC Smith. Did you see anything?"

"No." Chris answered curtly.

SGM Silver looked at me oddly and then told Chris to move forward slowly. As he did I could see him disturb the spores on the tree limbs causing them to glow.

"There. Do you see it?" I pointed at the bioluminescent glow coming from the spores.

SGM Silver looked around at Chris and the others in the area. Everyone shook their heads. "None of us see anything private. Are you sure of what you are seeing?"

"100 percent. I can see the spores glowing as they fall. I thought I saw it earlier too but wasn't sure. There is no discounting it now. I can see them." I was adamant.

"Ok, maybe this is something new to your abilities. Keep an eye on it and hopefully it will help us in our hunt." SGM Silver said this as he gave a hand signal for Chris and the others to continue. "Let me know if you see something that we don't. Maybe if the cat is moving it will cause the spores to glow too."

"Yes sir." I cringed as I said, sir. SGM just looked at me and shook his head. I would eventually get this wording.

We moved on and the evening progressed. A couple of our team members had night vision goggles. It would be so cool to use a set of these but I was not on the shortlist. It made sense since I had yet to train with them, but it would be cool to use them at least once. We had completely cleared the western part of the woods and had moved around to the pond on site. Most animals made their dens near drinkable water according to Lyla. I came up to the clear side of the pond and noticed that it had a sand volleyball court. It quickly passed through my mind to check and see if the cat used it as a litter box. Then common sense kicked in and I realized that a wild cat would not be litter trained, and if the cat was dead it wouldn't need to be.

As I was berating myself for being stupid Ragsdill called out for us to hold. We all dropped into a crouch and waited for more instructions. Lyla joined him and they spoke quietly. As I wondered what it would have been like when they had the proper radio equipment to communicate instantly, SGM Silver waved me to join Trey and Lyla. Trey had seen footprints in the mud around the pond near the treeline. Lyla agreed it could be near the area as she had seen scat along one of the trails. It was old but once bobcats made a den they did not move unless they had to. They were very territorial.

Evidence of the scat meant that the animal showed up in this area alive. Something must have killed it once in the area. Unless it was still alive and able to drain the people it killed. Did that mean it was kind of like us? Living, yet with the abilities of the undead. I guess we would have to find out when we found this cat. Also, we would need to see if one of us could drain the energy of a living being. That had not been one of Testerman's tests.

I was looking at the area Trey indicated and saw spores glow in a tree limb that was above the pond. It happened quickly and may have been from the wind, I needed to be sure. I crouched and kept my eye on the area. It was across the pond, but right on the perimeter. As I started to question what I had seen, I saw another branch bounce and shake the spores loose. I kept the trajectory from one to the other and watched another branch shake spores loose. I could not see the cat, but it made sense that it was moving lower and towards us. I motioned for SGM Silver to come by and informed him of what I had seen. He nodded and passed the information on to the others. Suddenly, there was a puff of spores in the weeds under the trees. The cat was on the hunt. I made a hand gesture to Silver letting him know it was down on the ground. He nodded. The squad closed in on the area that I had indicated. Unfortunately, I could only see the cat when it made a big move. If it slinked through the weeds I might not see it at all.

Cpl. Reid made his way to my side. He had a set of night vision goggles on. "You look for the spores and I'll keep an eye out with these.Maybe we can get the upper hand."

We settled in and kept each other apprised of what we saw. Neither of us saw the attack when it came. Veronica was turned away from us and tried to get Ragsdill to move to another position when she suddenly went down. Ragsdill called out and we all headed to her position. As we got there she was getting to her feet, only suffering a cut on her side from its claws.

"It shot in and took me down then moved away just as quickly." She informed us as she took her pack off for some medical supplies. Lyla helped her wrap the wound while the rest of us took up positions looking out and covering them.

Chris then reacted to a noise just in time to fend off an attack from the cat on the far side of the group. He was one of the squad members that had the night vision goggles, but they didn't help. He was able to get his gun up and get a single three-shot burst, hitting nothing as the cat flew by. It was able to knock his goggles from his face. As he tried to find his goggles and get reset the cat continued through the weeds and attacked Trey. He went down and wrestled with the cat. He cried out but was able to get a couple of shots off.

I saw the cat flee from Trey and followed the spore trail through the underbrush. Lyla had just finished with Veronica and went to help Trey. The rest of the squad formed up on me. Will came up beside me and pointed to the ground. He had taken off his night vision goggles and was waving a blue flashlight around. He spotted blood along the trail. He took the lead to follow the blood trail as I kept my head up looking for the spores.

We quickly found the cat hunkered in the crook of a tree about 5 feet off the ground. Trey had obviously wounded the animal, but it was able to make that jump so it was not that hurt. Will and I waited for the rest of the squad to catch up and surround the tree. If this cat was still alive it was seriously hurt and would feel backed into a corner. It would fight hard so we had to take it down quickly. If it was undead it felt the pain but would be able to ignore it. It would also be almost impossible to take down.

As we were about to get Lyla to take a shot at the cat with her rifle, I had an idea. I quickly stopped her and worked my way to Silver. I thought that if this cat was a deader it would also react to our emp grenades. We talked it over and he had everyone back up to a safe distance. I stayed to keep an eye on the cat and be the one to go through with my plan. Once it was safe I pulled the pin and tossed the grenade under the tree. The grenade went off too quickly for me to get away. I felt the wave come across me as it went off. The world spun and I fell to the ground. It felt like I had gotten drunk in seconds. The world went tumbling out of control.

I could hear the others running in. Lyla stopped to check on me quickly before she moved in to help the others. Apparently, my idea was right. The cat fell from the tree and couldn't get its balance either. The squad secured its legs and mouth before it could fight back. By the time I got my head right again, they had it tied up and in a net to drag back to the road. Veronica and Trey came to help me up and patted me on the back.

"Good idea rookie." Trey stated.

"Yeah it may have saved some ammo and some more injuries." Veronica told me as she grabbed her side.

I took it all in stride. One good idea did not make me a soldier, but it may help the others trust me and see me as a competent squad mate. We had a long walk ahead of us and a very irate deader cat to deal with. Hopefully someone had brought a couple of tranquilizers with us, and maybe a couple of aspirin. My head was killing me after that EMP shot.

More

The trek back to the trucks with the bobcat was not an easy task. No one had thought to bring tranquilizers and it was strong. It would twist and move in the net and cause the others to drop it on the ground. Once there, it would try and succeed to break the zip ties holding its paws together. Luckily, it never broke both sets at the same time.

Drew sent Trey and Will ahead to grab the trucks and bring them as close to us as they could get. As the others fought to control this almost rabid beast, I took some time to look it over and try and figure out what had happened to it. It was definitely dead. At some point, it had run into a large buck with an even larger rack. The sides and rear of the bobcat were torn up, infected-looking and oozing some kind of fluid. It had a couple of bullet holes in it from our fight, but they weren't even bleeding by this point. It also had a large caliber bullet hole in its head, just behind the right ear. The hole was much too large for our guns to make, so it must have been shot before. I am not sure if the deer or the headshot killed this thing, but either of them would have probably done the trick.

Once we reached the trucks we had a hard time getting the bobcat out of the net and into the large metal cage in the back of the truck. Veronica finally stopped everyone and had Will and Trey take the cat about 500 yards away from the truck. We moved back to the trucks and she then threw an EMP grenade at the bobcat. I got to watch this go off from a distance for the first time. There was not much to it from there. If you were up close you would think it was like a nuclear detonation. There was a pop and a small bit of smoke, but nothing else. Nothing that would clue you in on the massive world-spinning headache it created. The cat dropped and we were able to get it into the cage and locked down before it got its wits about itself again.

With that done we loaded up and hit the road back to the hospital. As we started off Lyla, Trey and Drew started talking about Lyla's concerns about the lack of other animals in the area. Not just close to the bobcat's den, but throughout our whole trek looking for it. She hadn't noticed any birds, squirrels, or other animal life along the way. This made tracking the bobcat easier, but it was still very odd even with a large predator in the area. I tried to listen in to their conversation, but I soon lost track and interest. I had nothing to add to the conversation so I just sat back and slept as we drove back to the hospital. The next thing I knew it was predawn light and we were pulling into the garage.

"Good morning, sleeping ugly. Have a good beauty sleep? You definitely need some more of that. Good timing though. You are going to help the doctors and Smith unload the bobcat NLB and take it to the labs." Trey giving me grief as he gave me orders, as usual. I just looked at him and nodded my head. No use in adding to it, usually only made the bullying worse. The cat really hated being in the cage. As we carried it to the lab area it would hit the side of the cage and cause the whole thing to tip over. We had to right it four times before we got it to the lab that Testerman wanted it in. Once that was done I started to walk off and head to my bunk. I needed the rest, the nap in the truck only seemed to make that more prominent.

"Matthew, wait up for a second." Testerman called out as he walked quickly down the hallway to me. "I wanted to talk to you about what happened in the field."

"I'll write up my report first thing after I get some sleep." I told him between yawns.

"That's fine, but I heard that you can see spores in the air?"

"How did you hear about that already." I looked at him quizzically trying to figure out how he could have known.

"Doesn't matter. I need to do some tests with you on that. Especially since no one seems to have that ability."

"Ok, but not now. We can do that tomorrow, or later today I think it's already tomorrow." I yawned as I turned away and headed to my bunk.

"Ok, but first thing. As soon as you wake up. I'll have my hands full with this NLB cat anyway." He stated as he turned back down the hallway.

I ignored anything else he might have said and headed to the bunk area as quickly as my tired legs would carry me. It wasn't until I passed the cafeteria that I realized I had no way to get into the bunk and military area. They hadn't given me a passcode or a card to get in. The soldiers I was with at the labs had already gotten into the area. Stopping to talk to Testerman put me behind them. I stopped and poked my head in to see if anyone on my squad or any other squad was eating. No one was there.

I continued on and made it to the double doors. I knocked and hit keys on the pad, but nothing seemed to be a doorbell and no one was answering my knock. Great, I had a bunk just a couple yards from where I stood but I had no way to get to it. Frustrated, I sat down with my back on the wall and hung my head on my knees. I must have fallen asleep right there because the next thing I knew my feet got kicked out from under me. My head fell towards the floor so I jerked it up so hard that I smacked the back of it on the wall.

"Sleeping ugly at it again. Damn man, go get some sleep." Trey again.

I quickly got up and shot him a look, but grabbed the door before it closed and headed through. I caught something about me not being able to make it in the military and being soft as pudding. I chose to ignore it completely as I found my way to my bunk and passed out properly.

Hours went by before Veronica came in and woke me up.

"Ok, enough rest." She said as she pulled my feet off the bed. "I need those action reports and I was told to send you down to Testerman for some more tests on your abilities."

"Which first?" I asked groggily not really hearing her.

"Testerman, is more important. All of the rest of our reports are done. Yours isn't going to add much. Now get up. Coffee is on your desk there. Along with an access number. Memorize it and stop sleeping in my hallways." Veronica laughed as she walked out of the room.

I got up and headed to the showers. Testerman could wait a few more minutes. After that, I got dressed and headed to the cafeteria to get a bite to eat. As soon as I sat down though Testerman walked through the door.

"I thought I asked you to head down to see me so we could talk about your ability to see spores?" he haughtily asked me.

"You did, but I needed sleep, a shower and some food. Nothing is going to change in that amount of time." I said through a mouthful of sandwich.

"Fine, we can just talk here. Tell me what you saw." He sat down across from me and took out a digital pad for notes. It was still odd to see ipads and electronics being used.

I took my time finishing my sandwich and then explained what I saw. He had a bunch of follow-up questions, most of which I couldn't answer because the words he used were confusing to me. This seemed a bit odd because I had always had a big vocabulary. I must have still been groggy. After what seemed like forever he ran out of questions. He told me that they had gotten some plants from outside. He had them set in a dark lab and wanted me to run a few more tests with him there. Others from the unit would be there too, just for a baseline.

I shook my head and got up to go do more tests. If I knew this was what would come out of dying and then living again, I might have chosen to stay dead. But that thought was fleeting. I still had work to do. I needed to find the girls and get us all back together. I then needed to do some good in this world with my second chance. If doing these stupid tests for Testerman were part of it, then I guess it had to be done.

We entered the lab area. Trey and Will were there waiting. We went to a back section of the lab area that we had taken the bobcat to. When Testerman said that they brought some plants in from outside, it did not encompass the sheer enormity or amount that he had brought in. People must have worked the whole time I was asleep to get this done.

"So can you see the spores in the light or only in the dark?" Testerman asked me standing by the light switch.

"Just the dark, I think." I barely got that out before the lights went off.

"Shit!" Trey exclaimed. Obviously not ready for the full dark of a closed-off laboratory.

"Ok, Tommy! Walk through the plants and let's see if Matthew can see you." Testerman yelled at one of the other researchers.

As soon as he started to walk I could see the spores floating in the air. At first, I could tell exactly where he was and when he stopped. I told Testerman so. But not too long after that, I think the HVAC kicked on and blew the spores all around the room. I lost where the researcher was, but the whole room lit up for me. I could not see the details of things, but I could see the outlines of everything and everyone in the room. I could see Will and Trey looking around trying to see anything. I could see Testerman tapping his pencil on his chin as I told him what I saw. He concluded the test and turned the lights back on. I blinked in surprise, even though I could see him reaching for the switch. Just as quickly as the lights came on they went off. The HVAC unit also kicked off. I could see the spores starting to settle in the air. It got darker for me as they settled and were no longer glowing in the dark. The generators or at least the generator for this area had gone out.

Will had his flashlight on him and lit the torch. It was a lot in this small space. We could still see lights on at the end of the long hallway.

"Uhh, Doc. Did you guys let the bobcat out of his cage to do tests on him back here?" Trey asked warily.

I turned to look at him and his eyes were set behind us in the plants that we had just been looking at.

"Yes, then we locked him in a mag-lock cell." Testerman replied. Still walking down the hallway toward the main labs.

"Well, I think I have a new ability too. I can't see the spore things that Washington can see. But I can tell you that bobcat is out and walking through those plants stalking us." Trey explained as he put his back towards a wall. Probably looking for an exit.

"Fascinating, tell me what you see."

"I see that cat is stalking us and is going to kill us unless we get help or get the Hell out of here." With that, he took off at full speed towards the doors to the main lab. Will and Tommy right on his heels.

I looked back and could see the spores being disturbed right at the edge of the plants. The bobcat was coming and it wouldn't be long before he leaped out to get us. I felt along the wall and found an open cell door. I grabbed Testerman and threw him in the cell. I then grabbed the door and took one last look down the hallway. The others were just reaching the door, I glanced back towards the plants and saw just a small bit of spores settling to the ground at the edge of the area. I quickly grabbed the door and slammed it shut, not seconds before the bobcat hit the door with the force of a Mack truck. I held the door closed, luckily it opened out. I heard the others yell something as they opened the outer door and slammed it shut behind them. The lights sputtered and then came back on. I could see the bobcat sitting in front of the door watching us, watching him. I let go of the door as I heard the electronic lock engage. We were safe in here and it was locked in this separate lab area.

"You know. Maybe with power being unreliable we should rethink mag-lock doors to keep deadly things behind. We lost power for a very sort time before this thing was loose." I told Testerman as I slid down the wall.

He said nothing. Just pulled out his pad and wrote something down. I hoped it was something about getting better locks. I hoped the others would not take long to get something to take this cat down. I did not want to be in this cell for very long with Dr. Testerman by myself. He might start trying to dissect my brain or something. I did have one question for him though since we were here.

"Hey, why does the cat attack us, even though it is a deader..."

"NLB." Testerman interrupted.

"Huh, Oh yeah. Anyway if it is a NLB and so are the humans we tested this ability on. Why is it attacking us and they don't?"

"I had thought about that too. Part of the reason we sent your squad was because we thought your abilities would make it safer for you. That didn't work out. " he now sat up straighter, to lecture me I'm sure. "I think it is the cats other instincts are stronger. It does not rely only on what the spores tell it to do, or whatever they see because of the spores. The cat would see you as either a threat or prey even before death. It may have been more wary before, but it would've still seen you the same. Now it lost the fear of you and responds as it would to any threat, or any prey. It is just more primal. That's partly what the spores do. They reactivate the primal centers of our brains. More aggression and more of a base instinctual thinking. Exactly what we are seeing in the bobcat. It's not so pronounced in humans initially so it is different."

"That actually makes a bit of sense. Thanks for explaining that. Also is the technical term for a bobcat a Robert Feline?" I asked trying to break the tension a bit more. I think I went too far though as Testerman hung his head and started writing again.

Luckily, a couple of minutes later, Will, Trey, Lyla and Chris came in with a few other soldiers and an armload of tranquilizer guns. Where were those last night? I few darts to the body and the bobcat was down for the count. As they drug it back to its cell Will looked at the doctor and me and moved to quickly open the cell and let us out.

As we wrapped up and headed back to the military area Will asked me if everything was ok. I nodded in the affirmative and kept on. I did stop and ask Trey what he saw when the lights were off. He explained that he could see the outline of the cat in the plants. He wasn't sure if it was spores or what it was just that he could see the cat moving. I could see the spores and couldn't see that. Hopefully, Testerman was going to pull him for some extra testing.

Empty

The next day was a typical day, back to training and the usual stuff. May 1st had come and I was still no closer to getting home. I had been gone for two and a half months at that point. It seemed like I was always getting delayed. I put this off my mind and tried to concentrate on my training. That was until Drew came into the room where I was learning about military bearing and rank structures while tearing down an M4 and told me that we were gearing up that evening and heading south.

"With everything going on, we lost another generator yesterday. We need to get back on the road and get some new fuel and parts. We don't have to go that far south for this, but I think you earned a little respect over the last couple of days. We all agreed to get you back home to get your family, if possible." I looked from Drew to Will. Will was just smiling and nodding his head. "Bonus for you, I guess, but a loss to the team. Pfc Ragsdill will not be joining us on this particular mission. Testerman wants to study his new ability more."

Finally, I would get the girls to safety. Bonus I wouldn't have to deal with Trey and his mouth during the whole trip. I asked what we needed and when we were leaving. He told me that Sgt. Hayes would come through in the next hour or so and tell everyone what to pack and when to be ready. We had to wait for low tide anyway so it could be a little bit of a wait. I understood and tried to go back to concentrating on my training. A minute later even Will gave up trying to instruct me and sent me on my way to get ready.

After hitting the bunk area and packing up my personal bag I waited in the staging area to see what would need to be packed for the trip. After a while I caught Veronica coming out of the girl's bunk area. She looked like she had just gotten out of the shower. It was odd to see her in sweats and a t-shirt and not in her uniform. She saw me sitting at a table trying not to look like I needed to rush over and ask her what needed to be done. Yet I think she got that impression.

"Easy, private. It will still be a couple of hours for low tide. It isn't that long of a trip on this side so we will have a long ride through the night. If you're this amped right now I am not sure you will make it. We aren't heading straight there. It may take us a day or two." She commented as she shook her head laughing at me.

"I get it. I just want to be ready to go. Plus I slept in today, which no one else seemed to have done."

"You know what. You're right. You will be the driver today then. Go get the SUV and F-150 packed up, fueled up and ready to go. The rest of us will handle the bags and weapons. We need as many fuel cans for diesel as the truck can hold. We will stop as often as we need to." She told me dismissively as she walked towards the double doors and out to the cafeteria.

"Yes, ma'am," I said and cringed. It must have either been ignored or low enough that she didn't hear me since she didn't react at all. Her head was probably somewhere else.

Getting the trucks geared up and ready to go was easy work, but at least it was work. We had mechanics that would fuel them up, check them out and pull them to the staging area's back doors. All I really had to do was find the gas canisters and anything else that would hold gas properly and get them in the back of the pickup. Doing this made me remember my trip from Florida where people were at the gas station fighting over gas. I smiled as I thought about the idiots trying to fill plastic bags with gasoline and take them home. It all seemed like so long ago. I am not sure what changed in me but I had no itch to be on a computer. I didn't get the errant buzzing in my back pockets like my phone had gone off like other people I saw reaching into their pockets for their phones and other devices only to realize they weren't there. Shoot, I bet Ava is still carrying around her old cell phone hoping for it to show a notification off some social media site. I liked my games and my computers, but my life had changed so much since the fall that it felt like it had all happened in another life or to another person.

I traded that life for life in the military. Not a life that I chose, those bandits chose this for me when they tried to kill me. Well, really when they successfully killed me. Games and computers were a way to pass the time in a life that had no real challenge. I mean life was challenging, don't get me wrong, but I always had food, shelter and a warm place to sleep. Most of the time that humanity has been on this Earth none of that had been guaranteed. We were wired to fight, hunt, gather and stress. That is why a lot of people enjoyed drama in their life, Ahem...Ava, even when they denied it.

As I thought about all of this I counted the number of diesel containers I was loading into the truck. It seemed like most of what we had were empty. How long had it been since a squad went out and got fuel? If this many were empty how much longer did we have running the generators? I would have to remember to ask Drew about that when I saw him. Once everything was loaded up I headed back to the staging area. The others had gotten together and were completing the bags and weapons checks for the trip. I tried to not get myself too excited. It would be a long trip south. I knew we were on a mission and I had to keep that focus, but it was really hard not thinking about getting home and helping the girls. As the squad finished up the checks they set the bags and weapons by the door. I grabbed what I could and loaded them up in the trucks. Lyla and Will would be in the F-150 and the rest of us would be in the SUV. I left the weapons inside so that nothing would happen to them. No one should be around to take the weapons, but it was better safe than sorry.

A little while later Drew came into the staging area and asked Veronica to give us the formal briefing. The whole thing was a little long-winded and used a lot of terms that I was not really fluent in yet. What is it with the military and acronyms? Basically, it was just as she had told me. We needed fuel. We were going to head south and stop by some of the lesser-known areas and towns to see if we could acquire it with the least amount of resistance possible. While out there we were to not risk our lives by testing our new abilities. If the situation called for us to have to engage the non-living then we would do what we had to. We would help civilians if at all possible and help them relocate if it was needed.

"No hero shit!" Veronica finished with. I guess to get it through our heads to make sure we come back home in one piece.

With that done we all gathered up our weapons and headed out of the door. Veronica was riding shotgun and leading the team today. I guess it was almost a training mission for her as the NCO. Drew was with us in case he needed to make a call, but it was her show. We always had to know the proper chain of command for each mission. That way there were no delays in following orders. Once we got underway and headed south I didn't think about anything at all until we hit the canal. I was the lead car and when it came into sight I started panicking. Was she going to make me make the call if we should cross? I had no idea if it was low tide or not. I had also never driven up or down these embankments or any embankments like them. Trey always did the driving when I was in the truck.

"Relax, Private." Veronica said while resting a hand on my shoulder. As usual, it extended calm throughout my body. "I'll make sure the tide is right and walk you through how to traverse the embankments. It's easy, just let the truck do the work."

We reached the edge and she got out with Drew. They made the call quickly and told us to stand down. We had another bit of time to wait before we could cross. I know Trey would've made it, yet I didn't feel comfortable trying it that way my first time. Also, we weren't in any type of rush, so there was no reason to risk the trucks and equipment. We turned the trucks off and waited while Lyla and Chris set up a quick perimeter. Will got out of the truck and got into the SUV with Drew, Veronica and me to talk while we passed the time. Nothing much in the way of conversation was interesting to me. I was thinking about getting home and what the girls had done in the time that I had been gone. So much had happened in my life in this short amount of time that I was kind of hoping their lives had been boring in comparison. I also still felt bad leaving them to deal with Dad's body without me.

"Do you think they will be happy when you get home?" Will asked suddenly.

"Huh? Oh, sorry you were talking to me? Yeah. Mostly surprised I'm sure. I have been gone a while and they probably think I am dead."

"Well, you were dead. Twice or three times was it?" Veronica piped in.

"It was four I think Sarge." Will countered.

"Ok, Ok. I get it. You all saved my life a lot. I will have to repay it. I know."

"Not at all. That is what we do. You don't owe any of us anything for that. Now saving your tail the couple of times since. That is something you owe us for." Veronica seemed very sincere in this.

"Well, I already saved you once. That should count for something."

We all laughed and they went back to some banter back and forth while I zoned out again. I hadn't thought about the fact that they may think that I was dead. I mean there were several people that died that day and others that had probably been run off to not return to the community. What if they wrote me off and left without letting me know how or where? Would I be able to find them again? I stopped going down that negative pathway as soon as I noticed that I was on it. The what-ifs would kill me. I had to lock it all down and concentrate. The future would be decided soon enough and I would have my answers, to these questions at least.

About that time I heard the rear door open and Will got out. Chris got back in at the same time and Veronica pointed the way forward. I guess more time had passed than I wanted to believe. I started the truck and put it in gear. I eased forward until the front tires were at the edge. Veronica told me to put the truck in 1st gear and let the transmission ease it down to the canal base. If I hit the brakes it could slide on the mud, especially at the bottom and cause the SUV to overturn. The embankments were not smooth and any wrong turn of the steering wheel could do the same. I white-knuckled the wheel and put the SUV in 1st, then eased it forward.

Instantly it felt like it was shooting down the hill. I almost hit the brake, trying to remember what she had just told me until the transmission caught and the truck slowed down. It whined like an RC car but kept a decently slow pace. The angle eased off and Veronica told me to put it back in drive and give the truck a little bit of gas as we leveled off. As we approached the other embankment I reached down at her instruction, and put the truck in neutral and 4x4 low. I grabbed 1st again and started the crawl to the top. At this point, Will went around me and ran up the other side faster than I would have been comfortable with. I shakily looked over to Veronica.

"Don't worry about him. He has done this plenty and knows the trucks limitations. Plus he always likes showing off for Cpl Oakley. She is a country girl and gets off on this stuff. I like it slow and steady. Especially for a rookie." as she said this she had ahold of the overhead and glove box handles for support. She may have tried to exude confidence in me, but I don't think she had any.

At least Drew and Chris sat back and exuded confidence in my skills.

A minute or more later we crested the top embankment and leveled out on even ground. I put everything back to where it should have been on the SUV and took the lead again. Our route took us along road 896 instead of the popular route 1. There was old aviation mechanics business nearby that we wanted to check out. Drew was hoping they would have similar generators to the ones we were currently using so we could scavenge parts and of course gas if they had any. When we got there we found that while all of the gas, especially diesel, was gone there were some parts that we could scavenge for things back at the hospital. We were boots on the ground for about an hour then back on the road and heading south.

We made a few more stops like this along the route. Once was happenstance as we found a group of big rigs that were all pulled along the side of the road. Chris hopped out and checked a few of the tanks while Lyla and Will provided security. Most of the tanks were dry, but we were able to get at least one full canister of fuel for the generators. Slow progress but progress all the same.

A little while later we came upon a blockade on the road. It was a small side road and it wouldn't take us long to get around, but Veronica wanted to find out what the blockade was about. We stopped back a ways and we all got out and weaponed up. Is that the term? I wasn't sure. It was how I thought about it anyway. Either way, we got ready and split up into two groups. One on each side of the road. I was happy to see that there was not an overpass for some sniper to take potshots at us while we were exposed.

As we approached the vehicles we could tell they were placed in a specific way. There was no way they had just wrecked or stopped where they were. There were a few small communities along this road. maybe one of them wanted to keep anyone with a vehicle away from them. It seemed plausible, but kind of meaningless. The roads here had a lot of room around them to go through fields or other side roads to get around. Thinking about this I stopped my group and walked off the side of the road. There was nothing where the cars were, so I backed up the road a bit and found what I had expected to see. About the place that a truck would pull off the road to go around the blockade, there were spikes, glass and wires laid along the ground. I called out and asked Lyla and Will to check their side, they found the same and noticed that their wires traced back to the cars in the blockade. Not knowing what these wires were connected to we backed up slowly and retreated back to the vehicles. Once we got back we talked about the issue. Veronica decided that it was not our mission for the day. We marked the concern on a map that Drew carried in his pocket and turned the trucks around.

The night wasn't a complete bust, but we had not found all that we had been looking for. The areas we were in had been picked over pretty thoroughly. New Castle and the upper part of Kent counties were pretty populated prior to the Fall. We figured that people had moved on before the bridges fell, but it seemed like if they did, they took a lot of the supplies with them. Veronica was getting a little frustrated and it was starting to show. The mission was hers and it was not going well.

"I know you wanted to get a lot of the gas before we got to my house. You wanted to work the mission south. But what if we head south and then work the mission back north. Get reset and maybe find what we need around all of the farm land in Sussex county?" I spoke up, probably out of turn or chain of command, but she seemed to be floundering.

"Sussex was pretty empty before the bridges went. At least that's what I heard." Drew spoke up. Was he on my side here?

"We haven't been down there much because there were so many small farms and communities that were protecting the supplies." Veronica countered.

"Yeah, but a lot of them are scared to venture out now. I know this because in my community I was the only one that really would. I think if we find abandoned farms, like where I found my bike before, we might have some luck. It may not all be safe but it may provide more resources."

"Plus you get back sooner?" She asked.

"That really is not the reason, but yeah. I also get back sooner." I added sheepishly.

"Alright private. Get us off this road and get us south. It is a couple-hour drive now. If you want to get home before dawn we need to get moving. Wave the others over so we can let them know what we are doing." She seemed resigned to the idea, though not really happy about it.

That done, I found us a side road and got us back moving south. I knew that this was what I wanted, but I really did feel that it would get us back on the mission too. There were a lot of farms and construction sites that had been active before the world stopped working. My dad had taken a lot of supplies to keep our community running, and he told me where a lot of those sites were and what they may hold.

The roads back were pretty clear so we cut a bit of time. I noticed that the fuel gauge was moving towards E a little faster than I thought it should have. I asked about this and Drew said that a lot of the gas was not lasting as long as it should because gasoline had a shelf life of about three to six months. As it went past that it didn't quite work the same. The gas that had been found around here had been shipped well prior to November when everything had started to shut down. Most of the gas that they had found had been siphoned from tanks in abandoned cars, so they were not properly stored. If they could find some in buried tanks it would be in better shape. I nodded as if I knew what he was talking about then just said that since we had a bit of time we should get some more fuel for our vehicles. It was late in the night anyway and a little delay would let the girls sleep a little longer before I woke them. Veronica nixed that idea and told me to get us south as fast as possible. I don't think she wanted anything else to go wrong tonight. The time seemed to drag and jump all at the same time. The next thing I knew, I was using my left blinker and pulling off the side of the road in front of my community.

"Did you just use your blinker?" Veronica asked me quizzically. So much so her eyebrows looked like a v on her forehead.

"Yeah. Sorry. Habit."

I stopped the truck and let the other know that I was going to try to see if there was still a watch set at the front of the community. Chris and Will got out to set security for the trucks, but let me go ahead alone. It seemed odd but I started looking at the high grass and seeing if there was any movement to the spores. There was no wind, so movement should mean some kind of body. Everything was quiet.

The front security area was vacant and seemed to have been for a while. I figured the watch had just pulled back to where it was really needed. I signaled the others and informed them that I was moving further in to see what I could find. Lyla jumped out of the truck and joined me.

"You ain't going alone that far in. I'll keep you covered."

"Ok, but can you hang back so it doesn't look like we are a threat?"

"If that's what you need." We exchanged quickly as we moved deeper. Lyla did as asked and quickly disappeared into the night. I felt alone, yet I knew she was there to watch my back.

I reached the outer houses and saw that a lot of them were open to the elements. I saw movement, I paused to see what it was. I noticed that Veronica was coming up to the side of the house to check it out as I moved deeper. I guess they all had my back. With this knowledge, I felt emboldened and moved deeper. I came around the bend where there should have been a watch set up. That post was empty too. This was becoming very concerning. I walked around the shed and found a body leaning against the back of the shed. The body had a gut wound, that might have been fatal. If that was the cause of death wouldn't he have risen to walk again? He must have been drained too. That means he was killed twice in a matter of minutes. It was dark luckily my night sight had gotten better after dying, four times? But I still did not recognize the body behind the shed. Hopefully, it was not one of the watch.

Shaking my head I moved on and worked my way around the outside of the community. I decided to skip trying to catch up with the watch and worked my way around them. If they continued on with the rotations that we had set prior, I could work my way into the field and hit the house without seeing any of them. I never realized there was this big of a void in our security before. Guess I had learned something in the time gone.

Finally, I had the house in view. There were no lights, obviously no power. Generators had caused an issue once before so I figured they wouldn't have any running. But there were no candles burning either. It was very late at night, or very early morning depending on your view so everyone might have been sleeping. I took a deep breath, looked back one final time at my back up and walked up to the back of the house. I knocked lightly on the glass hoping to get Andromeda's attention before heading in. The rear door should have been locked, but I knew where the garage key was. I wanted to let Andromeda know who it was so she wouldn't scare the girls too badly. Seconds passed and she didn't show. I knocked again and waited, trying not to worry. Andromeda should hear me unless Ava had her locked in the room. I couldn't see anything in the house since the blinds were pulled. More seconds passed and I sensed movement. Unfortunately, it was outside of the house. I spun quickly and had my gun at the ready. Seconds before pulling the trigger I noticed Lyla with her hand up telling me to settle. She walked up to the door with a sour look.

"Any luck?"

"No. I'm waiting to see if Andromeda will come to the door."

"You may want to get in sooner than that." She looked agitated. "There are bodies along the front yards and road on the way in. You skipped it all but it looks like NLB's got here and killed some people. Recently."

I had no words but I grabbed the door and pulled. It slid open easily, not locked. My stomach dropped and sweat beaded on my forehead. I tamped my fear down and headed into the house. I cleared every room and could not find anyone. I looked for their bags and it seemed like Ava's go-bag was gone, but Mom's was still there. There was food on the table that did not seem rotted or even bad. Whatever happened had not happened that long ago.

I looked at Lyla and she just shrugged and pointed to the door. She wanted to leave and head back to the rest of the squad. I agreed. The house was empty. No reason to stay here. Then I stopped and headed back into my room quickly. I didn't have time the last time I left to grab anything. There was only one thing I needed, so I grabbed it quickly and headed back out. Lyla and I looked at each other for a second. A look of pity went across her face quickly, then solidified into a stern look of determination. I decided to follow her example and do the same. I tamped down my fears and disappointment. I decided that I needed to get on with the mission. I had done what I needed to do. I checked on the girls. They were gone. Possibly just this morning or days ago. It was hard to say if the food I had seen had been theirs. I wanted to believe that they were still alive and out there together. I would never give up hope of finding them, but I needed to stay focused. Running into the night would not solve anything or get me any closer to them. I locked in on my team and headed back to the trucks.

I filled Veronica and Drew in on what we found. They nodded and didn't say anything further. Veronica did think about it and decided that the community was clear and that we should finish the night there. We moved the trucks in and the team found a house to secure for the night. It was not my house, I think they all thought that would be too much. Either way, I settled down for the first watch and was determined to sleep in the truck when it was my turn to sleep. Of course, that would be on the rarity that sleep would come tonight. Thinking about that I reached into my pocket and grabbed the one thing I couldn't do without. A picture I had on my desk of the four of us in Rehoboth, the summer before I left for college. We were all together, happy and smiling. This was how I needed to remember all of them. How I needed to remind myself to be.

It was not how I felt though. Besides the guilt and aggravation, I felt empty.

Onward

A couple of hours later I was relieved of my watch, and I decided against sleeping in the truck. I had driven most of the night and then had an emotional couple of hours worried about the girls. I needed to sleep in a bed and get some good rest. We weren't heading back to the hospital, we were following my suggestion of finding fuel and parts here in Sussex county. I needed to be sharp so I could do my job.

The house the squad was staying in was the house where the old watch captain had been killed in. Part of the reason it was so secure was that we had boarded it all up. A lot of the boards had been removed and the captain and the old man were not there any longer. I wondered what had happened to them. Were they released the day I left, or more recently? It really didn't matter but it had been something to ruminate on while I kept watch.

As I slept the others stood their time on watch. It was late morning by the time I smelled food cooking and woke up enough to get out of bed. I hadn't wanted to get up and make yesterday a reality, but I needed to. Staying in bed, especially a dust-covered one would not help my situation at all. I got up and walked to the bathroom to wash my face. It was after I pulled the handle that I remembered that the world had fallen and electricity did not work. Old habits and the time at the hospital had not helped that reality set in. For as much as I had endured, I felt lucky all the same. Lucky that I had been found by this team and then taken in to be a member. I knew there were a lot of others having a worse time than me. I had watched many others lose their lives in bad ways. I barely remember dying, any of the times.

I decided that the squad here had made my life better. They would be my new family. I would never give up on the girls, but I needed to keep my head and concentrate on what I could control. Even if I stopped everything and looked for the girls nonstop I may never find them or even have a clue as to where they had gone. As part of this group, I would move around the state and the peninsula a lot. I would encounter people and places that may never let me around if I was a vagabond on a mission of my own. This would be my best shot at finding the girls and doing something meaningful with my life.

All of that had gone through my head before I made it to the kitchen to see what was cooking. All thought stopped when I smelled the coffee. My head was groggy and the caffeine would be a great pick me up. I sat down and grabbed a cup as Veronica brought the pot over and poured the coffee for me. Her face was stern as usual, but her eyes had a softness to them that was unusual. The others seemed to have stopped talking when I entered the room too.

"So, I see everyone is here. Who is on watch Sarge?" I decided to break the tension myself.

She stopped and looked at me sternly. "No one. We all need a good meal before we hit the road. This house seems secure so we should be fine for a couple of minutes."

"Yeah someone boarded it up pretty well. Do you know why it is boarded up like this?" I looked around and everyone looked intrigued. They also started eating again and lost their pitiful looks. I decided it was story time and told them about the watch captain and his untimely death.

After my story, as everyone finished eating and sipping their coffee, we decided to figure out the plan for the day. There was no point in flying by the seat of our pants when we could take our time and plan it out. Will pulled out a map and I got to work marking the general areas of my dad's work sites. I knew what some had and what others should've had. I also circled a few family farms in the area that I knew would have in-ground gas tanks and tractor parts.

Shortly after, we loaded up and hit the road again. I was driving and in the lead car. I was the only person from Sussex county. Veronica, Will and Chris were all from Wilmington and the surrounding suburbs. Lyla was from Pennsylvania and Silver was from somewhere in the mid-west, he was a little dodgy on it when asked. They had barely even ventured into my county for most of their lives. Knowing the area had some disadvantages though, as I tried to use the roads that I knew a lot of them were blocked, overgrown, or too torn up to drive on. It took a few turnarounds, cutbacks and straight driving through fields to get us where I wanted to go, but the time it took wasn't too bad.

The first place we stopped was a dry hole. It was obvious that others had the same idea that I had and got here first. That was ok, we had expected a few holes to be dry. I decided to try a family farm that was close by before moving on to another construction site. As we pulled off the road you could barely tell that there had been a farm on the property. The plants were so badly overgrown I could not find the driveway. Luckily, I had been to this farm before and knew that there were no ditches on the property up to the house. I just picked a spot and started in.

"Whoa! Wait up a second private." Veronica shouted in my ear as I hit the property. It startled me and I hit the brakes a little too hard. Chris had to swerve in the truck behind me so he didn't hit me. With that, he just pulled up alongside and rolled the passenger side window down.

"What's up Sarge?" He asked.

"The private here was going to drive up into an unseen, unknown area with no security set."

"Oh, I thought you had talked about it and considered it fine since he had stopped then went to go. How do you want to set security? It is a long walk up to the house. They already know we are here if we wait for a couple people to walk up and check it out, they may be ready." I had not thought about any of what these two were talking about. A lack in my training so far. I had to start thinking of these things.

"Let's run and gun. Oakley take the truck. Smith, Reid on the tops."

Will and Chris were smiling as they opened the doors. I had no idea what run and gun were so I was trying to figure it out. Lyla took the driver's seat of the truck. Chris got in the back and Will hopped up onto the top of the SUV in a prone position. Chris locked in with his rifle forward and an arm around the rollbar. Then I figured it out, we were going to drive in and they would provide a mobile overwatch, fun.

"Fast or slow?" I asked Veronica once everyone was set.

She banged on the roof and shouted to Will. "Up or down Reid."

"Up Sarge. Take it all the way up!" He sounded excited. I was still confused.

"That means fast. Roll in hard and Oakley will weave out a ways and come in hard from another angle. Get us there without getting shot at."

I looked over to Lyla and nodded. She smiled and we put our trucks in gear and jammed the gas. I looked in the rearview mirror and Drew even seemed to be enjoying himself. He had been oddly quiet. I guess Veronica was doing fine. I came in at an angel to put us near the front door but not directly in front of it. There didn't seem to be any movement or any wearing of the weeds up to the house. Even if it was abandoned we had to be careful. If deaders were locked inside they could still be a threat.

As soon as we came to a stop, Veronica and Drew jumped out with their guns to the ready. Will stood up on the top of the truck and jumped to the top of the porch roof. I hadn't thought about that, but I parked close enough for it to be an option. I quickly turned off the truck, left the keys hanging in the ignition and grabbed my rifle. Within seconds we were stationed around the SUV. Lyla and Chris were on the other side. We couldn't see them but I heard the truck turn off.

Will walked the roof slowly and checked the windows on the second floor. He shook his head that no one was around. Veronica, Drew and I lined up at the front. We heard Lyla and Chris make entry in the rear so we followed suit. We cleared the lower floor, nothing out of place and it seemed like no one had been here for a while. We heard Will yell clear from the second floor. I hadn't even known he had made entry. Guess he found an open window. The last place to look was the cellar. Veronica looked at me, so I guessed that I was being volunteered. I cracked the door and turned on my flashlight. I ripped the door open and made a quick entry to the stairs. Nothing. I squatted down to get a better view below the stairs. I could see a lot but not everything. The backs of the stairs were open if someone was hiding behind there I wouldn't see them until it was too late. I gathered myself up and ran to the bottom of the steps and turned around like a kid that turned the light off in the hallway. Nothing, it was clear. I told the others the same and then took a second to see what was around. It was an amazing find. There were rows and rows of canned fruits and vegetables, smoked meats and dried herbs. The cooks would love this stuff. I yelled up to the others and told them what I had found.

"Leave it for now. It isn't going anywhere. We need to clear the rest of the property. Food is always good but we need gas and diesel. Parts would be good too. Get up here and lets get that done. We will clear this out before we leave." Veronica ordered.

The rest of the farm was clear. There were two outbuildings and a large open-air shed. No one had been here in a while. They probably bugged out before the lockdown. The good news was that I had been right, they had two underground tanks full of fuel. One was diesel the other was gasoline. Chris backed up the f-150 to the diesel tank and started filling the canisters. The pump was run by an old hand pump so there was no need for electricity. That got me a look of appreciation from Veronica.

Drew and Will went looking through the outbuildings for parts on the mechanic's list for the generators. That left Lyla and me to get the SUV loaded with the food supplies in the cellar. It looked like a good haul. If we could find a few of the parts we needed, we may be able to head back early. The canisters may be filled with this one-stop. I'd have to make sure to mark it on the map for us later in case we needed more, or I guess when we needed more.

Once everything was loaded up in the vehicles we huddled together to figure out our next plan. We found food, gas, diesel and a few spare parts. Veronica felt that the mission had been mostly a success, with a quick pity look at me, and that we should head back. Maybe make a small stop or two for some other foodstuff if possible. Drew seemed to agree so we loaded up to head north. As we were loading up Chris suddenly ran off back towards the gas tanks. He was only gone a second then came back smiling. He showed us the pump handles. He had taken them off.

"Gonna bury them under some stone by the house. They will be here if one of our squads need them, but may keep others from taking the gas."

Smart. It would leave us with a reserve and hopefully keep others from doing the same. A couple of minutes later they were buried and we were back on the road. The day was a success. Last night was not. I kept it in my rearview mirror and moved on.

North

We stopped just outside of Milford. There were a couple of broken-down vehicles on the road that had somehow wrecked into each other. There were only two vehicles, so it was odd. I read an article one time about the first two cars ever made. They somehow found a way to wreck into each other with no other obstacle in their way.

After a quick security sweep, we checked their tanks and saw that they still had fuel. Although we didn't have to top off it would never be a bad thing to keep the tanks full. I grabbed a hose out of the back of the truck and got ready to siphon gas out of one of the cars. I had inserted the tube and pressed my lips to it when Will looked at me and told me to stop.

"What are you doing?" He asked.

"Going to get the siphon started."

"By sucking on the tube. You like the taste of gas?"

"Not really. But how else do you do it?"

"Watch." he took another smaller tube and inserted it next to the hose. He then placed a rag around them to seal the air and blew into the smaller tube. The gas started flowing almost immediately. No coughing, gagging, or inhaling fumes. I wish I had known this earlier. Why was this never on TV?

Within minutes both trucks were fueled up again. We got back on the road and drove around the mess. We were headed to the outskirts of town to look for some food supplies. There was a small school that may be rife with opportunity. People didn't always think of schools having food, so the school may not have been touched for food supplies. We came in from Rt 36 and headed west into town. There were a few small communities along this path, but we didn't think that we would run into resistance.

Well, that did not go as planned. About a mile from the school, we noticed that a lot of the roadways were blocked. Not right at the intersection but a ways back from the main road. It was only one or two so we thought that maybe the communities down those roads were trying to keep people from heading their way. That was until we came to a bigger intersection and there was a wall in the middle of the road. Not just a wall of cars or a roadblock. It was a literal wall, made from metal fencing, wood fencing and car parts. We slowed down to assess the situation. About the time we thought about getting out of the car, a shot went off and a round went through our windshield. No one was hit, but I threw the SUV in reverse and tried to get away. Unfortunately, it took Chris an extra second to get moving than me and I had to stop again.

The second round hit the windshield and Drew grunted in pain. I did not have the time to check on him. Veronica and Will leaned out of the windows and threw rounds back at the wall. I got the SUV moving and pulled a sharp 180, kinda like in the movies, threw it in drive and headed back up the road. Three dirt bikes shot out of a small wooded area to my right. I swerved to get them away from the SUV and tried to keep them off the truck. They were faster and more agile than our big vehicles though and were able to maneuver around better. Veronica leaned out of the window again and shot at one of the bikes. She got lucky and took the rear tire out. The kid on the bike fell and slid off into the field. Unfortunately, the others were harassing Chris and Lyla. The bike on the driver's side was pointing a gun at Chris trying to get them to stop the truck. I revved the engine and tried to catch up. We had gone completely off-road by this point and it was hard to see to steer, let alone line up a shot. Chris was doing his best to keep his speed and direction erratic to keep them off guard.

"Stop! Now!" Will yelled at me.

Without hesitation, I jammed the brakes and looked back to see what he wanted. I was worried that the grunt I had heard from Drew was the reason. Was he bleeding out? Was he dying? Before I even stopped he was out of the door and jumping on top of the truck. It only took a few seconds but the others were almost out of range. What was he doing? Then the reason became clear. Chris must have seen us stop and was slowly swinging back the SUV and bringing the bandits around so they were coming back at us. Will set up and waited for his shot. Now that we weren't moving it would be easier to line up. Veronica saw this too and jumped out of her side using the door for cover. It seemed like everything was in slow motion. The bikes and truck were heading directly at us. Once the bikes were within range two almost simultaneous shots went off. The two bikes veered and went down. Will jumped down and Veronica jumped back in. As soon as Chris was passed we spun around and followed on their tail. We quickly hit a road and picked up speed to get out of the area.

If we wanted to stop and do more on this trip, it had just gone out of the window. Veronica and Will swapped positions as we flew down the road, so she could check on Drew. He had taken a round to the shoulder but otherwise seemed to be ok.

"Was it me or did we seem to be more in sync there than usual?" Will asked Veronica over his shoulder.

"It wasn't just you. How did you know that Chris was going to bring them back to us? We had never trained for that. We usually try to elude." She was talking to Will but trying to get Drew's shoulder to stop bleeding.

"Not sure. I think I just knew it. Maybe I saw something in the movements, but it seemed like he told me. I could see he wasn't going to shake them. It was so cool though. Our shots were almost perfectly timed too." Will was so pumped that I was excited for him.

"Do you think it has something to do with the spores?" I asked. I wasn't trying to ruin the mood but it was a new factor added. I looked back at Veronica as I thought about this being the cause. This caused me to career off the road slightly. I corrected and kept my eyes forward.

"We will have to talk to Testerman. He will probably want to run tests. Now please let her fix me up and keep your eyes on the road private. I hurt enough I don't need any more injuries." Drew ordered.

The rest of the trip was uneventful. We got Drew back to the hospital pretty quickly. Tide was not quite fully low, so Chris and Will took the trucks across. It gave me a break from driving, so I wasn't too mad. Two of the gas canisters took shots during the fire exchange. They were almost empty by the time we unloaded them. But we still had plenty for the near future.

The food made it back almost unscathed. The rough driving through the fields and hard braking did break a couple of the jars. Once we unloaded the cooks were happy to have new food introduced and fawned over the fresh dried herbs. We would have some good food coming our way for a meal or two. The mechanics told Will that the parts were usable for the most part and then placed them on a bench. They were a really emotional bunch of people.

Trey had come down to join us as soon as we arrived. He asked us all about the trip and what had happened. When we told him about the firefight I could see that he was mad that he had missed it. He did tell us that they had retrofitted the cage with the bobcat so it won't be able to get back out again if we lost power. But they had not done anything with any of the other locks. There had been more pressing issues. The generators had gone out again while we were gone. The mechanics didn't think that one of them would ever run again, no matter how many parts we brought back. That explained their mood I guess.

After everything calmed down, we had showered and eaten we met in the staging area to talk about the last battle. There was a lot of confusion and cross-talk but I think the gist of it was pretty clear. When the battle was raging and all of our adrenalin was pumping we could feel the others around us. It was small, but it provided a sense of what others were feeling and thinking. We tried to do it again while sitting in the room but nothing seemed different. We decided to test our theory by ourselves instead of involving Testerman at that time. I knew that I had enough testing done to me and Trey actually agreed too.

Over the course of the next couple of days, we trained hard and tried to work out how this new ability might work. We couldn't seem to get it to work at all. Maybe it only worked in life-or-death situations. Or maybe we all imagined it trying to come up with new abilities like superheroes. I was new and tried to help out where I could but I had not trained with them and did not have the same intuition during the training scenarios as they did.

I did walk through the NLB labs when we weren't training. I tried to find the alpha that Testerman had used, but I was not able to locate him. None of the other deaders seemed interested in anything at all. They were all probably starved or tested mercilessly every day. Even though we didn't figure out how this new intuition worked with our new training, we did learn to fight and work together better as a team. I was learning fast and able to help others with new ways of thinking about problems. Sometimes getting an outside perspective on things can be refreshing and breathe new life into a unit.

Drew healed up but nodded out of any further training with us. He actually decided to stop going out on missions at all, which was a shock to everyone.

"Look I have been in the military for 25 years. If the world still worked I would have been forced out or forced onto desk duty. I ran with your team because it was a good squad that needed some leadership and another member. Sgt. Hayes is now the leadership and Private Washington is the other member. You will work and operate fine without me. Look at how the training has been going. You are all working as a team and thriving under Sgt. Hayes' leadership. I can use my knowledge and abilities better here orchestrating all of the squads anyway. That's where my talents lie." he explained.

"What about being Unseen. You just did that and now you are getting out of the field?" I asked.

"I did that before I made my decision. I felt I would still be needed then. After this trip. The way you and Sgt. Hayes stepped up. The way all of you worked together. It was good to see. Plus, it can't hurt to be Unseen even here in the hospital. We found that it doesn't stop bullets, and I am too old to keep getting shot at." He laughed as he grabbed his hurt shoulder.

"Squad! Form up!" Veronica ordered. We fell into a quick two-by-three formation. "Hand salute!"

We all stood proud and saluted SGM Silver. He looked at each of us wistfully and then stood, albeit a little gingerly, and saluted back.

"Sergeant Major Silver. It has been an honor to serve along side of you. You have lead and taught all of us well. You will be missed on the squad, but will be a great asset to command."

"Thank you, Sergeant. Take care of this squad. You have a lot of missions coming up. You need to keep them safe and keep them working together. I trust that you can do that, possibly better than me from here on out. Otherwise I would not make this decision. Thank you all. Dismissed!"

-----Redacted-----

The story continued with how the squad worked together and saved lives. Ava apparently thought that I was going on too much about myself and my heroism and less about the NLBs and the effect the spores had on me and my team. Between her edits and some classified missions, I guess we should just move on to the important parts of my story. I would like to add a few notes that would have come out of these "hero" stories as she calls them.

1. The spore intuition is actually a thing. The more we fought together in life-endangering scenarios the more we noticed it. We can't read each other's thoughts but we can intuit what the other members intend to do and work together without speaking. This works great in an environment where radios aren't smart to carry. It is obviously an imperfect thing, but we have managed to get a handle on it. It does make it odd to be around other squads at times. They feel left out and do not coordinate as well with us. Lately, we have started only working with other squads like us, but the ability is not as strong with others that you do not work and live with all of the time.

2. The NLBs do ignore us for the most part. We now call ourselves "The Unseen". but that is limited. If we are attacked and they touch us they can still drain us. Cpl. Ragsdill, yes it is corporal now, found that out one day by accident. He was walking through a den and brushed his ankle up along the hand of a sleeping NLB. It came awake and grabbed his ankle, trying to drain him instantly. It was awakening. It meant we still had to be careful. Our uniforms are now all long pants, sleeves and high necks. Good to wear this in all black during the summer months, let me tell you.

a)Secondly, we have to be extra careful around water. Rain, sweat, or anything that can soak our clothes. With the conductive nature of water, per Testerman, it can transfer the electrical signal just like we touched skin to skin. It will awaken the NLB to our presence and open us to an attack.

3. The longer that we have these spores in our brain stems the more they affect our personalities. I had said before that I seemed to have more of a hair trigger. That I was easily angered. But it is worse than that. I have found that all of us have more basic

reactions to stimuli. Testerman has even tested this, of course. So if you think that becoming one of us is all glory, there are downsides. Higher functioning brain systems, like those that allow us to coordinate higher math and sciences, seem to be slipping away. I used to be a computer geek. I was learning to work on drones and UAVs in an elite college before the Fall. Now I can barely remember how they would work. Some of that may be from lack of use. We don't really use technology as we had before. But I can feel the pieces missing when I try to think about the past. Some of the others feel it, but I am not sure they were ever as tech-initiated as I was. It definitely takes turning the scientists off the list for a type of protection though.

4. Not all humans are capable of becoming an NLB or an Unseen. Seems like the spores would infect everyone and everything but we had found a few people that were killed and did not rise again, without being drained. We also had a new recruit. He was a guy that we found on a foray into Cambridge, Maryland. Dante was his name. He was a Navy veteran. When we came upon him he was surrounded by NLBs. he was holding his own, but the outcome was inevitable. We walked in right past them and saved his life. (yeah yeah hero stuff, but there is a point here). Well once we got him back he wanted to join our squad. He was vetted over a couple months and determined to be fit for the job. By this time we had two other squads of people like us, but they weren't full yet. Well, Dante went under the procedure. His heart was stopped for two minutes. He was brought back. The usual. Well, it didn't take. Even though he had the spores in his blood they did not coagulate in his brain stem after death. So even though we killed him, he was still just as vulnerable to the NLBs as he was before. Dr. Testerman took this as another opportunity to determine how to kill the spores or stop them from turning us after death. He took Dante for testing. I have not seen him since.

5. Each of us has adjusted to the new way of life differently. As I have stated before I can see the movement of spores in the air. It is hard during the day, but I have been able to identify it even then. Cpl Ragsdill has been able to identify the outlines of NLBs through the thick foliage. He says he can see them through walls too, but none of us have seen evidence of that, nor believe him. Pfc Smith and Cpl Reid have become tied to each other's thoughts that

we started calling them the twins. They almost have their own language and barely talk when it is just the two of them. It helps us out a lot because it does not seem to diminish with distance. It is an enhanced version of what we all share, yet they don't have to be in danger for it to work. Cpl. Oakley has the ability to track prints that are days old. Not just in dirt and grass, but on concrete and asphalt. She says that she can see where the print pushes the spores away slightly and leaves an impression. Everything is now covered in spores if you have the ability to see them as we do. It makes it hard to believe that we will be able to eradicate this plague as easily as our scientists think. Sgt. Hayes has not spoken of any ability that she has other than intuition. We all suspect that there is something that she has not shared with us as we have witnessed her do things that seem enhanced. If she doesn't want to speak of it that is her prerogative. She is the leader of our squad now and has pulled away just a bit with that role.

Family

Life became routine. We would spend time at the hospital working, strategizing and training. Then get sent out on missions for one reason or another. There were a few stories from the people that we saved that were quite interesting. Some of them had seen way more than we had and different things than we had. This one time we came upon this stoner, he was out of his mind on Blue Lightning. I had the satisfaction of interviewing him. The things that he told me about what he could see when high could be its own story.

As we spent longer in the bunker we started growing too large for our forays to feed everyone. We had to resort to hunting local game and game in the surrounding areas. We also lost a couple of generators. The fuel that we were getting was going bad. It wouldn't last as long and would gum up the mechanisms too often. We were almost always down one generator at a time to have it serviced and cleaned. Luckily, quite a few of the survivors were farmers and mechanics so they would pitch in to help out.

The scientists were coming close to what they thought would be a cure. I really hoped that it would work and we could get out of the basement. I wasn't sure how long this oasis in the wilderness was going to last. The fact that it had lasted this long was a miracle in and of itself.

For the last year and a half, I have been part of this squad and running missions. In the beginning, it was hard, but then it became easier even fun. But after so long with no end in site, it was starting to become monotonous and even a bit grueling. I mean I know we have work to do, and I love the work, but we don't even get a day off in this world let alone a vacation.

I guess it is not the job, but that the world may never get better. It may never recover. All of the work that we have done. All of the people that we have lost along the way wouldn't be worth it if nothing changed. I was starting to lose hope.

All of that changed on the day that I found Ava.

The mission we were on was a deader capture plan. Dr. Testerman liked to get new specimens at times to see if the spores have changed or evolved inside of their hosts. We had used the Dover Air Force Base before and had a decently easy setup to use. We would open the pen up and lure a few NLBs into the capture area then close it up. We would usually leave a couple of soldiers to monitor them for a few days to see if there was a captured alpha or just the minions. If there was an alpha we would usually try and take them for the study. One, it got them off the streets running their gangs, as we called them. Two, they were usually the strongest and would have the best health.

This mission went fine for the capture and set. We had a good haul that we lured in from the downtown area. It had taken us two days to get them there. Sure we could have just bagged and tagged one or two of them, but then we wouldn't know if we got an alpha or not. Testerman usually wanted to know. Once we had them caged in we set the watch with two newer guys on the team. Sarge, Ragsdill, Smith, Reid and I, Cpl Oakley had been left back at the hospital for some of her periodic testing, went back into the town to gather some supplies. We left the watch with a small radio in case of an emergency. I wasn't sure what that emergency would be but Sergeant Hayes insisted on it. It wasn't like the batteries would attract the deaders. We already knew where they were. If anything it made us a little more of a target. By this point, it was something we were used to.

We had been gone a little more than a day and had traveled south away from the airbase the entire time. We had been checking on farms and other outlying areas. We hadn't found much of anything and were about to start heading back when we heard from the watch team. They had seen a couple of people stalking about around the fence line of the airbase. They had disappeared into one of the buildings. No movement had been seen in about 20 minutes, but they felt that it should be reported.

"10-4. You made the right call. The rest of the squad and I will return to your position." Sgt. Hayes replied over the radio. "Shit! who is moving around the base and what are they looking for?" She said to us.

"Sarge, can't we just have the two watch hang out and keep an eye on them? We haven't found much and we need to get some food to the hospital. We are running low." Cpl Ragsdill interjected.

"I know, but let's make sure our team isn't in danger. The south hasn't worked much. we could head east after getting back to check that area."

"We did that area two times ago. That was what two months back? There wasn't much there then."

"But we did leave that small bit in that odd building out there. We could at least send a couple for you to go get that." Sgt. Hayes countered while glaring at Ragsdill. I hated it when she glared at me like that. "Besides, as usual I am in charge and this is what I say we will do."

So that is what we did. We had to travel slowly due to the road conditions, plus the watch team hadn't reported any new movement so we weren't really in a hurry. We passed some speculation around the few of us in the SUV about why someone would be coming through the base.

"It is most likely someone heading north looking for someplace safe to rest." I said glancing back in the rearview mirror. Yes, I was driving as usual.

"No, it is the first part of a raiding party. They have been watching us and want what we have. I told you we had used the base too much lately." Cpl Ragsdill spoke up with his ever-optimistic banter.

"Why is it always some raiders with you?" Reid asked him from the third row. "It is always raiders."

"We have run into our share of raiders, haven't we Smith?" Ragsdill pleaded.

"I'm not getting into this again. Washington, is there anything on the radio we can listen to?" Smith asked me while leaning through the middle of the front seats. He looked at Sarge and me with an eye roll and a smirk.

I turned on the radio and got a buzz of static.

"Ahh, that's the one. That is Washington's favorite song right there. He was jamming out to it when we found him." Ragsdill spewed.

I didn't react to him anymore. Especially with this type of banter. He was just looking to pull the conversation away from his raider theory and needle me at the same time. I just rolled my eyes in the mirror and shut the radio off again. It was good timing because the handheld went off at about the same time.

"Ahh, Sarge. Its the watch. Umm. the people. they are moving. we had to switch to night vision and move locations to get a better look at them. They are umm, heading right to the --static--- - what should we do?"

Sarge looked at me then at the others. "Did you hear what they said?"

Everyone shook their heads in the negative.

"Repeat. Watch this is Sarge. Repeat your last. We didn't get that clear." Hayes said back into the radio.

"We said that the ---static ---we are watching are --static-- to the NLB cage. What should we do?--static--"

"Do you have a description?"

"Two small women, probably ----static--- girls and a large dog." I smiled in the mirror. There went the raider theory. Mostly.

"Do not engage. Don't let them know where you are. Keep an eye on them and keep them out of that trap!"

"10-4, copy--static--"

"Do you think they heard us clearly? We obviously aren't hearing them correctly." Hayes asked the group while waving her hand for me to speed up.

"Probably not. I knew we shouldn't have left two newbies there." Ragsdill snarled.

"You still think I'm new. Anyone that wasn't prior military just can't muster up in your eyes Cpl. Ragsdill." I countered while glaring at him through the mirror. I don't think it chills him like the Sarge glare.

I hit the accelerator and pushed the SUV along the road. The bumps and noise all but ended any chance for conversation. We arrived at the fence to the base shortly after. The watch had reached out and told us that the "raiders" were two girls and a dog. The girls had walked into the NLB trap and had found the supplies that we had left there. They had just ventured out to check out the other buildings.

"Why did you let them get that far?!" Sgt Hayes yelled at them through the radio. We were all gearing up at the trunk of the SUV when she suddenly yelled into the mike. It was surprising.

"Get what your getting. We need to get inside that fence now. They are just two scared girls and a dog. They are probably going to get themselves killed." She then turned on her heel and jogged toward the trap. The rest of us looked at each other quickly, shut the door and ran to catch up. Sarge's jog was not a slow one.

I thought that we were too late when we reached the fenceline. One girl had gone down in a heap under a couple of NLBs. The other was still standing but had no idea her back was exposed. The dog was giving a couple of the NLBs a run for their money. It was jumping in to protect who I assumed was its owner. It was doing a good job too, but it wouldn't be enough. The girl that was down didn't have much time left.

Suddenly, Sarge called out. "Stop, throwing EMP." She paused and tossed one of the grenades into the fenced area. It rolled damn close to the girls and the dog. A few seconds later it went off. I could almost see the blast at this point. Unfortunately, we had used these things quite a few times over the last year or so. I had almost gotten used to the ensuing dizziness. We all blinked and then powered through. We jumped over the fence as the NLB's wandered around like they were lost.

Ragsdill and Smith shoot a couple of the NLBs to drop them and incapacitate them for as long as possible. Reid had taken to using a long-bladed machete and cutting the heads off of them to stop them permanently. Sgt. Hayes dropped down next to the downed girl while I protected the little girl that was still standing. Sarge rips an iv pack out of the pack and gets ready to insert it into the girl's arm when I realize who it was. The girl and the dog are instantly recognizable. As Andromeda lays down next to Ava I walk over to assist Sgt Hayes.

"This will help. It's just an IV." I hear her say.

I kneel down next to Andromeda and check her for open wounds. She has a bit of blood in her fur, but it seems to be from the NLBs she attacked, not her own. "Hello, there Rommy. What has she gotten you into now?" I say.

"How..? How do you know her name?" Ava asked dumbfounded.

"I was there when you named her you numbskull." I say as she passes out.

I walk back to the other girl. "Where are you coming from? How did you get here?"

"We were in Frederica, staying in the fire house." The girl answered.

"Before that. Did you ever see her mother?"

"Yes, we left a place called the Home of the Brave. We had stayed there with Ava's mom and a couple of others, but deaders attacked and we ran. Ava tried to save her but we couldn't find her. Why? Who are you?" She was looking around at all of us and the NLBs moving around, starting to get their senses back.

"Nevermind that. Where is this Home?" I said as I grabbed her shoulders to steady her gaze on me.

"Milford area I think."

"Yeah, It was a homeless veterans place if I remember right. Just outside of Milford." Smith pipes up.

"Sarge, I need to take a team and go there to see if she is still alive." I say turning about to Sgt. Hayes as she continued to work on my sister.

"Alright. Take the SUV. Ward and Adkins can stay with me and take the girls and their dog back to base. You take the rest and check it out." She said without looking up.

"Ok, you heard her let's get loaded up. Ward, grab that dog and help her. Then help Adkins with the other girl and get them both to the truck."

Reid, Ragsdill Smith and I jumped back over the fence and headed back to the SUV. Heading south again. Reid did take one more swipe and took another NLB's head off. He really seemed to enjoy that lately. I wonder if I should let Sarge know.

Bravers

The way down to Milford was a pretty easy trip. The question was, would anyone still be there? Smith had pulled out an old map and was trying to figure out exactly where the Home of the Brave was. It would take a little while to get into the area so he had time.

We reached the compound a couple of hours and a few wrong turns later. Everything was dark and the main gate stood open. That didn't bode well for it being occupied. We parked a little ways away and hoofed it up to the place. There was very little light since the moon had already set. Our night vision was pretty good so we went without our goggles. I kept watching for any spores being disturbed either near us or in the compound. I am sure Ragsdill was looking for his outlines. We were just back on mission and flowing as a unit. Smith did ask me if I was ok after finding my sister. I just nodded. We needed to find these survivors. Also, if they left this place that quickly there may be some supplies and food left over.

Once we entered the compound we could tell it was abandoned. We split up and checked the main buildings and thoroughfares. We found a bunch of rotten vegetables in a storage area, but not much else. It was late into the night. Nothing much was going to get accomplished. We all agreed to find some bunks and rack out for the night. We searched and found a building with rooms that were set up with beds, closets and desks. I found a room and opened the closet to make sure it was clear. The closet door had a mirror on it. I glanced at it quickly then shut it. I didn't need to look too deeply into that tonight.

In the morning we all met back up and figured we could conduct a quick search of the grounds before getting back on the road. It took about an hour but we found some small food stocks, some weapons and general supplies. Reid did come back with a handwritten note. The handwriting looked familiar but I wasn't sure until he started reading the note:

Ava, or whoever is reading this. We were overrun by a form of deaders I have never seen before. They are smart and set a trap for us during our harvest. A lot of people died near the farm. They were killed by these beasts. Right now we are hiding inside a building. We can't get to anyone that may be hiding in the basement. I hope you are there and we will be together soon. If not I know you got away and will find your way on your own as you have done before. The days of hiding are taking their toll on me. I am writing this in case something goes awry and I do not make it.

It has been a few days and we are going to leave this place today. We haven't heard anything outside in at least a full day. Most of us are delirious, all of us are hungry, and we only had a small bit of rations to sustain us. We cannot stay here any longer. We will stop by the basement before we head north. We are going to stay off the main roads to stay safe. If you find this Jessica tells me that we are going to go to the dual churches just north then work our way over to the DuPont Nature Center. We will hole up here for a while. I am not sure how long. I will try to leave a note at each as we move on. I hope you are safe. I love you and Andromeda. I still hold hope for Matthew too.

As I read the note I yelled for Smith to grab the map out of the van.

"Look for two churches that are north of our current location." I ordered

"Hey I am the ranking member here. I'll give the orders." Cpl Ragsdill piped.

"Stuff it Trey!" All three of us yelled at the same time.

When Smith got back with the map he found the churches that my mom was talking about. We loaded up and headed there. They were a complete bust. I am not even sure anyone had been here in the last year, let alone months, so we moved on to the DuPont Nature Center.

We had better results here, but not what I was hoping for. The nature center had the look of a way station. There were food wrappers, trash and old bedding. Unfortunately, we also found two NLBs walking around a back bedroom. Pinned to the shirt of one of them was another note. Smith walked up and removed it, then handed it directly to me. All to Ragsdill's chagrin.

Ava, Two of our people have died from sickness since we arrived at the nature center. We have to move on as it is not safe to stay here with them in such close vicinity since they became deaders. We are moving on but I wanted to leave you a note to tell

you our location. We are heading further north. To the South Bowers Fire Department. They should have fresh water there. We have gone without for too long now. A lot of our people are not doing well. They might not make the trip. To be honest. This has taken a lot out of me. I may not make another trip myself. Hugs and Kisses. Love to you two and Matt.

Mom.

I am not going to lie. Seeing the note that my mother wrote saying she may not be alive when I finally make it to her location pissed me off. I had worked too hard to find her for her to be dead when I arrived. We loaded up and headed north as Smith found the location of S. Bowers. The trip there was short. I don't think the others thought it was particularly smooth or relaxing but I made it in about an hour.

We stopped on the main street that led back to the fire hall. Ragsdill and Reid got out to walk the perimeter. Once they gave us the all clear we headed into the building. There was no one in the main bay where the trucks used to be held. We swept each room and found them in the old recreation room. There was still a pool table pushed to one wall. We looked around and saw about 10 people in different stages of dehydration and starvation. We quickly spread out and handed out our ration bars and some water bottles. I sent Reid out to the SUV to get more of each. I think that if we had not found these people in the next few days none of them would have survived.

As I passed out supplies I asked everyone I could about my mom. Asked if they had seen her. I finally came across a woman named Susie. She asked me if my sister's name was Ava.

"Yes it is." I replied as I knelt down next to her.

"God, was she always annoying or did she grow into it?"

I laughed and told her "Since birth."

"I am sorry but we lost her." She hung her head and looked away as she said this.

"My mother? Is she dead or missing?"

"No Ava. We lost her in the deader raid. No one seems to know where she went. Your mother is in the back room. She is watching the little ones."

I sighed and let out the breath I was holding. "Oh, we found Ava. She is safe. That room there?" I asked pointing to the door on the other side of the room.

Susie just nodded and looked relieved that Ava was safe too. I got up and walked to the door. I was almost afraid to open it and find Mom not there. My hesitation was short-lived, I opened the door and headed in. There were three kids huddled up around my mother as she read them a book. The kids looked healthy like they were getting most of the food and water that the group had. As the door opened my mother looked up and started to cry. She tried to get up but struggled a bit. I rushed to her side so she didn't have to get up. She grabbed me in a huge hug and refused to let go. I swear it was 15 minutes.

Eventually, she let go and took a water bottle and a protein bar from Reid. I wasn't sure when he even walked in. Mom drank the bottle and ate the bar faster than I had ever seen her eat.

"Mom, your last note said that you weren't feeling well." I stated.

"Oh, I wasn't we had gone so long without good water or food."

"Well we found you now. We have food and water where we are going."

"I am so glad you found me Matthew. I just wish I knew where your sister was." She said this with a sad glint in her eye.

"I can help with that too. I found her just about two days ago. She is already back at the hospital and waiting for you. She is who sent me after you." I explained with a smile.

Mom had nothing to say. She just hung her head, smiled and cried. I could just sit and talk to her but I had work that needed to be done. I patted her shoulder and told her to get the kids eating and drinking water. I would return when we figured out a plan.

"We have four of us, twelve other adults and three kids. How are we going to get all of these people back?" Reid asked.

"Sgt. Hayes was supposed to send us a transport once they got back to the hospital. They should be near us pretty soon. Smith, do you have that radio on?" Ragsdill asked.

"Yes. It has been on all day." Smith replied as he waved the radio at him.

"Reach out and see if you can contact the others. They should be in range. Let them know the situation. Everyone else, let's start getting these people ready to go. Is anyone infirm or too hurt to walk?"

"Just his mother. She has a bum leg." Susie piped in.

"Oh, yeah. Did you go in and find your mum. Cry on her shoulder like a little baby did you?" Ragsdill teased. I just ignored him as usual.

Reid came back in and told us that he had been able to reach the transport. They were actually a small bit south of us. They had been heading to the Home of the Brave thinking we were still there. It would take them just about two hours to get over to us. We took that time to get everyone another bottle of water and another protein bar. That was the last of our supplies but they needed it.

North

The transport came up a little earlier than expected. As we loaded the Bravers in the back we noticed that Susie was not quite correct with the number of people that couldn't walk. One of the older guys was so dehydrated that he passed out every time he went to stand up. I had Reid start an IV and ride in the back of the transport with him to give care as needed. That put Ragsdill, Smith Susie and me in the SUV with two other Bravers.

Once we were all loaded up we let the transport roll out first then set up to follow. Everything was going fine until our passenger rear tire blew out about an hour into the ride. We radioed up to the transport team and let them know to keep heading north. We would change the tire and catch up later. We most likely wouldn't hit the tide right anyway, so the worst case was we could meet up at the canal.

Smith and I got out and changed the tire while Ragsdill tried to flirt with Susie. He was not doing very well at it if her face was the judge. A few minutes later he got the hint and came back over to us.

"You got that tire on yet? We need to get on the road." he yelled.

"Not our fault your game is weak." Smith retorted. Ragsdill didn't respond. He just walked away and got into the driver's seat.

About fifteen minutes later we were back on the road. Ragsdill wanted to drive with Smith riding shotgun. All good with me since I didn't feel like putting up with his grumpy ass anyway. About an hour later we ran up on the transport where it was pulled over on the side of the road. As we pulled up one of the soldiers jumped out and started yelling.

"Reid is in the back with an NLB. One of the people died and tried to attack the others. We pulled over to get them out of the back, but Reid is stuck back there holding the thing down so it can't attack anyone." he exclaimed.

Ragsdill jumped out of the SUV and yelled at the soldier. "Then why aren't you in there helping him. You too damn scared?"

"Yes, we aren't like you or your team. We are just regular human soldiers. Not some super soldiers like you."

"We are not super soldiers. We are just better than you. Get the people ready. As soon as we get this dead piece of crap out of the back we have to hit the road." Although he said the words I feel like Ragsdill liked being called a super soldier. He had an extra hop in his step afterward.

We all jumped up in the back of the transport to help Reid. He was just sitting on the bench watching the NLB squirm. Its hands were tied down and its mouth was taped shut. It even had a blanket pulled down over it to stop any skin-to-skin contact.

"what is the emergency?" I asked.

"Oh, nothing now. They were all just scared out of their minds and people started to jump out of the back before we stopped. I figure this one can count as the specimen we were supposed to get." Reid said calmly.

I laughed and turned to give the order but ran directly into Ragsdill.

"Move this one to the SUV and Washington can ride up with it and Reid. The rest of the people will ride with Smith and me in here. Got it?" He ordered. Still a little high on the super soldier comment.

We nodded and made it all work. A little while later we were back on the road and heading north. The rest of the trip went without incident. After a small wait at the canal, we were able to cross and get back to the hospital. The place went a little nuts when we arrived. We didn't usually bring in an NLB with a bunch of survivors.

Once I knew that everyone was being taken care of and off of the transport I looked for my mom. She was in a bed with an IV in her arm. Most of the Bravers were getting IVs. I watched her until she looked at me and smiled. I gave her the thumbs up and headed to find Ava and her goofy dog.

I found someone to tell me where she was staying and burst into the door without knocking. I almost ran her over because she was trying to listen at the door.

"We found mom. She is OK." I stated.

"You found my mom?" she asked stupidly.

"Technically I found our Mom." I state as I removed my helmet and goggles. Both of which I forgot I was wearing.

She stared at me for what seemed like five minutes before reaching out and punching me. It was actually kind of hard. She must have been working out since I saw her last.

"How?"

"To which situation are you referring? How I saved our mother, or how am I here, or the big one. How am I alive?"

"Yes to all."

"Move over on the bed and I'll tell you." I said as I sat down on the bed.

We talked for a bit about what had happened to me since the last I had seen her. It was a quick overview and not in-depth at all. I just wanted her to know she was safe here and we would look after her, Mom and Andromeda. Nothing more really seemed to matter at the time. We would have plenty of time to talk about it all later. I did tell her that once everyone was checked out she would be able to see everyone we rescued. After that, I got up and headed out to find Sgt. Hayes and report what had happened on the trip. I also needed to find out if we had another mission. We were going to need more food.

Epilogue

As I said in the beginning. Please use this as a guide. Learn from what we have endured and accomplished. We need to be able to move forward as a species and stop this pestilence that is killing us and our world. Not just the NLBs, but the spores that make them function. In the two years since the fall, our world has become unrecognizable. The plants are huge and grow faster than ever before. Animal life is sparse and getting more affected by the environment every day.

This trip we are taking. This undertaking that we have agreed to do may change the world. It has to work because if it doesn't I am not sure if we will ever be able to stop this problem from spreading. We have had the best minds I know working on the problem for two years and this is the best answer they have come up with. With no electricity, no internet and no laboratory it is not going to be easy.

This trip is going to be rife with dangers. We are going into an area of the country that most of us have never been to before. We are going to have to blaze a path that will test us in ways that we have never known before. We will probably run into new problems that we never knew existed. That's usually how it works in the movies and comic books anyway. Add to that, we have to synthesize enough of the chemical for use while we move across the country. I mean what can go wrong with that, right? Waiting would have been better, but the incident at the hospital and consistently losing our generators have pushed our hand. There is no guarantee for success. Any number of things could stop us from reaching our destination and our goals. But we have to move forward for everyone out there that is just trying to survive. Even as I write this we have lost people and vehicles along the way.

All of us in the squad, the unit, and the group have lost someone to this pandemic. We have lost our homes and our way of life. Some of us, like myself, were lucky enough to find our family again and find a new direction in life. Others like Jordan were not so lucky. She had a hard life after the Fall and it ended just when it looked like it might get better. Mom seems to be on board. Ava seems to be lost. I am just hoping that we can reconnect on this trip and learn the ways that each of us has changed, for better or worse.

Even though it has been over a year I still think about Dad and the last few weeks we were together. He gave me a job to finish the greenhouse. Then on the day he died, he gave me a job to protect my mother and sister. It took a while and a lot of luck but we have been reunited. That does not mean they are safe. I started with the military and this mission through a lot of happenstance and coincidence, but I have come to embrace it. I have come a long way from the kid running all summer in the Daytona Beach heat training for cross country. I now have a very important job to help with. A job that is not done.

Author's note

A Dim Blue is a work of fiction, as should be perfectly clear from the subject matter. Many of the events occur in real places. While I have visited many of these places, I have not seen them all. No matter how much they resemble the real thing, please know that I have taken the liberty to change them to what bests suits the course of my story though. I hope that readers will not be too upset with my creative tweaks to reality in places that are dear to them.